FORTUNE TELLER

A Miss Fortune Mystery

I SEE DEAD PEOPLE.

NEW YORK TIMES BESTSELLING AUTHOR

JANA DELEON

MISS FORTUNE SERIES INFORMATION

If you've never read a Miss Fortune mystery, you can start with LOUISIANA LONGSHOT, the first book in the series. If you prefer to start with this book, here are a few things you need to know.

Fortune Redding – a CIA assassin with a price on her head from one of the world's most deadly arms dealers. Because her boss suspects that a leak at the CIA blew her cover, he sends her to hide out in Sinful, Louisiana, posing as his niece, a librarian and ex–beauty queen named Sandy-Sue Morrow. The situation was resolved in Change of Fortune and Fortune is now a full-time resident of Sinful and has opened her own detective agency.

Ida Belle and Gertie – served in the military in Vietnam as spies, but no one in the town is aware of that fact except Fortune and Deputy LeBlanc.

Sinful Ladies Society – local group founded by Ida Belle, Gertie, and deceased member Marge. In order to gain membership, women must never have married or if widowed, their husband must have been deceased for at least ten years.

Sinful Ladies Cough Syrup – sold as an herbal medicine in Sinful, which is dry, but it's actually moonshine manufactured by the Sinful Ladies Society.

CHAPTER ONE

I LIFTED THE CRATE OFF THE FLOOR AND WAS SURPRISED AT how light it was given its size. I looked over at Gertie, who was paying Walter for what felt like empty crates.

"Are you buying air?" I asked. "Doesn't feel like anything is in this."

"Jell-O," Gertie said.

I stared. "You're buying two crates of Jell-O? Why?"

"Nope," Ida Belle said. "That sounds like a question that will lead to things I don't want to hear about. I'm just going to assume she's about to visit fifty recent tonsillectomy patients and go on my merry way."

Gertie shot a sly look at Walter. "I bet Walter wouldn't mind hearing about my plans for that Jell-O. Might get some ideas..."

Walter turned an adorable three shades of red and fled the front of the store.

"See?" Ida Belle pointed at his retreating figure. "You've gone and scared the man."

"How scared can he be?" Gertie asked. "He's married to you."

1

Ida Belle and I grabbed the two crates, and Gertie tucked her receipt in her purse as we headed out to Ida Belle's SUV, loaded up the crates, and then climbed in.

"I need you to swing by Nora's place before you drop me off at home," Gertie said as Ida Belle pulled away from downtown.

"Uh-oh," I said.

Ida Belle gave her a suspicious look that quickly shifted to horrified as she put it all together. Nora was a Sinful local with lots of cash that she used almost exclusively to travel the world in search of the best buzz. At some point, she'd decided she could do a better job than her suppliers and had become an amateur chemist, which might not have been so problematic if she hadn't also tacked amateur pharmacist onto her many professional titles.

"Why do you need to stop at Nora's?" Ida Belle asked. "I thought your legs were better."

Just the week before, Gertie had put her legs through the wringer with a runaway horse ride and then this whole church/pigeon/catching-on-fire thing—Gertie caught on fire, not the pigeon. To help her out, Nora had hooked her up with some of her magic pills, consisting of something that everyone was afraid to ask about.

Gertie nodded. "My legs are better. I just need to pick up something for the party."

"The party is at Nora's. Why are you taking things away?"

"Because I'm making gummy worms with Nora's new home brew. I was going to use our new Sinful Ladies grape, but we sold it all at the Mardi Gras festival on Saturday and we don't have time to make more before tomorrow."

Ida Belle stared in her rearview mirror in dismay. "You're going to infuse children's candy with something from Nora's stash?"

"Children won't be eating them. Only adults are invited to the party."

"The word 'adult' is up for discussion."

I had to agree with Ida Belle on that one, although no way was I missing this show. Nora had decided that because her New Year's party had been such a hit—meaning no one had been arrested or died—she wanted to do it all over again for Mardi Gras. Technically, Sinful always held its Mardi Gras festival on the Saturday before Fat Tuesday. That way, if anyone was brave enough to venture into NOLA for the real throw-down, their Tuesday was open.

The Catholics mostly attended the Sinful festival on Saturday, used Sunday through Tuesday to recover, then confessed about it all and gave it up for Lent on Wednesday. The Baptists followed the same timeline, except they replaced confession with deniability. But I had zero doubt that both religions, and quite a few unapologetic, unrepentant sinners, would be represented at Nora's place tomorrow night.

"That woman is going to kill someone playing chemist," Ida Belle said. "You won't catch me eating or drinking anything there that didn't come straight out of the manufacturer's package. And I have to be the one who opened it."

"I'm eating a pizza before I go and bringing a protein bar," I said.

Gertie rolled her eyes. "It's just CBD. We're not loading up gummies with meth. Beer will pack a bigger punch, but the gummies might help with pain and inflammation. This is a blue-collar town. Lots of injuries walking around here."

Ida Belle laughed. "You're one of them."

She pulled up to the curb in front of Nora's house, and when we climbed out, I heard a ruckus inside. First there was a crash, then Nora yelling. As I took off running for the front door, Nora's cat jumped through the living room window and onto the porch, taking the curtain with him. The giant orange tabby, appropriately named Idiot, was clearly scared because his eyes were half the size of his face.

Or maybe he was high. Idiot had a bad habit of pilfering from Nora's stash.

At first, I thought the curtain was freaking him out as it was covering his lower body, but after only a second of hesitation, he leaped out from under the curtain and off the porch, and I could see that the real source of the problem was the purse he was tangled in. The strap was wrapped around his neck, and his back legs were stuck inside the open handbag. Every time he took a step, he felt the constriction on his back legs and likely choked himself a little.

Then the first shot rang out.

I dived behind the trash cans, pulling my weapon as I went, did a quick roll, and popped up to scan the area. Ida Belle and Gertie, who were farther behind me, had retreated to the SUV and were crouched near the front bumper, looking as confused as I was about where the shot had come from.

Idiot froze for a split second in the middle of the yard. Then a piece of paper blew across the sidewalk, and he jumped straight up in the air—as only cats can do—and another shot fired. This time, I saw smoke coming out of the handbag.

Good. God. There was a loaded gun in that handbag.

The second shot sent Idiot into another round of panic, and he took off across the lawn and did an impressive jump over the fence, firing off another round.

Nora burst out onto her porch, waving her arms in the air. "Don't shoot the cat!"

"I'm more worried about the cat shooting us!" I yelled back.

"I just need to get the purse off him."

"Neither the cat nor the purse is worth dying over."

4

Nora ran back inside—presumably to the back door—and I looked over at Ida Belle and Gertie and threw my hands up in the air. They both shook their heads, clearly with no better idea of how to handle the situation than me.

Two more rounds went off, and I heard sirens in the distance. If we didn't figure out how to get that purse off the cat, he was going to be occupying his favorite spot on Nora's mantel as taxidermy.

Gertie grabbed the curtain as we ran across the porch. "Maybe we can get him wrapped up in it and cut the purse off."

"I'm not getting near that cat as long as he's trigger-happy," Ida Belle said. "A cat with a loaded gun and the ability to fire it is what a lot of nightmares are made of."

We dashed down the hall, then paused at the back door to peer outside. The cat was on top of a storage shed, eyes still huge, and I could see him panting. If he didn't shoot himself, he was going to have a stroke. Nora was standing in front of the shed with a can of tuna, trying to entice the frightened animal down.

"How many rounds in that gun?" I called out.

"Six."

"That only leaves one," Gertie said.

"It only *takes* one," Ida Belle retorted.

"Tuna is never going to work," I said. "That cat is seriously stressed and likely high as a kite to boot. He probably doesn't even recognize Nora at this point."

Ida Belle nodded. "I know the odds are more in our favor now, but I'm not leaving this house unless that gun is empty or the cat runs back in here."

I studied the situation, trying to come up with a nonlethal solution for us *and* the cat. "I think our best gamble is to scare the cat into firing off that last round. If any neighbors were outside, they've retreated in by now, so the only risk would be to the cat. Assuming we can get Nora and her tuna back inside."

I leaned into the open door. "Nora! We've got a plan, but we need you to come inside."

"Not if your plan is to shoot my cat!"

"No one is going to shoot the cat."

Well, except maybe the cat.

"You promise?" Nora called out.

"I promise."

Nora looked up at the cat, who was frozen in place like an extremely odd, and lethal, weather vane, then back toward us as Gertie motioned for her to come inside. Finally, she lowered her arm and headed our way.

I knew I had to be ready to scare the cat as soon as Nora got inside because if she knew what my plan was, she'd be back out there with her can of tuna. I looked over at Ida Belle and she nodded. She'd gotten as good as my former CIA partner, Harrison, at reading my mind. As soon as Nora walked inside, Ida Belle pulled her off to the side and I put a round through a branch hanging above the cat. Nora yelled and the branch split and dropped onto the cat. He took a dive off the shed and onto a wheelbarrow next to it. I was hoping that final round would let loose when he bolted, but no such luck.

That's when I saw Carter and a man I didn't know rush into the backyard.

"Run!" I yelled. "The cat's packing heat!"

They stopped short and glanced my way, clearly confused, then the cat jumped out of the wheelbarrow and shot off across the lawn right toward them. Halfway across, the purse tripped him up and as he tumbled, that final round went off, hitting a bird feeder next to the two men. Birdseed exploded everywhere, and both men hit the ground.

"Last round!" I yelled and took off after the cat.

Idiot, now completely frantic from the last shot, jumped right over Carter and the other man, aiming for the top of the hot tub.

Except the top wasn't actually on the hot tub.

There was a big splash followed by another round of fire, and then water came streaming out of the hot tub and right on the two men. They both jumped up as I ran to the edge of the hot tub with Ida Belle, Gertie, and Nora right behind me.

"Look at that," Gertie said. "Cats can swim."

The plunge had freed Idiot from the purse, and he swam for the opposite side of the tub and climbed out. He took off running for the porch and after a clean leap onto it, came to a complete stop, sat down, and started cleaning himself as though nothing out of the ordinary had just happened.

"Sorry," Nora said as she peered into the hot tub. "I must have had one chambered. I wonder if the water is going to hurt my gun. Oh well, as long as the yard dries up before the party, I'll be fine. Gotta patch up that hot tub, though. I was planning on using it tomorrow night."

"I think you might need a professional for that," Ida Belle said.

She waved a hand in dismissal. "Got this stuff off the internet. It's amazing what you find when you're high at 3:00 a.m. Anyway, they used it to put an aluminum boat together, so the hot tub should be an easy fix."

She stepped through the slosh, getting her bare feet all muddy, and headed back inside, not even stopping to wipe them on the mat. The man standing next to Carter grinned.

Midfifties. Six foot two. Two hundred pounds. Good general muscle tone. Weak right knee. Stood like a cop.

"Gotta love these bayou towns," he said. "Morning, ladies. Since someone's forgotten his manners, I'll introduce myself.

I'm Andy Blanchet, and I'll be filling in for Carter for a bit. I have to say, looking after such lovely women is not going to be a hardship."

Ida Belle rolled her eyes and Gertie gave him a huge smile. I raised one eyebrow.

"Stop flirting," Carter said. "This is Fortune, Ida Belle, and Gertie."

He extended his hand, giving me a closer look. "Heard a lot about you."

"Really? From who?"

"Some from Carter, but also some grapevine sort of stuff. Cops talking."

"Uh-huh. And what are they saying?"

He shrugged. "Mostly it's a lot of whining about you messing in police business, but I figure that's just 'cause you're showing them up."

I looked over at Carter and nodded. "I like him."

Carter snorted. "Give him a week here and see if the feeling is mutual. We just got fired on by a cat."

"I would say it was a fluke, but Idiot's got issues," Gertie said.

Andy stared. "You call your friend 'Idiot'?"

"No, she named her cat Idiot. And it fits."

I nodded. "I assume you got a call about shots fired? Well, now you have a name for your report."

Carter looked over at Andy. "I clocked out when we left the sheriff's department. This ride-along was a favor. That bit of paperwork is all yours."

Andy looked around and nodded. "Did the cat hit anyone?"

"Just the bird feeder and the hot tub," I said. "And I took out the branch to scare the cat off the shed."

Andy shrugged. "Then no harm, no foul, I guess."

"You'll do," Ida Belle said.

Carter shook his head. "You're making me look bad. Just wait until you deal with shenanigans for a couple days and you'll be restructuring that relaxed thinking."

Andy looked at the three of us and narrowed his eyes. "You guys planning on doing anything questionable while I'm in charge?"

"Nothing any different than we'd be doing if Carter was here," I said.

Carter clapped his replacement on the back. "Good luck."

———

THAT AFTERNOON, I STOOD WITH CARTER IN MY LIVING room. His bag was packed, and he was on his way to the airport. And that was the extent of my knowledge on what he was about to do. But that's the way things were. I knew he wasn't going to be part of the infiltration team—at least, that's what he'd told me, and I believed him. But I also knew things could change on the ground, and if something went sideways and Carter thought he could help, he'd be right in the middle.

So I'd worry until I set eyes on him again. The same way I worried every time my father left when I was a kid. But not for the same reasons. I was a teen when my father left on the mission he never returned from. Back then, I was worried about my future if my sole parent didn't return, and then I got to find out exactly what that looked like. Now I was a self-sufficient adult with enough money, no debt, and steady income. I had a nice house, good friends, and a disgruntled cat.

I didn't *need* Carter, per se, but I wanted him.

More than I'd ever wanted anything.

Which is why I felt just a tiny bit queasy.

"Check in as soon as you can," I said.

He nodded. "With any luck, it will only be a few weeks.

Andy is a good guy and was an excellent cop, but I want you and Harrison to watch his back. Things have been strange here for a while now. I don't want him coming out of retirement to do me a favor and winding up in the middle of a big crap show."

"I could say the exact same thing about you."

He blew out a breath. "Point taken."

He put his arms around me and drew me in close. I could smell his shampoo and aftershave, and I took in a deep breath of him. When he released me, he lowered his lips to mine and kissed me...gently at first, then with a passion that I'd come to know so well.

"I love you, Fortune Redding," he said.

I felt my chest tighten, and I struggled with the overwhelming desire to ask him not to go. But we both knew I'd never do that. Just as he would never ask me to abandon what I felt was my responsibility.

"I love you too, Carter LeBlanc. Now, go save the world. I'll be here waiting with a cold beer when you get back."

"What will you be wearing?"

"My nine-millimeter."

He smiled. "The perfect woman."

He gave me another quick kiss and then he was gone.

I stood in the doorway and watched him drive away and said a prayer that he'd return to me soon, exactly the way he'd left.

CHAPTER TWO

THE REST OF THE AFTERNOON DRAGGED ALONG UNTIL IT crept toward evening. Carter had set Blanchet up at his house while he was gone because it was a lot nicer than the motel and closer to where the action usually occurred, especially given that Gertie lived across the street. So that meant Carter's house was covered and didn't need any tending. And Tiny was staying with Emmaline, who would spoil him rotten, so I wasn't needed on that front either. With no case and Nora's cat freed of weaponry, things slowed to a crawl.

My friends, sensing that I was downplaying both my concern for Carter and how much I missed him, made sure I was occupied. Ida Belle had talked me into helping her clean her guns. Gertie had insisted I learn how to bake a casserole because there could be a zombie apocalypse and her freezer would empty. Ronald gave me a manicure and while I had to agree that my nails looked nice, he was a hundred times happier about it than I was.

By the time my nails were dry, I was tired of my kitchen and trite tasks. Carter was going to be gone for weeks. I couldn't sit around every day wondering what was happening and when he'd be back. I wasn't made for this much inactivity. A single afternoon of it had me ready to climb the walls. So I moved the party outside to the hot tub.

The hot tub had several benefits—it was outdoors, relaxing, and just the right amount of heat for the cool night air. Plus, drinking with your friends in a hot tub was much more fun than drinking with them in your house.

"You know what we should do," Gertie said as she sipped wine from her tumbler. "We should go to the Swamp Bar."

Ida Belle shook her head. "No way. That Andy Blanchet might be saying the words of someone who plans on looking the other way when it comes to regular Sinful business, but I don't trust him."

"You don't trust anyone," I said.

"I trust Walter and you."

"What about me?" Gertie asked.

Ida Belle snorted. "When it comes to trouble, you're on the opposite end of the trust spectrum."

"I'll go," Ronald said, surprising me. "I've always wondered about the place, but it didn't seem like the kind of establishment that I should walk into alone. But if Fortune's there, then I don't have to worry because she could probably take the whole place out with a swizzle stick."

"That's true," Ida Belle conceded.

"So what exactly does one wear to the Swamp Bar?" Ronald asked.

"Anything you're okay with throwing away afterward," Ida Belle said.

Ronald stared. "Honey, nothing makes it past my doorstep unless I want to be buried in it."

"I'll lend you something."

Ronald sighed. "I'll just wear off-rack from my gardening stash. We can't both go looking like lumberjacks."

I had to smile. When Gertie had first suggested it, my immediate thought was *hell no*, but now I was rethinking my position. I hadn't seen the owner, Whiskey, in a while and it might be nice to catch up. And besides, it was the Monday before Mardi Gras. Everyone should be resting up for tomorrow night. How bad could it be?

Famous last words.

In anticipation of the Mardi Gras crowd the next night, the Swamp Bar had decided to host a 'practice' event. The practice included games like bead toss onto girls' arms for kisses and darts with the eyeholes in their Mardi Gras masks covered. Perhaps the most disturbing was the doubloon skeet-shooting contest, but at least it was over the bayou.

Ronald was enthralled by all of it, which surprised me a little because I'd figured he'd find it all pedestrian. Plus I thought he'd have a major fit over the hair, the makeup, and well, most everything about the way people looked. And I wasn't even going into how people were dressed. Or not quite dressed, as the case may be. It *was* Mardi Gras, so more cleavage than usual was showing, and I couldn't say that was a good thing.

Ronald, on the other hand, had on purple spandex pants and a glittery gold shirt. With his green feather boa, he looked like a '70s pimp. Then I remembered that he was wearing his gardening clothes, and the whole thing took on a whole other level of awe. Gertie had taken one look at him and had wanted to change, claiming her gold sequined miniskirt, matching tennis shoes, and tank that read *It's Mardi Gras—Don't Hide Your Crazy* was too tame. In an effort to save time, Ronald had lent her a spiky purple wig but had insisted she return it undamaged because it was one of his favorites. Ida Belle and I, who were dressed as normal, kept wisely quiet about the whole thing.

Whiskey was behind the bar and wore the expression of a man who was pleased with the profit but worn out on the people. I could appreciate his dilemma as I felt the same about my insurance clients. A couple of the regulars recognized me and made some room for us at one corner of the bar, and Whiskey headed over.

"This is a surprise," he said. "What crime did one of my patrons commit?"

"The shorter list might be which ones didn't they commit," I replied.

He laughed. "Got me there. Don't tell me you're only here for the festivities. That would be a first."

"Then mark it down on your calendar."

"Nice. Maybe I'll get away with no explosions, gunfire—except the doubloon shooting—and nothing stolen."

"Why did you look at me when you ran down that list?" Gertie asked.

"I wonder. What can I get you to drink?"

We all ordered beer, except Ronald, who ordered the best scotch they had in stock, and after Whiskey served us, he leaned over the bar toward me. "I heard Carter had to duck out for a bit."

I nodded. "Military consulting. Can't really say more." Mostly because I didn't know more.

"I'll say a prayer for him."

I raised one eyebrow.

"What?" he said. "I pray. I own this place. Wouldn't you pray?"

He gave me a grin and headed to the other side of the bar where some men were yelling for shots.

Ronald took a sip of his scotch and looked around. "This isn't nearly as rough as I expected it to be. I mean, it's totally a rustic vibe and there's more flannel here than at Walmart, but people seem to be having a good time. And it's clean. I wasn't really expecting clean."

"Whiskey runs this place right," Ida Belle said. "I'll give him that. It's his customers that derail things, but when this is the only place to drink locally besides your house, then you're ripe for hosting some questionable situations."

Gertie hopped off her barstool. "And this questionable situation is going to go volunteer for that bead toss."

"You want to kiss one of those girls?" Ronald asked.

"Heck no! I want to *be* one of those girls."

"But what about Jeb?"

"What happens at the Swamp Bar stays at the Swamp Bar."

"Unless it crops up in a police report," Ida Belle said.

Gertie headed off for the bead-tossing area and Ida Belle shook her head. "I know we should probably follow her and make sure she doesn't get into trouble, but I really want to check out that doubloon shooting thing. It's shoot until you miss. First prize is a bottle of Dom."

"Really?" I perked up. Dom Pérignon was an excellent prize.

"Good Lord," Ronald said. "You have to get out there and save that bottle from falling into hands that can't appreciate it. I'm pretty sure it's your sworn duty."

"Fortune might have a better chance than me," Ida Belle said.

"Ha! Who are you kidding?" I hopped off my barstool. "Besides, it will hack them off more if you do it."

Ronald trailed behind us as we left the bar, and he stood next to me as Ida Belle went up and dropped her ten-dollar entry fee at the registration table. The man taking the money grinned at her and a couple of men standing around groaned.

"This ought to be fun," he said.

Ronald leaned toward me. "How good is she?"

"Just watch."

Ida Belle pulled out her pistol and motioned to the guy slinging the doubloons.

"You don't want to borrow a rifle?" he asked her.

"Nope."

He shrugged and turned on the spotlight, which was giving off enough light to see mosquitoes from a hundred yards away, and then did the whole countdown thing. When he got to one, he flung the doubloon in the air. Ida Belle lifted her pistol and shot, blowing the tiny piece of metal into bits.

"Holy crap!" Ronald clapped. "That might be the most impressive shooting I've ever seen."

"Nora's cat shot a bird feeder and her hot tub this morning," I said.

Ronald stared. "If only I thought you were joking."

Ida Belle fired another round and another doubloon exploded. Eight more later, she dropped her arm and looked over at the slinger. "I can do this all night. What's the record so far?"

"Um, two?"

"Well then, there's no sense in wasting more rounds, is there? If anyone gets close to ten, come get me and I'll do some more."

"Impressive." A man's voice sounded behind me. A voice I knew.

I turned around and saw Andy Blanchet standing there smiling. He nodded toward Ida Belle. "I can see why you have her on your team. Can the other one shoot as well?"

"She's more lethal with her mouth," I said. "And she's handy with dynamite, but it makes Carter nervous."

He raised one eyebrow but didn't comment and I wondered just what it would take to get a rise out of the seemingly unflappable sheriff.

"You following me, Blanchet?" I asked.

"No, although I can see why men would. I'm merely checking out the locals in their natural habitat."

Ronald cleared his throat, and I remembered my manners and made introductions.

"We're pleased to have you," Ronald said, always with the impeccable manners. "Are you from this area?"

"Born and raised in Mudbug. Started off as a deputy there and transferred out twenty years or so ago. Wanted a bigger place. Got elected sheriff in my new town and retired just last year. I knew Carter's dad and I remember Carter from when he was little, so I was happy to do him a favor. He's a good man and a good cop. I wanted to make sure his leave didn't cause him problems with the election."

Ronald practically batted his eyes at him. "Well, Sinful is lucky to have such a handsome, helpful man at its disposal."

Blanchet didn't even blink. He was good.

"Thank you," he said. "I appreciate it."

Ida Belle stepped up and rolled her eyes. "If the Adoration Society is done, we should probably head back and check on Gertie. She's alone with beads, men, and alcohol. I'm not sure which one I give the best odds."

We heard the crowd roaring before we ever got inside, and I braced myself for whatever we were about to see.

"She's officially lost the plot," Ida Belle said as we watched the spectacle on the stage.

Gertie was wearing an enormous amount of beads, and the first thing I could think was *Good Lord, I hope she hasn't kissed all those men.*

Then I realized what the problem was. Gertie was the only sober one. The other women staggered around the stage, making them harder targets, especially since they also had trouble keeping their arms up. Then there was the added advantage that Gertie could easily step in front of them and collect the beads before they even realized they'd been thrown.

"Anyone ever got counseling for a bead addiction?" I asked.

"At least she's not flashing people for them," Ida Belle said.

"If she's got kisses from all those men, you're going to have to hose her down outside with peroxide," Ronald said. "Maybe go ahead and book a visit to the clinic for first thing in the morning...just in case her penicillin isn't up to date."

Ida Belle shook her head. "It's Gertie. She's had more penicillin than a brothel."

"Maybe we should get her down from there before those other girls decide to grab some of the bounty," I suggested.

"Ah, let her have her fun," Blanchet said. "She can't have that many years left in her to do such things."

"If she hears you say something like that, you'll be the one with limited years," I said.

Gertie pulled a fly-by on one of the other girls and snagged a big set of beads. The girl frowned, and Gertie might have gotten away with it if she hadn't started celebrating by twirling the beads above her head and cheering. All the girls stared at her and the one who'd lost the most recent bead battle lifted her beer, and it wasn't to take a sip.

Before I could call out a warning, she flung the beer at Gertie. And I mean the whole beer—can and all. I don't think that was the original intent, because let's face it, people in Sinful do *not* like to waste beer, even in a fight. She was simply too toasted to hang on to the can when she did the flinging.

The can hit Gertie right in the middle of the forehead and sloshed over all the other contestants. Gertie lost her grip on the beads she was twirling, and they went soaring into the darts area. I clenched my hands, praying for a miracle, but a second later I heard a pop and a scream. Then a bunch of people started laughing and pointing.

"I knew Sheryl wasn't packing that kind of heat in her caboose!"

"That butt's as fake as her teeth!"

"She ain't gonna keep those pants on the way her butt's deflating!"

I pushed through the crowd just in time to see a woman, who I assumed was the unfortunate Sheryl, sprinting for the door, one hand gripping her pants, which were already starting to droop. And sure enough, one butt cheek was as flat as a pancake. The other looked as though she'd stuffed a soccer ball in it, and heck, maybe she had.

By this time, a fight had broken out on stage among the remaining bead girls, and from what I could gather from the hurled words, they each thought the other was responsible for the beer dousing. Meanwhile, the guilty party had done the smart thing and crawled off the stage and was halfway to the front door. I scanned the bar, looking for Gertie, and spotted her sitting at the counter grinning as Whiskey passed her a beer.

"Oh my God!" Ronald said and clapped. "This is as exciting as I thought it would be. That woman's butt exploded. She should have sprung for the silicone. I could make some recommendations."

I heard someone snort behind me and looked over to see Blanchet leaned against the wall next to Ida Belle, sharing her peanuts.

"Aren't you going to do anything?" I asked.

"What would Carter do?"

I thought about it for a second, then sighed. "He wouldn't have even come out for the call."

Blanchet nodded. "I always said Carter was a smart man."

"Well, if everyone's had their share of excitement, maybe

we should collect Gertie and get out of here before they decide to have a wet T-shirt contest or a boat race."

"There's a story there," Blanchet said.

"You have no idea," Ida Belle said. "But she's right. Gertie's caused just enough trouble, so it's time for us to scram."

I headed to the bar to pay our tab and give Whiskey a big tip. He grinned as he stuffed the money in the jar.

"Never a dull moment when you guys are here," he said.

"That used to be a problem for you."

He shrugged. "Got bigger problems than you three...and a lot less entertaining."

He grabbed a bottle of champagne from under the counter and passed it to Ida Belle. "Ain't no one gonna beat you, so you might as well take this now. Next time you think you want to enter a shooting contest out here, let me know and I'll just have a bottle shipped to you. Saves everyone their rounds." He looked at me. "Same goes."

Ida Belle collected the bottle and grinned. "It always tastes better when someone else pays for it."

We'd just turned to leave when the door to the bar flew open, banging against the wall, and Kenny Bertrand staggered in.

"A girl," he managed, panting so hard he could barely get the words out. "Need an ambulance. Call Carter. Found her...in the bayou...boat." He pointed toward the dock.

Blanchet, all cop now, said, "Come with me," and strode past Kenny, who had collapsed in a chair and was hunched over.

"Who was that?" Blanchet said as we hurried toward the dock.

I gave him a rundown on what I knew about Kenny.

"Reliable? Drinker?"

"Everyone's a drinker," Ida Belle said. "But Kenny's no alcoholic and he's reliable, if a bit overly dramatic."

"He get upset like that often?"

"Not unless he finds a body, which has, unfortunately, happened to him more than once."

Blanchet frowned as we stepped onto the dock.

Ida Belle pointed. "His boat's the white one with the blue stripe at the end of the dock."

We hurried over and sure enough, I could make out something huddled in the rear of Kenny's boat, still partially covered by the net. I heard Ronald gasp behind me as I jumped in and checked for a pulse.

"She's still alive!" I yelled. "Call 911 and someone get me some light!"

Blanchet found the switch for the spotlight mounted on the top of the boat's cabin and pointed it toward the back to illuminate the girl. I gave her a couple quick breaths and she started coughing, then raised up a bit and spit up bayou water before dropping back down into unconsciousness.

"She's breathing!" I called out.

"Paramedics are on their way," Ida Belle said.

Blanchet stepped around me and looked down at the girl.

"Oh my God," he whispered. "It can't be."

CHAPTER THREE

I LOOKED UP AND COULD SEE THE SHOCKED EXPRESSION ON his face. He took one reverse step and tripped on a rope, then he pitched backward, hitting his head on the corner of a storage bench as he fell. I jumped up and bent over my second unconscious body of the night and could see blood trickling out from behind Blanchet's head.

I was afraid to turn his head in case he'd injured his back or neck in the fall, so I gently lifted his head and felt the back. Relief coursed through me when I realized it was only a surface wound, but the head bled so much, it always looked worse than it was. Still, he wasn't responsive, and that was always a concern. Even more concerning was why he'd tripped.

"Got two coming now," Ida Belle said as she, Gertie, and Ronald jumped onto the boat. "What happened?"

"I don't know. He stepped around me and got a look at the girl and freaked out a little."

"No Blood Pressure Blanchet freaked out?" Gertie asked.

I nodded and took a picture of the girl with my phone as I also mentally recorded her face, blue jeans, yellow T-shirt, and one red sneaker. "Do you know her?"

All three studied the girl and shook their heads.

"Never seen her before," Ida Belle said.

"How old do you think she is?" I asked. "Ten maybe?"

"Looks about right," Ida Belle said. "I wonder what happened to her."

"Maybe it's a Mardi Gras miracle," Gertie said.

Ida Belle sighed. "The saints come *marching* in. They don't float down the bayou."

"You all right there?" I heard Whiskey's voice from the dock and looked up to see a crowd forming.

"Got an unconscious, half-drowned girl and an unconscious temporary sheriff," I said. "Paramedics on the way. Where's Kenny?"

"I set him up with a couple whiskey shots. His nerves are gone."

"I can imagine, but the cops are still going to want to talk to him."

"The 'cops' are apparently laid out on the bottom of that boat. What happened to him?"

"Tripped and banged his head," I said, figuring I should leave out the reason behind it until I had a chance to talk to Blanchet.

"I called dispatch," Whiskey said. "Harrison is on his way."

I nodded. "If you wouldn't mind, can you get that crowd back in the bar and keep an eye on Kenny? Don't let him get too deep in that whiskey or he won't be able to answer Harrison's questions."

Whiskey gave me a nod and started waving at the crowd to disperse. They moved like a herd of cattle back toward the bar and I could hear some whining as they went.

"Maybe we should have let them take a look," Ronald said.

"The boat's already compromised enough with all of us tromping on it, and the paramedics as well. Not that I think there's anything to find here, but you know how cops get about the rules. The priority is making sure she's all right. Then the cops can figure out who she is. Likely, her parents have already reported her missing. She's a little young to be traipsing around the bayou alone, especially after dark."

I checked both of them again. Blanchet's pulse was strong. The girl's was still weak but better than before. Her breathing was shallow, but steady. I glanced back to make sure the dock was empty, then reached into her jeans pockets.

"Anything?" Ida Belle asked.

I shook my head.

"Well, this is a mystery!" Ronald said. "Good Lord, is this what happens to you all the time—bodies just appear in your path?"

"Seems like that sometimes."

"That's very exciting but also horrifying. No wonder you don't like to wear nice things or waste time and money on your hair and nails. You could be going to buy a loaf of bread and be in a shoot-out or have to tie off a compound fracture."

"It's a new adventure every time I step out my front door."

I saw the lights of the ambulance as they broke from behind a patch of trees close to the bar. "That was fast."

"They're keeping a unit in Sinful until after Mardi Gras," Gertie said. "They figure the savings on gas will outweigh the per diem for snacks since most people just end up needing bandaging or oxygen and not transport."

The ambulance flew into the parking lot and stopped near the dock. Gertie, Ida Belle, and Ronald climbed out of the boat as they hurried toward us with their bags.

"Unconscious female," I said as the two men jumped onto the boat. "Pulled out of the bayou by a local fisherman. Faint pulse and not breathing when I first checked. I administered three breaths, and she coughed up water."

One of the paramedics went to work on the girl.

I pointed to Blanchet. "This is our acting sheriff. He tripped over the rope and fell, hitting his head. There's a small bleed on the back, but I didn't move him."

The second paramedic was already checking Blanchet's vitals and then felt his neck.

"Second ambulance is about twenty minutes out," the second paramedic said. "His vitals are strong, and the head injury seems mild. I'm giving the girl priority. We'll take her now. Watch him until the other unit gets here."

By the time they got the girl secured on a board and into the ambulance, Harrison had shown up. He came straight to the boat, and when he caught sight of Blanchet, his eyes widened.

"Good God, Redding. You couldn't give the man one day on the job before you clocked him?"

"Funny." I gave him a rundown of the situation. "I'll wait here for the paramedics. You should talk to Kenny before too many people take pity and buy him a round."

"Let me get some pictures first."

He snapped some shots of the boat and the net, even though we both knew it was a file requirement and wouldn't yield any pertinent information. Then he headed off to talk to Kenny. The second unit arrived a couple minutes after and got Blanchet off to the hospital. He was starting to stir a little when they loaded him up, so I figured he'd be awake and able to explain his strange reaction soon. We headed for the bar and saw Harrison on the side porch, talking to Kenny, who was sitting on the railing and looking as if he needed a more stable perch.

Harrison motioned us over and Kenny gave me a grateful look. "Thank you for handling that," he said. "I've pulled a lot of things out of the bayou, and I found Hooch, remember? But when I hauled in my net and saw that girl there... Well, I just about fell apart."

"Whiskey is ready to help you fall apart just as soon as I'm done here," Harrison said. "He's even offered up the couch in his office, so you don't have to worry about how much you drink. You're sure you didn't recognize her?"

"No, sir. 'Course I don't have cause to be around kids a whole lot since my grandkids don't live around here, but I'm pretty sure she's not a local."

Harrison looked up at us, and we all shook our heads.

"Okay," he said. "And you didn't see anyone around? Didn't hear a boat engine?"

"Nothing like that. It was real quiet, which is why I went out. Figured everyone would be celebrating and I could get a good haul of fish."

"Can you tell me exactly where you were?"

"'Course. Red Rooster Cut just past the black cypress tree."

Harrison blinked.

"It's a bayou about a half mile up," Gertie said. "Old Man Partridge had this red rooster who kept getting out and one day he didn't come back. Hiked his butt all the way to that pass and took up residency. Partridge tried for years to catch him but never could. And he was too old to be decent eating, so shooting him would have just been petty. Anyway, people started calling it Red Rooster Cut and there was a big lightning storm—"

"I can show you," Ida Belle interrupted.

"Great. Whiskey said he'd lend me his boat. You think you can drive it?"

Ida Belle stared, and I struggled not to laugh. Ronald didn't bother to struggle.

"You might want to retract that question," Gertie said.

27

"Unless you want people pulling two bodies out of Red Rooster Cut tonight."

Harrison held up his hands. "My apologies. Still getting to know this place."

"Consider Ida Belle an older version of me," I said.

"And I'm a not-so-much-older version of Lara Croft," Gertie said.

"Somebody better pass me Kenny's hip waders," Ida Belle said. "It's getting deep."

"I'm going to go talk to Whiskey about that boat," Harrison said and fled, Kenny right on his heels.

"Do you mind if I take your SUV and head to the hospital?" I asked. "I want to be there when Blanchet comes out of this. I'd like to see what he has to say. Harrison will give you a ride home or to the hospital if I'm still there."

"I'll go with Ida Belle," Gertie said. "Someone has to document the scene."

Ronald clapped. "Oh my God! I'm in another investigation, and this time I don't have to worry about anyone's garments. Since this outfit isn't suited for swamp air, I'll go to the hospital with Fortune and see why the handsome sheriff took a dive."

"We're not on a case," I said.

Gertie raised one eyebrow. "So you *don't* want me to document the scene? I suppose you took that picture of the girl because you liked the color of her shirt."

"Fine, go document. Just don't let Harrison catch on to what you're doing. He can't afford any issues, being new on the job. And we all want him to stay here."

Ronald's face fell. "Does that mean I can't go with you to the hospital?"

"We're not investigating anything. We're just checking up on a friend."

———

OF COURSE I WAS INVESTIGATING. WHEN A VETERAN COP startled himself into unconsciousness over the sight of a half-drowned child, I was going to have questions. Heck, those guards at Buckingham Palace would have questions. And I was anxious to see what the good sheriff had to say.

The nurse at the ER desk recognized me when I walked in and pointed to the back. "Room 5. He asked me to send you back."

"He's awake?"

She nodded. "I can't say much as you're technically not family, but you can go back and see for yourself. But your friend has to wait here. Only one visitor at a time."

"Oh no!" Ronald cried, clearly disappointed.

"Do me a favor and go grab us some coffees," I said and handed him some money. "I could really use one."

Happy to be contributing again, he headed off for the vending machines. "I am your able assistant."

"How about the girl?" I asked.

"She's stable."

"Is Dr. Williams on rotation?" Harrison's fiancée, Cassidy Williams, was an ER doctor.

"Not until tomorrow."

The nurse buzzed me through, and I located Room 5. Blanchet was propped up in bed and the color was back in his face. Part of his head was wrapped with gauze, and he was frowning at the IV in his arm. When he caught sight of me, he straightened.

"Did they tell you anything about the girl?" he asked.

"Just that she's stable. I don't really have any grounds to know more. I would think they'd tell you, though."

He scowled. "That doctor wants to do tests. It's just a

whack on the head, I told him. I've had worse from my football days. Heck, got hit with a golf ball once and it was a line drive. Anyway, he said until he gives me medical clearance, I'm a patient, not the sheriff."

"What happened on the boat?"

He stopped scowling and tried to force a blank expression, not coming remotely close to succeeding. "I tripped over that rope and cracked my head."

"Uh-huh. And you looked like you'd seen a ghost right before you practically bolted backward, which is what caused you to trip."

He sighed and reached for his cell phone on the tray. He accessed his pictures, then turned the phone around to show me an old photo of a woman and a little girl. It was a digital picture but an old one. The quality was grainy. I didn't recognize the woman at all, but I could see why he'd been startled.

The girl in the old photo looked exactly like the one on the boat.

"Who is she?"

"The child was Lara Delgado. Her mother is someone I knew a long time ago. Her name was Maya."

"Was?"

He shook his head. "Lara and Maya disappeared twenty years ago. I've never known what happened to them. Obviously, the girl in the boat isn't Lara. She'd be thirty now, but you can see why I was surprised."

"Yes." Sort of. I mean, yeah, if he'd thought the girl and her mother died all those years ago when they'd disappeared, then that would be a bit surreal to see one of their faces on someone else. But his reaction was more than surprise; it was blatant shock, which led me to believe that this woman was more than a friend.

"So how long were you in a relationship with Maya?" I asked.

He blinked. "Carter said you were very intuitive."

"Doesn't take much to know that someone with decades of law enforcement behind him doesn't have that kind of reaction unless there is an emotional component."

"Three months. But the first time I spoke to her, I knew she was special. Most people would scoff at the idea that I knew she was the person that was meant for me, but that's the truth."

"I believe you." Men like Blanchet didn't make those sort of declarations unless it was the truth.

"Maya was a wonderful woman...the kind of person that people enjoyed being around. She made everyone feel included and important and interesting, and I think she was absolutely perfect."

"How did she disappear?"

"One day, she was just gone. My dad was killed in a robbery in New Orleans just two days before, so I was already on the ledge, trying to insert myself into that investigation and cope with my mother, who fell completely apart."

"I'm sorry. That's horrible."

He nodded. "Then Maya disappeared, and the one light left in my world went dark. The apartment she'd rented still held all her belongings except for the clothes she and her daughter had been wearing that day. Her purse and the keys to the apartment were on the counter. There was a half-eaten peanut butter sandwich on the table along with an empty glass of milk. No sign of forced entry. Neither her landlord nor the neighbors reported hearing a struggle. She simply vanished."

"This was in Mudbug? You were a deputy then?"

He nodded. "Sheriff Lee told me I shouldn't be part of the

investigation, but he knew that wasn't going to stop me. He said it because he had to and then looked the other way. But there was nothing to be found, and you best believe I turned over every leaf in the parish. No one saw her go. And no one ever saw her again."

"I know this is a stupid question, but I assume you checked in her hometown, with relatives?"

"She didn't have any."

I blinked. I mean, I didn't have any, so it wasn't as though it didn't happen. But it still wasn't the most common thing in the world, especially in the Deep South where family roots tended to grow stronger than other places.

"No one at all? What about friends? A former neighbor or coworker? She didn't materialize out of thin air. Where was she from?"

He looked away, and I could see a tinge of embarrassment in his expression. "She never really said. I mean, she said a small bayou town outside of NOLA, but that's it."

He looked back at me and sighed. "And before you ask, no, I didn't push. I was young and in love and all the things I would have yelled at someone else for ignoring, I ignored myself. So as far as me and law enforcement were concerned, she *did* appear out of thin air, and she disappeared the same way."

"What about her credentials? She was renting an apartment, right?"

"Her identification was fake, and the apartment was above a widow lady's garage. She saw a woman with a young child and took cash, no questions asked. She had no bank account, no credit cards, no car. I don't even know how she got to Mudbug. I searched every database I could access and came up with nothing. The NOLA papers put her picture in a story about missing persons, and a local news station covered it."

"Nothing came of that?"

"Tons of calls—which is normal—but after wading through them all, we were still left with nothing. Maybe some of those people had seen her on a sidewalk or in a store, but even if they had, it didn't get us anywhere. And not one credible sighting happened after she disappeared from Mudbug."

I shook my head. "I know I don't have to tell you the stats."

"No. I'm more aware of them than 99 percent of the population, I'd guess. But I'll admit I've never let go of the idea that she was still out there somewhere. I wasn't too young and inexperienced to know she was running from something, even before she disappeared. But whatever she was running from, it wasn't me. I loved her. Hell, I asked her to marry me."

I blinked. "You did?"

He nodded and I could see just how miserable he still was. Then suddenly it struck me.

"You never married, did you?"

"No. I got close a couple times, but I couldn't seem to step over that line to forever. I knew they weren't right. None of them were Maya."

My heart clenched as I thought about this man, still in love with a woman after two decades. No wonder he'd been startled by the girl. All that longing was just bubbling below the surface every day and suddenly, it had been ignited.

He reached over and clutched my hand. "You have to help me. Carter said you have a mind for puzzles that rivals the best detectives he knows, and Carter doesn't hand out compliments unless he means them."

"Carter and I are in a relationship. He's going to speak better of me."

"He also said you were stubborn, a professional liar, and were probably going to put him in an early grave."

I smiled. "Okay, so maybe he meant it. But the thing is, I'm not a cop and don't have access—"

"But I do. That girl...she's the connection. I know she is. I can feel it as strongly as I feel that gash throbbing on the back of my head."

"What if her parents come forward? What if it's just a freaky coincidence? For all you know, Maya could have been adopted or separated from her family by her own parents and others aren't even aware of her. Some family lines have super-strong DNA. We have generations of kids in Sinful who, I swear, look just like their great-greats in photos I've seen."

"All possible, but if she *is* related somehow, maybe I'd finally get some answers. If not, then nothing's lost because I don't have anything to lose."

Except hope.

I blew out a breath. Of course I was intrigued. Who wouldn't be? And that Hallmark moment part of me that I mostly liked to dismiss was touched by his obvious feelings for a woman who had been gone from his life eighty times longer than she'd been in it. But what if I couldn't find anything, either? What if that tiny flicker of hope that he'd clung to all these years was finally extinguished? Would that be a positive thing or a negative one?

I looked at his expectant, hopeful face and knew it was pointless to refuse. He was going to look into it with or without me. I was going to look into it with or without him. Might as well combine resources. That gave us the best chance of finding something.

"Okay," I said. "Give me a dollar."

He looked a bit confused but grabbed his wallet from the nightstand and handed me a dollar from it.

"Now you're a client. I'll draw up a contract when I get home."

34

He smiled. "So I've got confidentiality and your butt is covered."

"Well, it's not shining bare, but covered is probably still a stretch. It's Swamp Bar covered. But just so you know, the ADA isn't a fan of mine."

"That's got to sting a little considering he's up for the DA position only because you exposed the DA's crimes."

"He was more polite than usual when he questioned me, but there's still no love lost."

"Foolish man. He'd do better to have you on his side."

I shrugged. "I'm only on two sides—truth and justice. Although I will occasionally wander over to some good old-fashioned revenge."

He laughed. "You know, when Carter told me he'd settled down with someone, I thought, no way it will last. That man will never find his counterpart. But I was wrong. If you'd been around twenty years ago, I might not have gone for Maya."

"Sure you would have."

He sniffed. "Yeah. I would have."

"I'll do everything I can to help you get some answers, but I'm going to need a lot of help from you. I'm coming at this completely blind—no knowledge of the missing persons, not a clue as to her real identity."

"I know. It's the longest of long shots, but we have the girl."

"What if she's not related? We can't know for sure that she is, and we don't have a sample from Maya for a DNA test, even if we could get one done."

"Actually, we do. I have a hairbrush. She used it to brush her hair at my place the day before she disappeared. We'd been...well, and she had to get back to Lara, who was baking with her landlord. I kept the brush. I know that sounds weird, but back then, I'd go through bouts of shaving my hair off military short and wouldn't use the brush for months. After she disappeared, I didn't care as much about things like regular haircuts, and when I grabbed the brush one day, I saw the long hairs and I bagged them. Just in case…"

He didn't have to finish the statement. Plenty of bodies were pulled out of the swamp in less-than-identifiable conditions. DNA was the go-to if you wanted certainty. But in this case, all they would have gained was the certainty that fake identity Maya had died. They still wouldn't know anything else.

"Okay," I said, feeling encouraged with the possibility of hard evidence.

If the girl wasn't related to Maya, then I would try to convince Blanchet to let the whole thing go. If she was, then I'd have a starting point just as soon as we knew the girl's identity.

"As soon as I get out of here," Blanchet said, "I'll make a trip to my house and get that hair sample. And I'll get the appropriate permissions to get a sample from the girl."

"What if you can't get them? If her family comes forward, there's no reason to run her through CODIS, so your request for DNA goes out the window."

He frowned. "We'll cross that bridge later, but you're right. It might take some time to go through proper legal channels, and surely by then, we'll know who the girl is. I don't suppose… No, I can't ask you to break the law."

I grinned. "I'm pretty sure you didn't."

CHAPTER FOUR

I HEADED BACK TO THE LOBBY AND SPOTTED RONALD PACING one side of the room. He looked over when I exited the hallway and threw his hands in the air.

"It's about time! I've already drank my coffee and yours and just got refills. I'm going to have to detox tomorrow, or my skin is going to just up and leave my body, or worse, wrinkle."

"I drink at least a pot a day and don't even moisturize."

He gasped and held up one hand. "I don't know why we're friends."

"Because of my sparkling personality, which could use some help. I need a wig."

"And what? These pants are so tight they'd show a freckle. Where do you think I have a wig?"

"In that huge purse you have in the SUV... You know, the one that looks suspiciously as large as Gertie's?"

"Hmmmm. Well, I might have an emergency wig in there."

I had no idea what kind of situation Ronald got into that called for an emergency wig, but I knew what kind of situation I had. And committing a crime in a hospital at the sort-of bequest of the acting sheriff definitely fell under emergency status.

"What is the wig for?" he asked.

"I need to get into a room and can't be seen."

"Well, good Lord, it's not a magical wig. It can't make you invisible."

"I'll take care of that part. I just need two things from you —the wig and a distraction."

"Well, you've come to the right place for both. Give me a minute."

He returned and shoved the purse at me. I held my breath as I opened it and looked at the emergency wig. I was afraid it was going to be something akin to what he'd lent Gertie, but when I saw the shoulder-length brown hair, I gave him a surprised look.

"What?" he asked. "Sometimes I need to blend, just like you. Do you know how hard it is to get service at some places when I go as myself? Took me three trips with different wardrobes to get those punks at the phone store to sell me the new iPhone. Debbie the Commoner, which is what I call the wig, can accomplish anything. Ronald the Awesome tends to scare salespeople. Except in NOLA. They don't even blink in NOLA."

I slipped the wig out of the purse, rolled it up, and stuffed it into my bra, causing Ronald to make the sign of the cross.

"I'm going to have to wash and restyle that when you're done."

"Are you even Catholic?"

"It depends on the situation."

"Okay, I cased the ER before I left, and I need to access the room at the end of the hall. Halfway down that hall is the nurse's station. I'm not getting by there unless they think I'm an employee. There's an employee locker room before you get to the nurse's station. I can lift some scrubs from there."

"Do I even want to know why you know all this?"

"No."

"Alrighty then. What do you need me to do?"

"The nurse already told me that she can't allow visitors anymore, so she won't unlock the door. That button is on the back side of the desk wall, right next to her computer. I need you to pretend to ask a question and spill your coffee, then when she's grabbing paper towels, let me in."

Ronald perked up. "That's it? I can do that. I thought since Gertie wasn't here, I was going to have to shoot someone or blow something up."

I wondered briefly what those other zippered bags inside his purse contained but didn't have time to dwell on it. I needed to get this handled before that girl was identified and out of here. And the night shift was the time to pull this kind of stunt because during the day there were far more eyes around.

I waited until the front desk nurse was turned slightly away from the lobby and slipped behind a fake rubber plant near the ER access doors. Ronald headed for the desk and plopped his coffee on the counter on the side farthest away from me.

"I'm sorry to bother you," he said when the nurse looked up. "Fortune had to take a call, but she wanted to make sure you had her contact information in case anything happened with Mr. Blanchet. He's a friend of Carter's, and she feels responsible for him with Carter out of town and him filling in."

"Of course," the nurse said. "I'll be happy to take her number down, but my guess is Mr. Blanchet will be leaving us tomorrow. The tests are routine in this type of situation, so as long as everything looks good, the doctors will let him go in the morning."

"That's excellent news," Ronald said and threw his arms out, knocking his cup of coffee over the counter and onto her desk, where it splashed in all directions.

"Oh no!" She jumped out of her chair and ran for a cabinet on the rear wall.

Ronald leaned over the counter and pressed the button while half-yelling his apologies to cover the click of the door opening. "I'm so sorry! Oh my God! I'm such a klutz. Let me clean that up for you. Do you have a mop?"

I could still hear him offering condolences and janitorial services as I slipped inside the employee locker room. I located a set of scrubs that would fit over my jeans and T-shirt and yanked them on. Then I pulled the wig from my bra and stuffed my ponytail under it. I checked myself in the mirror and smoothed the hair out a bit, then hurried into the janitors' closet and grabbed a box of tissues and used it to cover my chest, where my access card should be hanging, as I passed the nurse's station in the middle of the ER.

One doctor and two nurses were at the station when I walked past, but they didn't even look up. I figure as long as they got a glimpse of scrubs in their periphery, they didn't take a closer look. I located the girl's room and slipped inside. She was hooked up to a bunch of monitors, but I was relieved to see she was breathing on her own and her heart rate was a little weak but steady. Unless she had issues I couldn't see, she was probably going to be all right. I took a quick picture of her whiteboard with her vitals on it, then hurried to the bed and took another of the girl, now that she'd been cleaned up a bit and I had better light.

I could tell by the rise and fall of her chest and the flickering behind her eyelids that she was dreaming. But her expression told me the dreams probably weren't pleasant. Either that or she was in pain. I felt just a sliver of guilt as I reached up and plucked a couple strands of hair from her head. Then I wrapped them in tissue and shoved them deep into my jeans pocket and prepared to leave.

That's when she woke up.

And grabbed my arm.

And screamed.

A nurse bolted into the room. "What happened?" he asked as he rushed to the girl, who'd collapsed back on the bed.

"A nightmare, I think. I'll go get the doctor."

I practically ran out of the room and *did* run down the hall. I could hear footsteps scrambling behind me, but they were going in the opposite direction, so I assumed the other nurse had issued the call. But when I didn't return, they were going to come looking for me, and that was going to happen quickly.

I had a split second to consider my options. There was no way I could make it out of the building without them seeing me go. And that would invite all kinds of problems, especially for Ronald, who was still in the lobby and didn't have the car keys. And even if I made it to the locker room, they'd definitely check there since they were looking for a nurse.

My plan devised—sort of—I bolted into Blanchet's room and threw my cell phone at him. He gave me a startled look and I remembered the wig. I pulled it off and tossed it on the end of his bed. Then I yanked off the scrubs, jumped onto his bed, lifted a ceiling tile, and flung the garments as far back as I could. The hospital speakers sounded with what must have been the equivalent of a hospital code red for intruders, and loud voices sounded in the hallway. I jumped down and had barely gotten the wig stuffed back in my bra when the door flew open and the front desk nurse burst in.

"What are you doing here?" she asked, frowning. "I thought you left."

"That's my fault," Blanchet said. "I'm staying at Carter's house while I'm filling in for him, and we changed the alarm code. Fortune needs it so she can feed the dog since I'm in here."

"The door to the wing was open so I thought it would be okay to just pop in and get it."

The nurse narrowed her eyes. "Why didn't you text it to her?"

Blanchet gave her a horrified look. "You don't *text* alarm codes. Please don't tell me you have. You don't even *say* alarm codes on the phone. Those things are listening. Why do you think we're whispering and our phones are under my butt?"

He made a big show of lifting his hip and pulled both phones out from under the blanket. Then he passed mine back to me.

"Is something wrong?" I asked. "Is the girl all right?"

"She's fine, but we're trying to locate a nurse who was attending. Have either of you seen a nurse in green scrubs with shoulder-length brown hair?"

We both shook our heads.

"Okay, well, I need you to leave, Ms. Redding. I have a situation here to handle, and this man needs his rest if he expects to be released."

I gave Blanchet a nod, and he barely managed to contain his smile as I followed the nurse out. She gave me a pointed look and I headed straight for the exit door. I didn't need an invitation. The sooner I got out of the hospital the better.

Ronald was pacing the lobby again and ran over as soon as I exited. I gave him a look that said, 'not now,' and he was practically bouncing by the time we got in the SUV.

"Good Lord! That was exciting! What happened?"

I backed out of the parking space so no one could see into the front windshield and finally freed my bra of the itchy wig.

"I'm afraid you're definitely going to have to style it again," I said as I passed him the rumpled hair.

He waved a hand in dismissal. "It was worth it. At least I assume it was. Now tell me what happened!"

I filled him in on the events as I drove, and he shook his head. "You're a marvel. Truly. How can you think that quickly and not only come up with a plan but execute it? It's a gift. It takes me twenty minutes just to decide on breakfast. And the execution...please, there's flatware to choose and do I go with the daily ware, the stoneware, the collector's stuff...and then there's plating the food."

"It sounds like a real problem."

"Now you're just making fun."

I grinned.

"So did you get what you were going for?"

"Yes."

He stared when I didn't elaborate, and then his eyes widened. "You broke into that girl's room, didn't you?"

"Well, the door was unlocked, so no."

"Did you steal her medical records?"

"Not exactly."

He threw his hands in the air. "Are you going to tell me or not?"

My phone buzzed and I passed it to Ronald. "That's Blanchet. Can you read it please?"

If I were twenty years younger... I understand why Carter settled down.

"Good Lord, the man sounds like Gertie," Ronald said. "What exactly did you do for him?"

"Took him on as a client."

Ronald sighed. "And now you'll have the whole client confidentiality thing, and you won't tell me any of the good stuff."

My phone signaled another text.

You're clear to share my story with your trusted circle.

Ronald clapped and then looked over at me. "Please tell me I'm in the trusted circle. I'm not asking to go investigating, because honestly, the times I've been involved have been a little stressful. And keeping wrinkles away is a delicate balance. Plus, I already live next door to you. I've had to add an extra Botox session since you arrived."

"You're in," I said. "Text him back and ask him to forward me the picture. He'll understand. Then send Ida Belle a text and tell them to meet us at my house. I'll fill you all in there."

Ronald sighed. "An entire car ride of anticipation. Can we at least discuss a nightly skin care routine for you? Nothing big. Maybe just a moisturizer before bed and a mask once a week?"

"You can talk about it, but it's going to be a monologue as I have nothing to add. And I don't make any promises on listening."

"That will do. Now what do you clean your face with?"

"Shampoo?"

"Good. God."

IT WAS CLOSE TO MIDNIGHT BY THE TIME WE GATHERED IN my kitchen. Ida Belle, Gertie, and Harrison had beaten Ronald and me home and already had coffee brewing. Ronald took one look at the pot and went for a bottled water. He'd probably had enough of coffee to last the rest of the week. When we'd gotten our drinks and Harrison fetched a chair from the dining room, we all crowded around the kitchen table.

"First thing," Harrison said. "How are the girl and Blanchet?"

"Blanchet seems fine," I said. "Got a crack on his head, but he's talking normal. They're going to run some tests, but the nurse seems to think they'll cut him loose in the morning, assuming everything comes back okay. The girl is stable and breathing on her own."

Harrison nodded. "That's good. Is she still unconscious?"

"Mostly, but I'll get to that in a minute. Did you guys find anything?"

"Nothing," Harrison said. "I'll go back in the morning, and I've asked Ida Belle to go with me since she knows the area so well. We didn't see any boats or signs that someone had been in the area, and no signs on the bank that people had passed there recently, but you know how hard it is to see out there in the dark, even with spotlights."

"I don't like it," Ida Belle said. "There's no easy way to walk out to that area and the nearest camp is at least half a mile away. That girl must have come from a boat. But who the hell loses a kid from a boat and isn't out looking for her?"

"Someone who was trying to lose her?" I suggested.

"Exactly why I don't like it."

"I stopped off at the sheriff's department on the way over," Harrison said. "There's no children reported missing who fit her description and none reported missing within the last two days in the area."

"That doesn't sound good," I said. "So let me tell you what I found out. And before I start, I have to say that Blanchet is an official client, so everything is confidential. That goes for you too, Harrison, so if you'd rather leave to avoid any conflict, that's fine."

"What? No way. Just consider me Carter on this one. Well, except for the relationship part."

"We never tell Carter anything," Gertie pointed out. "He doesn't want to know."

Harrison shrugged. "He's got a stricter moral code. I was CIA. I can spin it to suit me."

"I think you and Gertie must be related," Ida Belle said. "So what's the case?"

I told them Blanchet's story, and when I was done, I produced my phone and showed them the picture I took of the girl in the hospital. Then I showed them Blanchet's picture from twenty years ago. They all stared, then looked at one another.

"Wow," Harrison said finally, breaking the silence. "I can see why he had a reaction. They look like the same person."

I nodded. I was sure the CIA lab could find differences, but both Harrison and I had been trained to recognize features such as cheekbones and jawline and the shape of the forehead and how the eyes were centered. Basically, we had needed to be able to recognize people in disguise. Sometimes, our lives had depended on it.

Ronald asked for my phone and flipped back and forth between the pictures. "Definitely the same structure. Even the shape of the eyebrows is the same and the set point as well." He handed the phone back to me. "When you're dependent on makeup to achieve the look you want, you learn all about facial anatomy. If these two people aren't related, I'd be shocked."

"I agree," Harrison said.

"So is this why you created all that drama at the hospital and rumpled my good wig?" Ronald asked. "Because I thought you took a picture of the girl on the boat."

I shook my head. "Before we descend on this girl and her family, we have to be sure. Blanchet has a hair sample—"

Ronald covered his mouth with his hand. "You stole that girl's hair, didn't you?"

"Just a couple strands."

"Was that her who screamed? It sounded like a horror movie."

"She woke up after I took the hair. She was in REM state. I'm pretty sure she was having a nightmare."

"My wig has been part of a theft and an assault. It's really made the rounds."

Harrison looked a little pained.

"See," Gertie said, and pointed at him. "That look is why we don't tell Carter things."

"You could have just waited until she woke up and asked," Harrison said. "Or asked her parents when we locate them."

"Really? And would you willingly give samples of your minor daughter's DNA just because she favors someone who went missing long before she was ever born?" I asked. "And since the missing woman claimed she had no family, that might include giving up family secrets in order to answer questions."

Ida Belle nodded. "But if you have proof, then the cat's out of the bag, and denial is a waste of time. It's messy, but I would have made the same call. On the plus side, if it's not a match, we can all write this off as one of those weird doppelgänger things that happen and worry about what kind of heat Nora's cat will be packing at her party instead."

"Nora's cat is in heat?" Ronald asked. "Or Nora? Because the second sounds completely plausible if not somewhat daunting."

"Packing heat," Gertie said. "Didn't you hear about her cat shooting a gun?"

Ronald looked at all of us, as if trying to determine if we were punking him. I was waiting for him to check for a television crew.

"It's true," Harrison said, chuckling. "Blanchet elected not to file charges against the cat, so there was no official police report, but it was a darn good story over lunch."

Ronald sighed. "As if it wasn't enough that the wildlife here is always trying to kill me, now I have to worry about the domesticated fare as well."

"Maybe you could design a fashionable bulletproof vest," Gertie suggested. "I'm getting Madonna cone bra vibes, especially given the extra storage capacity."

"Hmmm."

"So back to the case, how is Blanchet going to handle that DNA test?" Harrison asked.

"He's not," I said. "I'm going to use a friend of a friend and get it done."

"Good. So what do you need from me?"

"I don't need anything from anyone yet. I'll get the DNA processed and then we'll see what we see."

"And if it's not a match?" Gertie asked. "Are you really going to leave Blanchet hanging with no answers? It's his one true love. We can't just forget about it."

I smiled. "You're such a romantic, Gertie. But I will admit, I feel sorry for the guy. So no matter what this test turns up, I'll probably still do some asking around. The original police reports would be a good starting point, but I think it's best if Blanchet pulls them, given that he's the one who made the connection."

"And because you don't want me in trouble," Harrison said.

I nodded. "I'm afraid that target on my back is now built for two."

CHAPTER FIVE

I WAS UP EARLY THE NEXT MORNING, READY TO GET GOING on the investigation. I placed a call to the Heberts first—my friends with a friend—and asked if they'd call in another favor from their contact at the DNA lab client who'd processed a test for me before. Little called back in a matter of minutes letting me know the whole thing was arranged and I was welcome to drop off the samples at any time. So the only thing I was waiting on was the other sample from Blanchet.

He'd already sent a text this morning asking if I wouldn't mind picking him up from the hospital when they released him, which was fine by me. The sooner he got that sample, the sooner I could get this ball rolling. And once he got me that original police report, then I'd be able to see if anyone was still around Mudbug from back then that I could question.

The big one, of course, was identifying the girl, but that was Blanchet's purview, and I knew he'd be on that the instant he walked out of the hospital. Harrison and Ida Belle were planning a run into the bayou again at first light, so if there was anything to be found on that end of things, she'd let me know. So unfortunately, after I finished my call with the

Heberts, I was left with absolutely nothing to do and the energy to move mountains.

Story of an investigator's life.

I made use of the free time by feeding Merlin and unloading the dishwasher and spent all that time wondering where Carter was and how things were going. My biggest concern was that the military hadn't been up-front about the mission. I had personal experience with government agencies and their 'need to know' policies, and they were never favorable to the person who didn't get to know.

My phone rang as I put the last dish away, and I saw Blanchet's name come up on the display.

"You need to get down here and straighten this doctor out," he said as soon as I answered.

"What's wrong?"

"He won't release me! That's what's wrong. My head is just fine. I've had worse cuts from a house cat. Hell, that cat yesterday almost shot us."

"So why won't he let you out?"

"He'll let me out of the hospital, but he won't release me to work. Says he has concerns about my heart. Some irregular rhythm BS he's pushing. Wants to do more tests, and all that takes time. Time I don't have."

He sounded stressed enough to give himself a heart attack, so I grabbed my keys and wallet and headed for the door. "I'm on my way. Just hold tight and we'll figure it out. Don't go shooting people."

"They took my gun when they admitted me. Communists."

I made the drive to the hospital in record time—not Ida Belle record time, but fast for me and my Jeep. Blanchet had been moved to a regular room and was stomping around like a soldier going to war when I walked in.

As soon as he saw me, he threw his hands in the air. "That

doctor still hasn't made it in here. What kind of hours do these people work? I've got a parish to protect, and they're holding me here like I'm going to keel over in the next ten minutes. If it was so serious, why isn't he here already?"

"Let me go check."

I headed for the nurses' station and found a harried-looking nurse who gave me a suspicious look. I had a feeling she'd recently been on the receiving end of Blanchet's anger.

"I'm a friend of Andy Blanchet and was wondering if there's a way to contact his doctor."

She sighed. "I've already told Mr. Blanchet that his doctor is in surgery and will make his rounds as soon as he's out."

"Any estimate on that—one hour, ten? Just trying to get an idea how long I need to contain him because I know he's not making this easy on you. In his defense, he's been appointed temporary sheriff while Carter LeBlanc is out of the country, and he's worried about not fulfilling his job duties, especially as he just started yesterday. You know how these old-school guys are about responsibility to the public."

She softened a little and gave me a grateful look. "Reminds me of my father a little, which is both a good and a bad thing. I know it's frustrating, but it was an emergency surgery, so no parameters were set as far as time beforehand. However, given what the doctor's specialty is, and the fact that he's already been in there for two hours, I'm guessing that he'll finish up soon, maybe within the next hour. I'll make sure Mr. Blanchet is first on his list to see."

"I really appreciate it."

"Good luck with the containment, and God bless you."

I smiled and headed back to Blanchet's room, bracing myself for the next round of complaining.

At least he'd stopped pacing and was sitting on the couch. I sat in the chair nearby and explained the emergency surgery situation, that it should be soon, and that the nurse had assured me he was at the top of the list.

"I'm sorry you had to start off your morning dealing with me," he said. "I know you've got bigger things to do than handle middle-aged man drama."

"Don't tell Gertie that. She thinks *she's* middle-aged."

"Ha! No way I would want to live that long. Especially if visits like this one are in my future. You get past a certain age and doctors always want to run some test and question your eating habits, exercise, and work-life balance. Meanwhile, the only guy I know who dropped dead in his forties was a marathon runner, a vegetarian, and a trust fund baby. DNA speaks louder than lifestyle."

"Probably true. And you're in good shape, and retired mostly, so the doctor shouldn't have a problem with you. I'm sure it's just a cautionary thing."

"The darned attorneys have ruined simplicity."

I heard a knock on the door and a second later, the door opened and a young man walked in.

Five foot ten. A hundred seventy pounds. Excellent muscular definition and low body fat. His purposeful stride said doctor, but his face said he was thirteen, max. High threat to Blanchet. Zero threat to me, except by way of not releasing Blanchet.

"I'm Dr. Yoshida," he said as he approached. "I'm the head of the cardiac unit at the hospital."

Blanchet blinked, and I knew what he was thinking but hoped he didn't voice it.

"My tennis shoes are older than you."

And he voiced it.

Dr. Yoshida looked slightly peeved, and I guessed that he probably dealt with that perception a lot, especially given that heart issues lent themselves to older generations more than younger.

"I assure you, I have the education and experience necessary for my job," he said. "I've reviewed your tests and stats from the ER, and there's an irregularity in your heartbeat that concerned the ER doctors. That's why they asked me to take a look. Have you been informed of that irregularity before?"

Blanchet shook his head. "I get a physical every year and no one's ever said a thing. If it was a problem, shouldn't I have symptoms?"

"Have you experienced any light-headedness or felt tightness in your chest or difficulty breathing?"

"Not at all."

Dr. Yoshida frowned. "But you were brought into the ER because you passed out."

"I didn't pass out. I tripped over some rope and banged my head and knocked myself out."

Dr. Yoshida nodded. "That's good. It wasn't clear in the report. I'd like to do a stress test and an EKG just to rule out anything serious."

"Great. So can I come back for those in a few weeks?"

"No. I'd rather get them scheduled today before you're released."

"Fine. But then you'll release me for work."

"I need to see what the test results are first."

The door opened and I looked over as Vince Hermes, a deputy in a neighboring parish, entered the room. We'd never met in person, but Carter had shown me a picture while he'd described just how big an a-hole the guy was.

Midforties but looked older, six foot tall, two hundred sixty pounds, muscle tone sketchy, bum right knee and left shoulder, wearing a superior look that even Dr. Yoshida probably couldn't manage. Physical threat level practically nonexistent for me. Threat level extremely high for Blanchet and everyone else in the parish given Blanchet's current non-released status.

"Blanchet," he said with a nod. "You've looked better."

"I've *always* looked better than you, Herpes."

Vince's jaw flexed.

"Oh, sorry," Blanchet said. "Air-pez."

Dr. Yoshida looked at the two men and apparently decided he was done with the room. He gave me a nod and headed out. Hermes looked over at me and raised one eyebrow.

"Are you part of the package when someone is sheriff?"

"You couldn't even handle me in an arm-wrestling match."

Blanchet chuckled and Hermes gave him a death stare.

"Well, I'm here to relieve both of you of your duties," he said. "My understanding is you're not released for work, and we can't let the sheriff's position go unattended."

"I'll be released this afternoon," Blanchet said. "And you don't even live in the parish."

"Don't have to when the governor makes a phone call, but then, you know that. And the parishes finally ended a dispute over the area where my house is, so technically, I *am* a resident of the parish now."

He grinned. "That makes me eligible to run for sheriff in the upcoming election, so I figured getting some saddle time in early would set me up nicely for when I take the position."

I desperately wanted to slam him in the face with the bedpan, but I knew I couldn't. For Carter's sake, I had to be on my best behavior. But it was taking every bit of self-control not to shoot off my mouth, which would probably be worse than the bedpan maneuver.

"You'll never beat Carter in that election," Blanchet said. "I don't care who your friends are. The residents of this parish know who has their best interests in mind. The only interests you have are your own."

"Really? If Carter is so concerned about the residents of this parish, then why did he leave?"

I clenched my jaw. "Because unlike you, he has abilities that no others possess, and those who have them sometimes have obligations larger than themselves or their parish."

Hermes shrugged. "His loss, my gain. Anyway, I just figured I'd stop by here on the way to Sinful and let you know your services are no longer needed." He gave me an up-and-down. "If you're interested in providing any services, you know where to find me."

Blanchet grabbed my wrist and squeezed, and that was the only reason I didn't clock him. Hermes gave me a smug smile and then headed out.

"Why didn't you let me hit him?" I asked. "He was sexually harassing me, and he's in a position of power."

"He's also buddies with the ADA. They play golf every Friday. And he's a distant cousin of the governor."

"You've got to be kidding me! Although I don't know why I'm surprised. He and the ADA are cut from the same cloth."

Blanchet nodded. "Butt cloth."

"What are we going to do?"

Blanchet shook his head, clearly miserable. "I don't think there's anything we can do. If the governor handed down the edict, then your mayor has been overruled. This is the last thing Carter needed. I feel horrible about it. If I hadn't banged my head, none of this would have happened."

"Maybe, maybe not. I mean, you just banged your head last night and Hermes has already got the slot. My guess is he was working that angle long before yesterday."

He blew out a breath. "You're probably right. As soon as he heard Carter was leaving, I'm sure he was in his cousin's ear. But my situation hasn't helped matters. It just made it easier for him to grab the seat. Let's just hope the governor didn't agree to anything more than a temporary fill for Carter."

I bit my lower lip. "Do you think he'd replace Carter until the election?"

"I guess that depends on how much Hermes has on his cousin. No one holds a high political position without some skeletons."

"God, I hate politics."

Blanchet nodded. "I'm going to stick around even though I can't officially do the job. I want to keep an eye on Hermes and be on hand to help with the investigation. But you and your friends need to watch your back. Warn Harrison. Hermes will be more concerned with getting the dirt on you to use against Carter than policing the parish."

"Do you want Harrison to risk pulling the old case file on Maya and Lara?"

"No. Tell him not to go anywhere near that case for his own protection. I kept my own book, and it's got everything the police file had plus my thoughts. We'll work from that. Hermes will be watching, though."

"He'll have to find me first. I have a guy lined up who will do the DNA test. I just need your sample."

"Okay, then let's get that done first. Maybe we'll find out all of this is nothing."

I nodded but didn't think that was the case. I had that feeling I got when something big was about to break loose.

That familiar and unsettling feeling that nothing was what it seemed.

———

BECAUSE HE WAS STUCK IN THE HOSPITAL UNTIL ALL THE tests were completed, Blanchet gave me the keys to his house and combination to his safe, which was where the hair sample and his notebook were. I headed there straight from the hospital, calling Harrison on the way to fill him in on the situation with Blanchet and Hermes and warned him not to even peek at the old case file. Blanchet lived outside the city limits about twenty miles north of the hospital, so it was a good hour and a half before I made it to the lab and dropped both samples off to the Heberts' guy.

He promised to put a rush on it and said he'd call as soon as he had results. I headed home, eager to crack open Blanchet's notebook. I should have figured he'd have his own file, but he'd been so worked up the night before, I guess he hadn't thought to mention it or figured I would assume he had one. Either way, I was glad to have it because there was no way I wanted Harrison sticking his neck out on anything now that Hermes had taken over.

I'd just sat down at my kitchen table with a water and the notebook when my front door opened and Ida Belle called out. Then I heard the stomping of multiple sets of feet down the hallway and seconds later, Ida Belle, Gertie, and Harrison walked in. I took one look at Harrison's red face and clenched jaw and knew he'd met Hermes.

"I take it you've met our new sheriff," I said.

"I swear to God it took everything I had not to shoot him where he stood," Harrison said. "He's put me on traffic duty and restricted my access to everything, so it's a good thing you didn't want those files."

I shook my head. "If it makes you feel any better, he asked if I came along with the sheriff's position. And I don't think he wanted me for traffic duty."

Ida Belle whistled and Gertie let out a strangled cry.

"I'm surprised *you* didn't shoot him," Harrison said.

"Well, I was in the hospital and there was oxygen. Plus, Blanchet grabbed my wrist before I could clock him. Blanchet also called him Herpes, which I appreciated."

I filled them in on what Blanchet had told me about our new nemesis and his connections with our esteemed governor and the ADA. I was sure if anyone snapped a photo of the moment, we all looked like we'd just come from a funeral. I prayed that wouldn't end up being the truth.

"This is the worst possible outcome," Ida Belle said.

"Is there anything we can do?" Harrison asked.

"*You* are going to write traffic tickets and avoid me like the plague, at least for all appearances."

I held up a hand before he could start shouting. "It only helps Carter's case for the election if he can point out that Hermes reassigned a former CIA operative to traffic duty when you were far more qualified to handle serious crimes. It's a gross allocation of human assets."

"She's right," Ida Belle said. "And that's a really good spin for Carter, especially if anything happens and Hermes isn't able to handle it because he assigned everyone who was a threat to him to entry-level jobs."

"Maybe we should commit some crimes that Hermes can't handle," Gertie said.

I stared. It was an absurd and totally Gertie suggestion.

Also, not the worst one I'd heard.

"I'm fine with it," I said. "But I don't think we'll have to go out of our way to create trouble. It usually presents itself. So when it does, instead of attempting to defuse, we up the ante."

"Given Nora's party tonight, I'm sure opportunity will present soon," Ida Belle said. "What about the Blanchet investigation?"

"Still moving forward, just obviously without any official help."

I told them about the DNA tests under way and showed them Blanchet's notebook.

"Did you even get to do your bayou search this morning?" I asked.

"We were out there when his lordship Hermes called me in and told me I was off the case," Harrison said.

"Did you find anything?"

"We didn't get a chance to look for long," Ida Belle said. "But I figured you, me, and Gertie could head out and do our own check. Hermes can't tell us where to fish. I printed off some aerial shots of the bayous there and marked the nearest camps."

"Good. And I want to talk to Kenny."

Gertie grinned. "Can't stop us from taking a casserole to a friend in need either."

I looked at Harrison. "Do you know if there's been any progress on identifying the girl?"

He shook his head. "I checked before we headed out into the bayou but there are still no kids reported missing that match her description. At this point, we need her to wake up and give us a name."

"Worst case, if they can't find her parents, what do they do with her?" I asked.

"The hospital will release her to a Children and Family Services caseworker when she's got medical clearance. They'll place her in temporary foster care or a group home, depending on where they have a space."

"And who makes the decision to release her?"

"I'm guessing, given she's a minor and this could involve a crime, they're going to pass that call up the line at the hospital. Maybe even to the chief of staff. But they're probably going to rely heavily on what Cassidy says to make that decision. They always rely on her when it's calls about children."

I nodded, feeling a tiny bit of relief that Cassidy would have some input. "I'm not going to borrow trouble on that one. Until we know something happened to her parents, we'll assume the best."

Harrison nodded, but I could tell by his expression that he was worried about the parents as well. The girl wasn't a teen who'd lied about her whereabouts so she could sneak out and drink with her boyfriend. This was a young child who had no reason or means to be where she'd been found. And so far, no one had reported her missing.

Which begged the question—where were her parents?

CHAPTER SIX

HARRISON LEFT FOR TRAFFIC DUTY, AND IDA BELLE, GERTIE, and I decided to pay a visit to Kenny first to make sure we had all the details from him, then we'd head out into the bayou and see if we could pick up anything new. Gertie always had a casserole on hand, so she grabbed one from her freezer and we stopped off at Ally's bakery to pick him up a box of cookies. Kenny's middle section gave away his sugar addiction, so I figured we'd be well received.

It took Kenny a while to answer his door, and I wondered for a minute if he had even made it home yet, but finally, we heard shuffling inside. When the door swung open, I saw immediately what the problem was—Kenny had been treated to too many rounds the night before at the Swamp Bar. He stared at us and blinked a couple times before appearing to focus. Then he gave us a tiny smile, which looked like it hurt to manage, and gave us a slow and deliberate wave inside.

"We brought you a casserole and some cookies from Ally's bakery," Gertie said.

He grimaced. "I appreciate it, but it might be a bit until I get around to them. The boys took care of me a little too well last night, I'm afraid. At least Whiskey gave me a ride home this morning."

We followed him into the kitchen, and he waved toward the counter. "I just put on a pot of coffee and got out a bottle of aspirin. Can I offer you either?"

We declined both but insisted Kenny sit before he fell over. Gertie stuck his casserole in the refrigerator, and Ida Belle got him a cup of coffee and the aspirin bottle.

"I really appreciate you taking over with the girl," he said. "Didn't get to thank you last night. What a shock...I keep wondering if God is trying to tell me to stop fishing."

"Fish are one of the most popular dishes in the Bible," Gertie said. "I think maybe God's just using you because you're there and you're a good person."

"That makes me feel a bit better. Have you heard anything about the girl? Is she all right? Do you have any idea what happened?"

"The girl is stable but still unconscious. But no one has come forward to claim her, so we have no idea what happened."

"That's the darnedest thing. How do you just lose a kid that young and you're not looking for them?"

"We're a little concerned about that as well. We're going to head into the bayou after we leave here and see if we can find anything—maybe the parents were using someone's camp or something? Anyway, we wanted to check with you first to make sure we have the locations right and see if you remembered anything else since you talked to Deputy Harrison."

He described the location where he pulled the girl in, and Ida Belle nodded. That was the same location he'd given last night.

"Did you see any other fishermen? Any boats at all? Someone who might have seen something?"

He shook his head. "I mean, I saw several of the regulars a couple hours before, but not many are going to choose night fishing over a good party, and there's plenty of that going on right now. I can drink any time and figured that meant the good spots wouldn't be crowded. Guess it would have been better if they had been.

"But now that you mention it, I did hear a boat right before I hauled in the girl. Not sure how far away it was. Sounded fairly close, but you know how sound carries."

"You couldn't see any running lights?"

He frowned. "No. And I should have. The trees don't start until farther up that bayou. Everything in front of me was open marsh, and the light reflects back off the water pretty good, even small lights."

Someone had been running without lights, which was fool-hardy at best, deadly at worst.

"Do you know any of the people with camps in that area?" I asked.

"Probably know them all, or the families at least, since those places get passed down. But I didn't recognize the girl. Not that I know every child or grandchild attached to someone in Sinful, but grilling out is a big deal around here in the summer. You see a lot of peoples' extended families over a hot dog and a burger."

I nodded. Even though I was people-averse and rarely had reason to be around kids, I still knew I'd never seen the girl before. And with Ida Belle, Gertie, and Ronald all agreeing, I was convinced she wasn't related to any locals, at least not close enough to make the summer rounds.

I was just about to wrap things up when someone banged on Kenny's front door, causing him to grimace.

"Who the heck is knocking like that?" He rose from the table, and we followed since we were done talking with him.

"Everyone I know has better manners than to bang on the door of a man with a hangover. That's the problem with the world today—we've lost all sense of propriety."

I nodded. There was plenty wrong with the world outside of a loss of manners and propriety, but it was definitely a contributing factor to the decline.

The banging started again, and he threw his hands up in the air as we headed for the door.

"Whoever this is better have something good to make up for all that racket."

I glanced back over at Ida Belle and Gertie and could tell we were already on the same page. And I didn't figure the man on the other side of that door had anything but attitude. Kenny didn't manage the angry door swing he was going for—his balance was still off—but he did accomplish an Oscar-level dirty look.

Hermes barely glanced at Kenny before his gaze settled on me.

"I'd heard you were always in police business. Well, since you're not sleeping with the guy in charge anymore, that's all going to change. Unless you want to adjust our relationship."

Kenny puffed up his already somewhat puffy chest and for a minute, I thought he was going to slam the door in Hermes's face. Something I would have paid good money to see.

"Who the hell are you?" Kenny asked. "You've got about two seconds to apologize to my guest, then leave."

"Didn't they tell you? I'm Sheriff Hermes, so you can't order me anywhere. And if Ms. Redding has a problem with my assessment of her inappropriate insertion into police business, then she can take that up with the ADA or perhaps the governor. I have both of them on speed dial."

Kenny glanced over at me, clearly confused and still more than a little angry.

"I don't give a crap who you are," he said finally. "You're not going to insult a lady in my house. And I don't know nothing about your police business nonsense. These people are my friends, and they brought me food because I'm not feeling well and that's what good Baptists do. So you can take your insinuations and that attitude about women that's from the Stone Age and get it off my porch."

"Go, Kenny," Gertie said.

"Thanks, Kenny," I said. "But you can't fix stupid. I hope you get to feeling better."

Ida Belle nodded. "As soon as fake Sheriff Herpes releases your boat, Walter will make sure it gets back to your slip."

Kenny started laugh-choking at the 'herpes' comment and barely managed a nod. Hermes glared at all of us, then whirled around and stalked off.

"What the heck is going on?" Kenny asked as Hermes peeled out like a petulant teen as he drove away.

I gave a brief description of the situation, and Kenny frowned. "I hope he don't cause any problems for Carter. We don't need the likes of him around here."

"Well, I'm afraid you're going to have to deal with him sooner or later, as he's in charge now."

Kenny shrugged. "Then when my headache's gone, I'll head down to the sheriff's department and give a statement. But that man is not setting foot in my house. My daughter is one of those New Agers—always talking about positive and negative energy. I just ignore it mostly as I think it's a load of crap. But that guy—he makes me think there's something to this negative-energy thing."

"Thanks for talking with us, Kenny."

"You let me know if I can do anything else. I'll be praying for that girl and her family. And you guys, because if anyone is going to help her, it's going to be you. Assuming that idiot doesn't get in your way."

I nodded. I had the same worries.

———

THIRTY MINUTES LATER, WE HAD COLLECTED RAMBO, IDA Belle's super-smelling bloodhound, and were flying across the water in my airboat. What Kenny had said about hearing but not seeing the other boat bothered me, and Ida Belle and Gertie had agreed. The only reason to go without lights after dark was because you were an idiot, and the one thing people in Sinful weren't idiots about was boating after dark. Everyone had a backup light of some sort. Your buddy might be sitting on the bow with a flashlight, but by God, you didn't navigate these channels blind.

So it was far more likely that someone was intentionally running dark, and there was only one reason for that—they didn't want to be seen. The question was, did the girl fall out of the boat? Was she tossed out of the boat? Or were the people in the boat out looking for her? Then there was the other thing to take into consideration. The one that bothered us the most.

Only someone very familiar with these channels could successfully navigate them in the dark.

Ida Belle got us to the area where Kenny found the girl in record time, and I could see what he meant by the expansive view. From the entry to the bayou, you could easily see a good mile or so across marsh grass. A small craft might not be visible in the tallest of grass, but if it had lights on, the glow would have reflected up off the water and moved with the boat.

I looked down the bayou where the trees started. "Are there camps on this bayou?"

Ida Belle shook her head. "No. The ground on either side is too wet. No one wants to deal with the hassle of setting pilings in it. If you go up farther where it's firmer, the tide gets so low when it's out that you'd be dry-docked."

"And was the tide going out when he found the girl?"

"Should have turned about an hour before."

I nodded. "So unless she went into the water here and he found her quickly, we have to assume she went in farther up this bayou and floated down until she hung on something."

"My guess is the second. See that little offshoot just to your left—looks like the embankment reaches out a foot or so? There's a shrimping barge that got blown over here in a big storm and got stuck against the bank. The tide ripped the foam right off it and it sank. Would have taken a crane to get it out, so the owner just left it. That was back about ten years ago and since, erosion from the bank has built up around it. She was probably stuck there and his net pulled her loose."

"That makes sense. Well, the tide's in now, so let's head up the bayou and see if we can figure out an entry point."

Ida Belle directed the boat slowly up the bayou, and Gertie and I each took a side, scanning for any indication that the girl had passed that way.

"There!" Gertie shouted, and pointed. "I saw a flash of red."

Since the girl had been missing one red sneaker, I felt a sliver of hope pass through me as Ida Belle pulled up to the bank. I stuck a pole out to locate the ground in the watery grass and to make sure no alligators lurked nearby, then jumped over the muddy part to the solid bank. The water was up to my ankles when I landed, but I stepped away as soon as my feet connected, so they didn't have an opportunity to sink into the mud.

"A little more to your left," Gertie called as I walked.

I veered over a bit and spotted what had caught Gertie's eye and smiled. It was the missing red sneaker, partially embedded in some mud. I held up the shoe and Gertie cheered.

"Time for Rambo to do his thing," Ida Belle said.

Rambo, who'd been watching patiently from the side of the boat, smelling the air, must have felt the change in energy and now stood and started baying and wriggling. Ida Belle snapped his lead on, and I waded close enough to the boat to take the puppy from Ida Belle as she handed him over.

At four months old, Rambo was already a solid forty pounds, and his wriggling didn't make the transfer easy, but he'd already proven his ability as a tracker. If Rambo couldn't figure out where the girl had come from, then no one else would. I waded back to solid ground, then headed over to where the shoe was and let him take a good whiff.

"Rambo, track," Ida Belle called out, and the dog took off at a steady trot right through the center of the marsh. We were going too fast for me to spot many indications that someone had recently passed this way, but I didn't doubt the dog's abilities for a second. Every once and a while, when he slowed, I'd spot an area of bent or broken grass, until finally, we reached a small clearing and he paused.

Trails extended out from the clearing in every direction, which was normal as the nutria that lived in the swamp were huge and created their own pathways. I figured Rambo now had competing smells, so I gave him another whiff of the shoe. He walked around the clearing, smelling every path, then let out a long bay and set off down one of them that led toward the tree line.

Rambo stuck to the path as we progressed, and it occurred to me that the girl must have been fleeing someone through the marsh. At first, she'd been able to follow the nutria trail but at some point, she'd lost the light or had panicked and run off the trail. The shoe had likely gotten stuck in the grasping black mud and she'd run out of it and kept going. Which meant she hadn't had the time to stop and retrieve it.

Which made me all kinds of angry.

I scanned the marsh, but as far as my eye could see there was only grass until the cypress trees began. No camps were in sight at all yet. So either the girl had come from a boat or she'd managed to run a good distance. Either way, I couldn't imagine how terrified she must have been and prayed that she'd wake up soon and could tell police who was behind this. Because unless she could name names, maybe even give an address and phone number, I had my doubts that Hermes would accomplish anything.

Ida Belle had been tracking me parallel on the bayou but she was too far away to yell, so I pulled out my cell phone.

"Rambo has picked up a trail that heads toward the tree line, but it's veering away from the channel you're on. Where's the nearest camp?"

"About a hundred yards over is the next channel. The nearest camp is off that, maybe thirty yards into the tree line."

"Okay, I'm going to stay on the ground with Rambo to make sure we don't lose the trail. But go ahead and move the boat to that channel. Sounds like that's where we're going."

Ida Belle spun the boat around and took off as Rambo and I continued down the trail. He was young and full of energy and certainty, so I let him move at his own pace and relaxed into a slow jog to keep up with him. When we hit the tree line, we were about thirty yards from the bank of the second channel, and Ida Belle was already there, slowly coasting so she and Gertie could scan for clues. When we reached the trees, I motioned for her to continue and I followed the hound into the woods.

It didn't take long to reach the first camp, and Rambo set up a howl as he tried to scramble up the steps to the structure. This was definitely where the girl had been hiding or held. I looked toward the bayou and could just make out a dock through the trees. I managed to pull a frustrated Rambo away from the steps and headed for the dock. Ida Belle had already stopped there, and she and Gertie gave me an expectant look.

"This is the place," I said as I tried to console the upset hound.

Ida Belle nodded. "I figured since he's pitching a fit."

"Who owns it?"

"Nickel."

"Really?" Nickel was Whiskey's brother and also part owner of the Swamp Bar. But his penchant some years back for electing trouble over work got him five years in prison, hence the nickname.

He'd been out a while now and seemed to be toeing the line as far as the law went. In fact, he'd even been a client of mine. He was helping at the bar now, but my understanding was that he spent most of his time taking care of their father, who was terminal but still hanging on despite doctor's predictions to the contrary. Either way, it was a load off Whiskey, who'd carried it all for too long.

I pulled out my cell phone and Nickel answered right away.

"Did you dump Carter and you're calling me for a date?"

"Not yet."

He laughed. "Just as well. I'm pretty sure I'm more scared of Carter than I am attracted to you. So what can I do for you?"

"You heard about Kenny finding that girl in the marsh?"

"Whiskey called me while he was pouring up shots for Kenny, asking me to put some feelers out. I called everyone I could think of, but no one has heard about a kid going missing. Whiskey said he didn't recognize her."

"No one has so far, and Ida Belle and Gertie were there with me."

"Well, if those two don't know her then she's definitely not from around here. I wish I could help, but I'm afraid I don't know anything."

"You might be able to help. I'm out in the marsh now trying to figure out how she arrived at the location where Kenny found her, and Ida Belle's bloodhound led me straight to your camp. Do you mind if I poke around?"

"Go for it. There's a fish cleaning station under the camp with a sink. Got one of those magnetic box things on the bottom of it with a key. If that girl was there, I want to know about it."

"When was the last time you were here?"

"Hmmmmm, been a while. I was there after Thanksgiving and meant to go around Christmas, but never made it. I'd say two months or better. Let me know if you find anything you shouldn't."

"I will. I appreciate it."

"Any time."

By the time I finished the call, Ida Belle and Gertie had gotten the boat secured and were on the dock with me.

"Nickel told me where to find the key and said help ourselves. Said Whiskey called and filled him in last night and he made some calls, trying to get a line on the girl, but came up with nothing."

Gertie nodded. "That boy sure has done a turnaround for the better."

"Seems like," I said as we headed for the camp. "He hasn't been to the camp since December, best he can remember."

"Then let's see if anyone else has."

Nickel had built a wooden walkway from the pier to the camp, so there was no way to tell if someone had passed there recently. I located the key where he'd indicated, and we headed upstairs to the camp, Rambo setting up a howl before we ever stepped inside. As soon as I opened the screened porch door, I knew why. The front door to the camp was open. Not swung fully open, but opened even a crack wasn't what I was supposed to find.

Ida Belle quieted Rambo as she tied him to a porch post. I pulled out my weapon and motioned for them to take position behind me. I slipped across the porch to the side of the door, my back against the wall, then mule-kicked the door all the way open before peering around, gun leveled.

Nothing moved inside the camp, and the only sounds I could hear were the rushing water of the bayou and Gertie breathing behind me. I stepped inside the door, flicked on the lights, and scanned the big room that appeared to serve as kitchen, dining room, living room, and bedroom. But unless someone was hiding in a cabinet, it was empty.

I waved toward the kitchen, and Ida Belle and Gertie headed that way to make sure it was clear. I crept over to the door on the back wall, assuming it led to the bathroom. I didn't hear anything as I approached, but the light from the front room filtered into the opening. I whirled around the doorway into the bathroom and lowered my weapon. The shower curtain was pulled back and the tub was empty. The vanity cabinet was an open style with shelves and the hamper was open and contained a single towel.

I walked back into the front room. "Anything?"

"There's wrappers for frozen burritos and pizza in the

trash," Gertie said. "There's more of the same in the freezer and I assume by the dates on them that it was stuff Nickel stocked here. There's a six-pack in the refrigerator that hasn't been touched."

"Any clothes?"

Ida Belle had been checking under the bed and rose, shaking her head. "No clothes, bags, nothing personal."

"There's one towel in the hamper," I said.

"Nickel would have hauled laundry out with him," Ida Belle said.

Gertie shrugged. "He's a man, and a young one at that."

"Not even young men like the smell of mildew or throwing away perfectly good towels," Ida Belle argued.

"You'd be surprised at what young men will choose over doing laundry," Gertie said, "but he wouldn't have gone without taking the trash with him. Those wrappers will attract ants at best. At worst, other things."

I stepped back to the door and squatted, checking the doorframe. "No sign of forced entry. And there's no scrapes on the lock. Did you check the windows?"

"They're all locked and all the blinds are down," Gertie said. "But then, if someone came in an open window, they could have locked it behind them and drawn the blinds."

"Twenty bucks says you couldn't open one of those windows if you wanted to," Ida Belle said. "Looks like they've been painted over more than once."

"Let's give it a try."

The room only contained four windows and the bathroom none, but a quick check showed that Ida Belle had been correct. Even if all the windows had been unlatched, it would have taken a crowbar to get them up. Which meant that whoever had entered the camp had done it through the front door. And there was every indication that person had used a key.

"Get Rambo in here," I said. "Her smell is probably everywhere, but maybe he can find something we missed."

Ida Belle nodded and went out to retrieve the hound. As soon as she brought him in and released him, he scrambled around the camp, sniffing every inch and baying as he went, signaling that the girl had been inside. Then he went into the bathroom and really set up a howl and started digging the bathroom rug.

Ida Belle called him off and I rolled the rug back. It looked like the same worn wood slats as the rest of the camp, but then I spotted what appeared to be a knothole but was a little too precise. I stuck my finger in and triggered a latch and then pulled the piece up. As I suspected, directly below it was an old wooden ladder I'd seen leaning against a piling that stood behind some sheets of old plywood. It looked as if it was simply stored there, but now we knew better.

"Why would Nickel have an escape hatch?" I asked.

"Drugs," Ida Belle said. "He probably kept things stored here or did them here and figured if the law rode up, he had a way to get out and dispose of everything so they couldn't find it."

Since he did five years over the stuff, I guessed it wasn't as successful as he'd originally thought. But he also hadn't gone to the trouble of closing it up, and Rambo's response made it clear that the girl had exited the camp this way. The question was, why? Who was coming in that forced her to flee?

I closed up the door and put the rug back. "Wait here. I'm going to go downstairs and see if I can trigger that door from underneath."

The keyhole hadn't appeared to go all the way through, which wouldn't have been optimum from an insect and mouse standpoint, but I wanted to make sure there wasn't a second way to trigger opening. It only took a quick look at the bottom of the trapdoor to see there was no release underneath. So it was definitely constructed to be a one-way sort of deal. I headed back inside and told them what I'd found.

"Let's lock up," I said. "I want to check farther up the bayou and see if we can find a boat. That girl might have gotten out of the camp through that hatch, but she didn't come in that way. And she didn't walk here."

Gertie nodded. "I'm going to grab that trash and the towel. Nickel's got his hands full with his dad, and we're already here."

"I'm sure he'll appreciate it," Ida Belle said.

We got secured in the boat and then cruised slowly up the bayou until the water got too low, but we hadn't spotted anything along the way.

Ida Belle shook her head. "That girl did not materialize in Nickel's camp, and she was clearly running from someone to have wound up where she did. And the only way she could have gotten there was by boat. So where is the person who brought her? And why did they leave her?"

"Maybe the girl got away and that person didn't," I said. "And if the people looking for them found them here, then they would have taken their boat as well. But we have one answer—where she was staying."

"But a million more questions," Gertie said. "Story of our lives."

"Sure seems that way," I agreed. "We've found all we can out here. Let's head back in. I need to be ready to pick up Blanchet when he calls. If I leave him waiting too long, he might burn the place down."

I pulled out my cell phone and called Nickel. He was shocked to hear what we'd discovered.

"How many people know where you keep the key?"

"Everyone and their cousin. I ain't ever had no problems out there. I mean, sure, people have stopped off when they got out in a bad storm, but most people leave a note and a couple bucks if they eat or drink anything."

"And the hatch? Does everyone know about that too?"

"Heck, I don't know. It was mentioned in a police report from one of my arrests, but that's some deep digging on someone if they found it. Guess I should nail it up, right? And definitely change the lock. But then, if that girl was trying to get away from someone, sounds like that hatch got her gone."

"It does."

"Man, I don't want any part of this. Do you know what kind of hassle it is for a young, single guy with a criminal record to be linked up with anything to do with an underage female? Might as well tie an anchor around me and toss me in the bayou."

If Carter was here or Blanchet was still in charge, I would have disagreed, at least from the police perspective. But with Hermes running the show, I had no doubt that he'd zero in on Nickel just to save himself the hassle.

"Is this guy filling in for Carter going to be a problem?" he asked.

"Loaded question." I explained the situation with Blanchet and Hermes, and he launched into a ranting and cussing fit that was both creative and impressive.

"I know that a-hole Hermes. A buddy of mine got two years because of him and his trumped-up 'investigation.' That guy is lazy and corrupt, and he'll throw someone under the bus to fluff up his résumé."

"Yeah, I got that impression, and I'm not breathing a word of what we found. I'm already in neck-deep taking that shoe, and Hermes is just looking for a reason to arrest me and score some points with his buddy, the ADA."

Nickel launched into another round of impressive cursing.

"Look, I know you had nothing to do with this situation," I said. "So unless Hermes gets his lazy butt into the bayou and pokes around, he's not going to find out the girl was at your camp. Gertie got the trash and the towel, so there's no signs that anyone has been there. The only way he'd know she was there is to take prints."

He blew out a breath. "Okay. That makes me feel a little better. I appreciate it. I knew you were a good one, Redding, but you always seem to be taking things up a notch."

"I have the luxury of only being interested in the truth. But just in case Hermes surprises us, do you have an alibi for last night?"

"What time?"

"Honestly, I have zero idea. Say a couple hours before the girl was found maybe?"

"That was around eight, right? I was with Pop. The day nurse that makes rounds left around six, maybe. I talked to a buddy about fishing a bit after that, then fixed dinner for Pops, but he dropped off before I was even done cooking."

"Could anyone else vouch for you being there?"

"Don't see how. Can't see his place from any others, and even if someone came by and saw my truck out front, my boat's docked out back."

"Then the nurse and the phone call will have to do. Try not to worry about this. If things take a turn with Hermes, there's plenty of people who'd say straight out that there's no way you'd leave your dad there alone."

He sighed. "Once you've been inside, that seems to be the only thing everyone sees. Man, if I could go back in time and kick my own butt... Thanks for checking on this, and tell Ms. Gertie thanks for taking that stuff out."

"I will. And in the meantime, you stay put and pretend this conversation never happened. If for any reason your phone records come into question, then you say I called you to check on your dad and then called back to ask you about your fried fish batter recipe. Go ahead and text it to me, just in case."

"Got it."

I disconnected and slipped my phone into my jeans. That was, at least, the beauty of small-town living. No one needed much of a reason to drop by a house or make a phone call, so cops had a much harder time making implications based on location, conversation, or the company you were keeping. It was often like one big family reunion. Unfortunately, every family had those members who spoiled things for the rest of the group. I'd already unearthed a few of them since I'd arrived in Sinful and had no doubt others would come. I just hoped this case didn't involve my extended family.

Especially with Carter gone.

CHAPTER SEVEN

WE HAD JUST DOCKED THE BOAT WHEN MY PHONE WENT off, signaling a call from Blanchet. He sounded as peeved as ever, but said his tests were clear and I needed to come get him the hell out of that place. I couldn't blame him for being upset. If he hadn't been in the hospital, Hermes might not have had the ammunition to get the placement. But we couldn't exactly go back and redo things. If we could, I'd be tempted to ask Carter to turn down the military altogether, but then, that wouldn't be fair. Carter's sense of responsibility matched my own, and I knew his decision hadn't come lightly.

I made a quick change of jeans, socks, and shoes since I'd gotten my feet wet wading around with Rambo, then we headed for the hospital. Because the ER doctor was ordering the tests, they'd kept him in that wing, figuring it would probably take just as long to get him moved to a regular room as to get the tests done and let him go. When we walked into the lobby, I could hear arguing down the hall and recognized Hermes's and Blanchet's voices. Then Cassidy chimed in, and I rushed up to the desk.

"I'm here to pick up Andy Blanchet."

The nurse at the desk gave me a grateful look. "Good. Then maybe you can get him out of here. Dr. Williams has her hands full with that Hermes guy and Mr. Blanchet is making things worse. I've already called the chief of staff."

I gave Ida Belle and Gertie a grim look as we hurried through the door. Blanchet, Hermes, and Cassidy were all in the hallway, and it was clear from the red faces that no one was happy. Hermes looked over as we walked up and pointed a finger at us.

"You have no business here, so leave now or I'll arrest you."

"We're here to pick up Andy," I said. "If you can figure out how picking up a friend at the hospital is breaking a law, let me know."

"Then take him and leave. Because he's interfering in my investigation and that *is* against the law."

"This is not about your investigation," Cassidy said. "In fact, this is not about you at all and from my standpoint never will be. This is about the patient."

"Exactly," Hermes said. "And given her circumstances, she's a ward of the state. So someone from child services will be picking her up."

Cassidy took a step closer to Hermes and stared him right in the eye. "And I've already told you that girl is not leaving this hospital until I release her. And that will not be happening until I'm certain she is medically clear."

Hermes waved a hand in dismissal. "She's fine. She woke up, had breakfast... What else do you want?"

We all stared. She'd woken up?

If Cassidy had been armed, I was pretty sure she would have given the finger to the Hippocratic Oath. "She almost died," she said between clenched teeth.

"But she's fine now."

"You and I have very different definitions of fine. Fortunately, since you're not a doctor, yours isn't relevant."

"We'll see about that."

I could tell Blanchet was a second away from clocking Hermes when a man in a suit rounded the corner at the end of the hall and walked right up to us.

"This discussion is highly inappropriate to have in the ER hallway," he said, giving all of us dirty looks.

"This discussion is inappropriate to have at all," Cassidy said. "This 'man' is insisting I release the girl who was brought in last night to child services."

He stared at Cassidy for a moment, then blinked. "This is the emergency I was called out of a board meeting for?"

Hermes nodded. "And a good thing since this hospital is breaking the law. That kid is a ward of the state."

"The *child* needs medical supervision and is under my care," Cassidy said. "She's not going anywhere."

"I don't think you have the juice to make that call, little lady," Hermes said.

Suit guy cleared his throat as his gaze darted uncomfortably back and forth between Cassidy and Hermes.

"Sir, I don't care who you are and what authority you think you have," he said. "Dr. Williams is a pediatric specialist. Her assessment on this issue ranks higher than mine, and I'm chief of staff. But if you require someone with a more impressive title to draw that line in the sand for you, then hear this—I reviewed the child's case this morning both before and after she regained consciousness, and at this time, there's no way I'd release that girl to *anyone* except her parents. And even then, *not* until we've run more tests and are absolutely certain she's stabilized."

Hermes smirked. "Really? How much are you charging the taxpayers for her stay in the ER?"

"I'm certain the hospital can handle the cost of not throwing a child to the wolves."

"The system is not the wolves."

He gave Hermes a pointed look. "It's also not a hospital. Inside these walls, I am cop, judge, and jury. If Dr. Williams determines the girl can be released, then I'll review the situation with her, and we'll let you know. Until then, you have no further business here. So please show yourself out or I'll call security."

Hermes stared at him, his frustration, arrogance, and anger so clear, but he also knew he'd overplayed his hand. He had no authority here. If the chief of staff said no to something concerning patient care in a hospital, and it was in line with hospital policies, then that was final.

"You're going to regret this." Hermes gave us all a dirty look, then whirled around and stomped off.

The doctor looked over at us. "I'm sure your reach doesn't extend any further than his, so if you'd please make your way out so that we can get back to our jobs, I'd appreciate it."

Cassidy gave me a nod, and I motioned for the others to follow me as I started off. Cassidy and the chief of staff stood talking, their voices too low for me to hear what they were saying, but I felt relief course through me that Cassidy had prevented the girl from leaving the hospital. Unfortunately, I knew she couldn't divulge any information about the girl to me and not even Harrison, and neither of us would ask her to, but I knew the girl was conscious enough to have eaten—assuming Hermes was to be believed—and that was huge.

We remained silent until we climbed into Ida Belle's SUV, and then Blanchet launched into an explosive rant about Hermes and the seven hundred ways he needed to die. The rest of us just nodded until he finished. We all agreed with him.

"So did the girl really wake up?" Gertie asked when he stopped to take a breath.

"That's what I overheard some nurses saying in the hallway. I asked my attending and she said that she wasn't allowed to say anything but that since she knew I was the cop assigned when we brought her in, she'd just say that the girl seemed medically okay, at least physically, but that she had no memory at all. Not her name, parents, where she lived, how she got into the bayou. It's all gone."

"She could have banged her head on something in the water and gotten a concussion," Ida Belle said.

I nodded. "Any swelling could cause that problem. The almost-drowning could cause brain complications as well. I'm sure Cassidy will be thorough on the medical end of things and a mama bear when it comes to releasing her."

"Cassidy?" Blanchet asked. "You know her doctor?"

I smiled. "That's Deputy Harrison's fiancée, and trust me, she is no pushover."

Blanchet relaxed a bit and nodded. "That makes me feel a lot better. I got the immediate impression that she was going to protect the girl, but knowing she's Harrison's fiancée, which means she'll have heard all about Hermes, that takes a huge weight off."

I nodded. I felt the same way. But the reality was, once certain medical markers were met, Cassidy would have to relinquish custody to the state. And if the girl had no serious physical injuries, that time was probably going to be way sooner than any of us were comfortable with.

"I think we figured out where the girl was hiding." I told him what we'd found in the bayou, leaving Nickel's name out of it but telling him to make sure he never repeated any of it, as Hermes would definitely go hard after the camp owner, who I was certain wasn't involved.

Blanchet said as far as he was concerned, he didn't know nothing about anything and we'd never spoken. I figured as much, but a reminder is never a bad thing. We dropped him off at the Swamp Bar because that's where his truck was. He promised to head straight to Carter's house and stay there, but I had my doubts as to how good he'd be at actually doing it. Since he was sticking around Sinful but no longer had a job, I figured it might be better if I had eyes on him at least part of the time and invited him to Nora's party.

He said a cat with a loaded gun seemed appropriate at the moment, and he'd see us there. I felt bad for him as we drove off. I knew what it felt like to have your hands tied, but I also knew what might happen if you cut the ropes and did whatever you wanted. I'd managed to make it out of the CIA with my personal file glowing, but Director Morrow was definitely balder because of me. Blanchet had a pension on the line and couldn't afford to stick his neck out, or Hermes would chop it right off.

"What now?" Ida Belle asked as she headed back to town.

I shook my head. "I don't even know. The girl not having any memory is a huge curveball. We've got some time before we have to get ready for the party, though. In Blanchet's notebook, he had the name of the person who rented Maya and her daughter the room—Lottie Pendarvis. Do you guys know her?"

"I kind of know her," Gertie said. "Through knitting channels mostly. She's about my age, born, raised, married, and widowed in Mudbug. I haven't had a lot of dealings with her, and none in a couple years at least, but she's always seemed nice and on the normal side for these parts."

"You think she'd talk to us?"

"I don't see why she wouldn't. I probably have her number. Do you want me to give her a call or do you just want to drop by?"

I usually preferred the drop-by because then people couldn't prepare a lie and get it to a convincing point if they didn't know what was coming. But I couldn't think of anything this woman would have to hide, so I told Gertie to give her a buzz and ask if she could visit but not tell her why. Gertie made the call, and Lottie was happy to see us that afternoon.

We made the hike over to Mudbug and parked in front of Lottie's house. It was a two-story farmhouse build that sat close enough to downtown to walk if you were so inclined but on a street with big lots and huge oak trees that provided a ton of privacy for the residents. A detached garage sat off and back slightly from the house, and a staircase led to a door on the second floor. I assumed that was the place that Maya had rented.

The whole house and lawn were neat as a pin. Not a single weed in the flower beds or a speck of peeling paint on the white clapboard siding. The shutters were painted a soft yellow that I imagined matched flowers in the beds in spring. We headed onto the porch and knocked and a few seconds later, the door swung open and a woman peered out at us, smiling.

Eighty-ish. Five foot five. A hundred thirty pounds. Thick glasses. Inclined head to right side after greeting, so a bit hard of hearing in left ear. Stance showed signs of back and knee issues, but overall, in good health. No threat. But then, people who didn't know any better thought that looking at Gertie.

"Ladies, it's so good to see you. Please come in. I had just pulled my last batch of chocolate chip cookies out of the oven when you called and I made a pitcher of sweet tea this morning, so we're all set for our chat."

She looked at me as I stepped inside, and Gertie waved her hand at me. "This is our good friend, Fortune Redding. She's fairly new in Sinful."

Lottie's eyes widened. "That CIA gal? Well, this is a treat. Our knitting group has talked about you a lot. It's exciting to have a woman doing so much to keep us safe. And you not even on the city payroll. Come on back. I've got everything ready."

We headed back to a bright and cheery kitchen with light green cabinets and white countertops. Wallpaper with daisies hung on the rear wall of the dining area and fresh flowers graced the buffet and the center of the table. We all took seats, and Lottie hurried over to remove the arrangement from the table so it wasn't blocking our view, then started pouring the tea. A huge platter of cookies was already on the table and little plates and napkins were laid out.

"I spend too much money at the florist in the winter," she said, noticing Gertie admiring her flowers. "I put my own in here during the season, of course, but I miss having them when it gets all rainy and gloomy in the winter."

"They definitely brighten up a room," Gertie agreed. "I buy some myself every couple weeks or so. It will be spring before we know it, though. I'm already getting the catalogs."

Lottie nodded as she sat. "I've been working on my layouts. I like to change things up every year. Keeps it interesting. So I'm just dying to know why you wanted to visit. I know good and well you didn't just think of me out of the blue—and I mean no offense by that—just that we're more acquaintances than good friends, and Fortune here can't possibly want to spend her afternoon talking flowers with a bunch of old ladies."

"I'm horrible at gardening," I said, "but I am trying to learn. At least enough to keep my stuff alive. I like pretty things as long as it doesn't involve hair, makeup, or painted nails and toes."

Lottie laughed. "Well, there's flowers and there's weeds.

Whether they're pretty or not depends on who's looking at them. But the flowers usually require the most care, whereas the weeds are not only survivors but conquerors. There's beauty in that as well."

I smiled. "That's an interesting way of putting it. You seem like a very observant person, Ms. Pendarvis."

"Please, call me Lottie. And yes, I'd say I notice plenty. And the longer you're on this earth, the more you notice and the clearer it is what it means. Which is why I found myself excited after Gertie's call, because I'm hoping that you're on a job and I can help you make this town a better place. So what did you want to ask me about?"

I explained the situation with the girl and told her that the girl's appearance had shocked someone and I wanted to get her take on it. Then I asked if I could show her a picture.

"She's alive, though, right?"

I nodded. "She was unconscious when the picture was taken. She's a little bruised, but the image shouldn't cause you any distress. Now she's awake and appears to be okay."

I pulled up the picture I'd taken in the hospital and pushed my phone across the table. She lifted the phone up and gasped as she jerked her head up to stare at me, eyes wide.

"It can't be," she whispered.

"You recognize her?" I asked.

She shook her head. "It can't be her because the girl I knew would be a grown woman now, but it's like looking back in time." She studied the image again. "If you hadn't told me this was a recent picture, I would have sworn on my prizewinning azaleas that this was Lara Delgado."

She pushed the phone back over to me, and her expression shifted from astounded to sad. "You showed this to Andy Blanchet."

"Actually, he was there when the girl was found, but how did you know?"

"I heard he was filling in for Carter, and he would have seen what I see. And assuming he explained the extent of his relationship with the girl's mother, you would have wanted to make sure he saw what *was* and not what he wanted. Am I right?"

"Corroboration always helps, but he did have an old picture. And yes, the resemblance is uncanny. I hoped you could tell us about Maya and Lara."

"You think this girl is related?"

"We don't know, and unfortunately although she's under the hospital's care, she's technically a ward of the state because she has no memory and no one has stepped forward."

Lottie's eyes narrowed. "Her parents haven't been looking for her?"

"No children have been reported missing locally—at least not recently—and she doesn't match the description of any missing children already in the database."

Lottie shook her head. "No memory...how horrible. I can't imagine how frightened she must be."

"Plenty, I'm sure. And given the circumstances under which she was found, I'm worried about her safety when the hospital releases her. I know she'll go to an approved foster parent or a group home, but those people aren't really set up to cope with a potential kidnap situation."

Lottie's eye widened. "She was found in the bayou? Do you think she fell off a boat? Or jumped?"

"We have reason to believe she was hiding out in a camp, unbeknownst to the owner. But we have no idea why she was there, how she got there, or why she wound up unconscious in the bayou."

"Lord, what an ordeal. When I think about all the things that girl might have gone through."

"Andy Blanchet is convinced she's related to Maya, but then, he's got big personal stakes involved. I've agreed to look into it for him and for the girl's sake, but we don't have a lot of information on Maya and Lara. Blanchet tried to find them after they disappeared, but he was never able to dig anything up, which is strange, given the access he had to data back then."

Lottie nodded. "I always assumed Maya wasn't who she said she was. I had a cousin who had that look Maya wore when she knocked on my door and asked me about the rental. She was running from something. And it was clear that Lara was scared as well and had been coached not to give any information. She was the quietest child I've ever met."

"Did you ever get the impression she was scared of her mother?"

"Lord no! Maya doted on that girl, and you could see how deeply they loved each other, even when they were just playing outside in the yard. Whatever was going on in their lives, Maya was trying to fix it."

"And she never gave you any indication of where she came from?"

"No, but I don't think she was local. I mean, not originally. Maya's English was great, but she had a bit of an accent— which most people probably passed off as regional Creole or Cajun or just Southern drawl, but it wasn't any of those. If I had to guess, I'd say her first language was Spanish."

"What makes you think that?"

"Well, Delgado is Spanish, and even though surnames don't mean what they used to, sometimes she turned the letter *j* into a h. She was quick to catch herself and not make the same mistake again, but I think sometimes she just slipped into her default. It happened more often when she was really tired. I have a cousin married to a woman from Mexico, and she does the same thing."

"So an immigrant, maybe."

"Or first generation born here, and she learned Spanish before English. Lara didn't have that accent like her mother. Her speech was definitely from this area. If her last name had been Dupont or Laveau, everyone would have assumed she was Creole with that almost-black hair and darker skin tone."

"She never gave you any indication where she was from?"

"No...but I had my suspicions." Lottie looked over at Ida Belle and Gertie. "You ever heard of the Brethren?"

Ida Belle and Gertie glanced at each other, then nodded.

"But it's been ten years or better since I've heard anyone mention them," Ida Belle said.

"Who are the Brethren?" I asked.

"A religious group that lived or still lives deep in the bayous," Lottie said. "I mean, so deep that only their own people know where to find them. Most of what we heard about them was rumor because only one or two of them were allowed to come into town when they had to conduct business, and it was mostly always men. A woman only came twice that I heard of, and it was to buy women's supplies—material and women's products. I heard she didn't speak a word either time."

"Sounds like a cult," I said.

Lottie nodded. "That's what most people thought, which only made them more interesting to young people. I can't tell you how many times everyone headed out in their boats for a search-and-rescue over young people who thought they were going to find the Brethren and got turned around deep in the swamp."

"We had some of that in Sinful too," Gertie said. "It came

and went like a fad. For a couple years, it was all the rage, then it would die off and people wouldn't even talk about it. Then someone would tell a story to one of their kids and they'd get a group all fired up again."

"Did anyone ever find them?" I asked.

"Not that I'm aware of," Gertie said.

"You mean to tell me that somewhere out in the bayou, there's an entire village of people, and no one knows where to find them?"

"Probably more than one," Lottie said. "But the Brethren is the only one I've ever heard of around these parts."

I shook my head. "That's incredible. And you think Maya might have been part of that group? Why?"

"Her clothes, for one thing. They were several years behind current fashion. And before you say, maybe she was too poor to afford new clothes, that's exactly what I thought as well. Maybe they were hand-me-downs or purchased at Goodwill or the like, but the fabric was newer patterns and colors—it was just the style that was off. And that's when I realized they were all homemade. One of the first things Maya did after she started working was buy bolts of fabric and she'd sit out back in one of my lawn chairs and sew every evening. Made clothes for her and Lara completely by hand and beautifully done. And they were all current style."

I nodded, understanding her point. "So if she'd been kept away from society, she would have continued crafting clothes to match the last things she'd seen. When she was back among people, she brought their clothes up to current specs. You really are an excellent observer, Lottie."

She flushed a bit. "Always thought I would have made a good detective. Of course, women didn't do such jobs back when I was a girl." She nodded at Ida Belle and Gertie. "When these two and Marge went off to Vietnam, I thought hard on it for a bit. If those women could go to war, why couldn't I be police, especially as there was a shortage of able-bodied men at the time?"

"So why didn't you?"

"They say life is what happens while you're making other plans. I'd just married, and my husband was about to be deployed. I realized I was pregnant right before he left. That shifted everything."

"That would. So do you think the Brethren are still out there in the bayou?"

"No one's seen any in a decade or more that I'm aware of, but then, things along the bayou have grown up. They've got other options for shopping besides Mudbug. And I'm guessing they figured out that all they needed to do was head to a bigger city for the things they couldn't make for themselves, and no one would even look twice at them, which cut down on all that schoolboy hunting nonsense."

"That would mean they'd have transportation," Gertie said. "Can't take a boat everywhere. And what about gas for the boats and parts?"

Lottie nodded. "All good questions and things I've asked myself. But my momma insisted the Brethren were real and so did her friends. My nephew worked at the General Store here in Mudbug years ago and said he used to pack up boatloads of supplies for them a couple times a year. And that included a lot of cans of gas."

"What else did they buy?" Ida Belle asked.

"Stuff for sewing, medicine, tools...the kind of things you can't find out in the bayou. You know what the second thing I noticed about Maya was? Right after I locked in on her clothes?"

"What?" I asked.

"That she didn't have a cell phone. Maybe she couldn't

afford it, but a young woman on her own with a young child usually sprang for one as soon as she could, even twenty years ago."

"So how did she rent the place? If she was part of the Brethren, she couldn't have had much money, unless she took it when she left."

"Had cash. Didn't look like she had much, but I wasn't charging much either, especially after I laid eyes on her. I would have offered her the place for free, but I knew she wouldn't go for it. Probably would have just made her wonder what I was up to. I wanted her safe, so I rented for half what I was asking, but then she'd never seen the ad in the paper, so she didn't know any better. Stopped because she saw the sign in my front yard."

"She might have stolen it," Gertie said.

I nodded. "Might have been the only way to get her hands on money."

"She got a job as a housekeeper at the hotel right away," Lottie said. "They were always shorthanded and she was a good worker, even repaired a lot of their drapes so you couldn't even tell they'd been torn. People talk about such things."

"And neither her nor Lara ever talked about family or where they lived before?"

"Not a peep. And plenty of people tried to get it out of her. Not me, mind you. I already had my own ideas and didn't want to spook the girl. I have to say, I was happy when she took up with Andy. He was a good man, and I figured she needed some extra looking out for and couldn't do better than a cop. Still feel bad for him the way things turned out. I've never seen a person so wrecked as he was when they disappeared, and given I've lived through my share of wars, that's saying a lot."

"Did you tell him what you just told me?"

She frowned. "No. I considered on it long and hard, but if

that girl had left a bad situation and then ended up going back to it, sending Andy after her would have just made matters worse for the both of them. I did my best to help save her and obviously it wasn't enough. I didn't want him lost to whatever she was involved in as well. Those cults don't take kindly to people trying to help members walk away."

"Especially the women," Ida Belle said dryly, "who are expected to be servants."

Lottie looked out her kitchen window and sighed. "There's not been a day go by since then that I haven't wondered if I did the right thing."

Gertie reached over and squeezed her arm. "Even if you'd told him, the chances of him finding the Brethren would have been slim. And if he'd gotten obsessed—and seems like he would have—he'd have spent all his time in the bayous, neglecting his work, friends, and family. There's no doubt he still loves her, but he managed to make a life for himself. If he'd believed she was out in the bayou, just a boat ride away, he'd have never moved on."

Lottie gave her a grateful look. "I know you're probably right, but guilt is a powerful thing. Almost as powerful as love."

"I agree with Gertie," I said. "I've spent most of my life working with men like Andy. Some might even accuse me of being the same way. You did the best thing for him at the time. But now maybe we can get some answers. Do you think there's anyone who would know more about the Brethren?"

She rubbed the side of her jaw as she considered. "Might be. There was a hermit—lived off Chapel Bayou just north of here. Can't say where exactly. I haven't seen him in years and he wasn't young back then, but he might still be around. He probably knew these bayous better than the tide, and I saw him talking to one of the Brethren at the dock behind the General Store one day."

I nodded. It wasn't much—in fact, it was practically nothing—but at least we had something to pursue tomorrow. I thanked Lottie for the information and gave her my card in case she remembered anything else. She gave me a big hug and said she was going to pray for the girl and for me, so I'd get answers for everyone.

We were halfway back to Sinful when my phone rang. It was the lab tech.

"Ms. Redding. I've got the results of your test. There's a 25 percent match between the two samples. That usually indicates a twice-removed relationship. So a cousin or grandchild or great-niece or -nephew."

"But they're definitely related."

"Without a doubt."

CHAPTER EIGHT

WE HEADED STRAIGHT FOR CARTER'S HOUSE WHEN WE GOT to Sinful, and I was relieved to see Blanchet's truck in the driveway. At least he'd done as promised and was staying put. Granted, it had only been a couple hours, but I knew all too well how hard it was to sit on your hands when you had a personal stake in things. He must have heard us pull up because he had the front door open before we even made it to the porch. I could tell by the expectant look as he waved us back to the kitchen that he was about to burst from wanting answers.

"I'm going to owe Carter a new rug in the living room, I've been pacing so much," he said. "Do you ladies want anything to drink? I haven't even checked stock, but Fortune probably knows it as well as Carter."

Since we were all still full from Lottie's tea and excellent cookies, we declined, then Blanchet asked, "Do you have news?"

"Yes, and you should probably sit. You can pace later."

He nodded and walked over to the refrigerator and took a

bottle of whiskey down, then grabbed a tumbler. He pulled out a chair and sat across from me, poured a shot, and then looked straight at me.

"Hit me with it."

"The DNA test was a match."

He'd poured the whiskey for just this reason, but apparently, taking a shot was far too passive for such a huge statement. He jumped up from his chair, sending it tumbling over backward, and let out a choice few expletives as he went. Then he paced the kitchen, which was more like a stomping-mad march, so his comment about Carter's living room rug made sense. Finally, he stopped at the table and righted the chair, then ran one hand through his hair and looked at me.

"I knew it. I know you weren't sure I was right, but you took my word and moved forward with it anyway. I can't tell you how much I appreciate that. Most people wouldn't have."

"Carter speaks highly of you. He doesn't of most people. And yeah, I had some doubts but only because I was afraid emotion could be influencing you to see more than what was there. But that was before you showed me your picture. You weren't imagining the similarities. Not even by a tiny bit. And you were right. It was a 25 percent match. I'm sure I don't have to tell you what that implies."

He nodded and sat down again, then grabbed the tumbler and tossed back the shot of whiskey. "I knew it. I knew it in my bones and my heart but hearing it is still stunning on some level."

"I'll bet. We also spoke to Lottie Pendarvis. I showed her the picture I took in the hospital and she was shocked as well. She said if she hadn't known when the picture was taken, she would have assumed it was Lara."

His eyebrows went up. "You talked to Lottie already? You definitely get right on with things, don't you?"

"Unanswered questions make me itchy, and when they involve the safety of a child, they make me feel like I rolled around in poison ivy."

"I did that once," Gertie said. "Not on purpose, of course, but you know how things happen."

Blanchet smiled. "I had some concerns when Carter described the three of you. That whole cat-toting-a-gun thing didn't help negate any of his warnings, either. But he also said you're honest, loyal, and direct, and that if a person ever needed someone they could count on, they couldn't do better than the three of you. I can't even tell you how much I appreciate what you're doing. Especially now that I've been cut out of things by that aaa—butthead Herpes."

Gertie chuckled. "Herpes. That makes me laugh every time I hear it."

"It's the only legal way I can punch him, so to speak. So you had a visit with Lottie. What was your impression of her as a witness?"

"Solid, honest, reliable," I said. "And her observation and listening skills are stellar. So is her ability to draw conclusions from both."

I told him about Maya's clothes when she arrived versus what she sewed after arrival and the other 'off' things that Lottie had noticed. He remained silent the entire time I talked, but I could tell by the way his jaw flexed that he was getting worked up again. When I finished, he slammed his hand on the table.

"Why didn't she tell me all of that? I could have been out in the bayous looking!"

"And that's exactly why she didn't tell you. Because she was afraid you would have wasted your life in those bayous finding nothing, or worse, finding something and putting you all at bigger risk. I don't know for sure what circumstances drove

Maya into Mudbug, but I think Lottie is right in her assessment. She was running from something. And if she made the decision to return to that something, then you showing up wouldn't have been good for either of you or for Lara."

He threw his hands up. "I would have protected her. Why didn't she believe that? I must not have—"

"Don't do that," Ida Belle interrupted. "Don't start thinking that there was something you could have done differently that would have changed the situation. People always said the Brethren were a cult. If that's the case, then you know if they didn't want to let her go, they had all kinds of ways to get her back and make her stay. If you'd headed out into those bayous looking for her, that's where they'd have buried you."

He slumped back in his chair and blew out a breath. "I know. I know. I worked a case involving a cult once. I've read the studies, seen the worst of them play out on the five o'clock news. I get it, but if it meant leveling the place, I would have done it for her."

"Maybe she didn't want you taking those risks," I said quietly. "I have a tiny lead—I'm talking thinner than a hair—that might be able to help us locate the Brethren. And I was all set to head out tomorrow, but before I do that, I have to ask you, given what we now know and also what we suspect, do you still want to pursue this?"

He frowned. "You're saying if we go poking around, we'll probably be putting people at risk."

"Yes."

He shook his head. "If that girl in the hospital wasn't part of the equation, I think I could be convinced to let it go. It would kill me, but I'd manage. But that girl *is* here, and she went through something in that swamp—something bad enough that she risked her life to get away. And someone risked their life to get her to that camp. I can't let her go back to wherever that was. And I can't let the state put her with a family knowing that she might carry risk to everyone around her if the wrong people are looking for her."

I nodded. "I agree. Then tomorrow morning, we'll head into the swamp to try to track down a hermit who might know where to start looking for the Brethren."

"Needle in the marsh grass?"

"Pretty much."

———

HARRISON PULLED UP IN MY DRIVEWAY JUST A COUPLE minutes after Ida Belle dropped me off, and as expected, he was still fuming. He went straight to my refrigerator, pulled out a bottle of water, and flopped into a chair.

"I wish this was beer," he said as he guzzled down half the bottle. "Or whiskey."

"Why not just go for liquid cocaine? Cyanide?"

"If I have to put up with Herpes much longer, I'll be opting for the last one, but it won't be for me. Although I guess I shouldn't complain. At least I'm out of the building. He has Deputy Breaux cleaning the place—I literally mean scrubbing toilets and mopping floors."

"There's a cleaning crew who does that."

"Exactly."

"Jesus. He's trying to run anyone off who's loyal to Carter."

"Which is everyone."

I nodded. "Have you talked to Cassidy today?"

"She called me right after the hospital showdown, mad enough to spit, as they are fond of saying here. She might be up to figuring out an untraceable option for that whole cyanide idea."

"I know she can't tell you stuff, but I assume she told you

as much as I heard standing there for the doctor-versus-idiot showdown."

"Oh yeah, I got an earful and he's lucky I wasn't there when he pulled that crap. She told me to let you know that the girl appears fine in every way except the memory. She didn't go into details and couldn't, of course, but she said to tell you not to worry about things on that front. That you needed to spend all your efforts on finding her family before that clown shoves a traumatized child off into a group home."

"Not to mention that given how she was found, she's probably in danger."

He nodded. "Not to mention."

"Did she give you any indication of how long she can hold her in the hospital?"

"Yeah, and it doesn't look good. Loss of memory alone isn't enough to keep her there. Cassidy says she can probably stall for another day, but that's starting to push it. The chief of staff has her back, but we both know if Hermes runs this up the pole, then that's subject to change, especially if her condition has improved to the point that he can't medically justify it."

"I imagine all it would take is a call from the governor to convince him to err on the side of less conservative if it comes down to it."

"Bet on it. Hermes is determined to get his way, and I'm sure he already knows who Cassidy is and her relationship to me. That's why he's pushing so hard to get the girl out of the hospital. He doesn't want to risk you having access to any information."

"God forbid I do his job and a little girl is saved."

"The girl isn't important—not to people like him. His big concern is you showing him up when he's making a play for the sheriff job. You've got a good reputation around here already, and if you take care of this on his watch, people will take notice, especially now. Then they'll assume that you wouldn't continue doing what you do if Carter isn't elected sheriff."

I frowned and he held up a hand.

"Before you start—I said, 'they'll assume.' We both know that you're not doing this for Carter, or at least not only for Carter. It's that horribly burdensome and frequently inconvenient need of yours to make things fair and right, which is why you were both a blessing and a curse to the CIA. Bottom line is you'd be doing this even if the Antichrist was sheriff."

"Hermes isn't that far off."

"Please tell me you have some leads."

"Maybe. I definitely have some news."

I told him about the DNA test and our conversation with Lottie. Harrison listened intently, then whistled when I finished.

"Boy, you weren't kidding about things here. They definitely major in unusual. A twenty-year-old missing persons case and a secret cult? If that girl and her mother or any other adult escaped from a cult, then she needs to be in police custody, not a group home."

"Yes, but that order would have to come from the sheriff, and we can't even ask for it without telling him what we've found out."

"Which means putting Blanchet and you on the chopping block. Jesus H. Christ. What a mess. Man, the Marines couldn't have picked a worse time to need Carter."

I nodded. I couldn't help but agree.

———

NORA'S PARTY OFFICIALLY STARTED AT 7:00 P.M. BUT SHE'D asked us if we'd come over an hour beforehand to help her get set up. I decided that included frisking her cat and ensuring all her handbags were stored. Ida Belle intended to sort the food on the table based on things that came out of packaging versus things that Nora had made. That way, we knew for sure what we could eat without rolling the dice into the psychedelic unknown.

Gertie, as expected, was planning on testing the other end of the table.

I took a quick shower and pulled on jeans, a purple T-shirt, and tennis shoes, blow-dried my hair and pulled it back into a ponytail, then declared myself fit for society. Ida Belle swung by to pick me up and I was surprised to see the front seat empty.

"Isn't Walter coming?" I asked as I climbed in.

"Yes, but he didn't want to go early when the 'Nora versus the rest of the crowd' odds were lower. She scares him a bit."

"Probably because she's always flirting with him," Gertie said. "She's not serious, but then Walter is an old-fashioned guy."

"What about Jeb and Wyatt?" I asked.

Gertie grinned. "They'll be there at the official start. Wyatt is trying to play it cool, but I know he's excited about seeing Nora again."

"He hasn't seen her since the New Year's bash?" I asked.

At Nora's previous throw-down, she and Wyatt had gotten more than a little cozy.

"He's talked to her on the phone, and he says when she remembers who he is, they have great conversations."

I laughed. "I'll bet."

"Anyway, I'm figuring she either sees him and remembers or she sees him and doesn't. Either way, he'll get lucky if he wants to. I don't think there's a big line of contenders in Sinful looking to take up with Nora. She scares more than just Walter."

Ida Belle parked in front of Nora's house, and we could see she'd already been decorating, of sorts. Purple, green, and gold condoms were blown up and attached to the front porch posts. As we walked up, Nora threw open the door and beamed at us.

"Isn't it great?" she asked, waving a hand at the condoms. "Party favors. People can take one on their way out, and I'm doing my part with that whole safe-sex movement I just heard about."

"Nora, what year is it?" Ida Belle asked.

She frowned. "Let me get back to you on that one."

"I'm convinced she thinks this is still the '70s," Ida Belle said as we walked inside.

"She would have been a little kid in the '70s," I said.

"Who was probably raised by hippies."

Nora was practically bouncing as we headed into the kitchen, and I studied the spread. Not a single inch of space was left on any surface in the room, and Nora had a decent-sized kitchen with a big island. It was loaded with bags of chips and boxes of crackers, and a bunch of boxes of cookies, brownies, and cakes, and I let out a breath of relief when I saw the logo for Ally's bakery on them. Eating brownies at Nora's was always a roll-the-dice sort of thing, but if Ally made them, we were good. Two kegs of beer were in the corner.

"I have a whole fridge of cheese and sliced meat in here, and the one in the garage has dips, salsa, and a ton of fruit juices for those who want to rock my party mimosa-style. Then there's the wine and champagne fridge, of course."

"You have a whole refrigerator for wine?" Ida Belle asked.

"You don't?"

"What's this?" Gertie asked as she picked up a dainty

teacup and smelled the contents. A matching white pot with pink roses on it sat on the table with more cups and saucers and looked completely out of place in the rest of the fraternity party setup.

Nora hurried over. "I've started reading tea leaves. I met this incredible herbalist in Holland... Well, incredible in the romance department, but he couldn't mix a good muscle relaxer to save his life. Anyway, he did a reading for me, and I was hooked. I gave it a whirl and he said I was a natural."

Ida Belle snorted. "You're telling me you look at leaves and tell people their future?"

"I have a gift. Finn said so. Let me do your readings."

"No way in hell," Ida Belle said.

Gertie clapped. "I'll do it!"

Nora studied us for a moment, then shook her head. "Not yet. The spirit is guiding me to do Fortune's."

I stared. "You don't strike me as the kind of woman who can be led around, even by a spirit."

"Guided is not led. I have this overwhelming feeling that there's something important for you in the tea. Please? I won't feel right if I don't get this out."

"Like eating a bad hot dog," Ida Belle grumbled.

I gave the tin of tea leaves a suspicious look. "What kind of tea is that?"

"Kratom."

"Don't drink that," I said to Gertie as she was just about to put the cup to her lips.

Only Nora would be brewing opioid-adjacent tea.

Nora waved a hand. "A sip won't hurt anyone."

"You're not serving tea at the party, right?" I asked.

"No time for all that brewing and reading, and I imagine it will be too noisy. Plus, I only have one five-pound bag, and my

Indonesian supplier won't make rounds for another two weeks. I'm going to be selfish on that one."

"I think you should be," I said, struggling to imagine just how big a five-pound bag of tea leaves was and how she could possibly consume it in less than two weeks. Ultimately, I decided it was safer not to know.

"But I *must* do your reading," Nora said. "The spirit is not going to give me a moment's peace until I do. And I'm a peaceful soul. I can't live in turmoil. It ages you."

Since Nora's lifestyle already had me guessing her age at ten years older than she was, I didn't think a little stress was going to send her tipping over into Crypt Keeper territory, but I also didn't want her harassing me every time she saw me.

"Fine," I said as I sat. "What do I have to do?"

She put a small spoonful of the leaves in an empty cup and poured hot water on them. "First, formulate a question."

"What kind of question?"

"Something specific that you desire an answer to. The thing that is pressing on your mind the most."

I held in a sigh. "Fine. Am I going to solve the case I'm currently working on?"

Nora nodded, then motioned to the cup. "Pick it up with your left hand and contemplate the question while you sip the tea."

I put the cup to my lips and pretended to sip, but I wasn't about to consume it. Fortunately, she hadn't poured much in the cup, and given her usual vague state of mind, I didn't figure she'd notice the oversight.

"Okay, now swirl the cup around three times, then put the plate on top of it and turn it upside down with the handle facing south."

I raised an eyebrow but followed her instructions to the letter. Ida Belle stood behind Nora, shaking her head.

"Now, we wait one minute," Nora said. "Think about the question while you let the tea assimilate into your system."

The only thing that tea was going to do was bounce off my lip balm, and I'd make sure I wiped my mouth as soon as I had a chance. It seemed like forever, but finally, Nora told me to turn the cup back over and remove the plate. Then she slid it over in front of her, leaned over the cup, and studied the mess of tea leaves inside.

"There's a cross," she said. "That signifies unforeseen trouble ahead."

"We're at your house and Gertie is still holding her purse," Ida Belle said. "Your cat could have made that prediction."

"My cat doesn't have this skill."

"He can shoot people."

Nora's face screwed up in concentration. "You're right. I'll need to contemplate that later. Back to the tea. I see a life-changing event in your near future. It has to do with someone close to you. There are factors beyond yours or this person's control."

I frowned. "Is this a good or bad life-changing event?"

"I can't tell. The spirit isn't clear. Maybe because he doesn't know how you'll receive it."

She straightened back up, staring at me with a concerned expression. "I think you're at risk."

"Me? I'm probably the safest person in Sinful. I sleep with one eye open and a loaded weapon practically in my hand."

She shook her head. "I don't see your heart stopping. I see it breaking. Be very careful, Fortune."

"Careful about what?"

"You have to decide. When the time comes."

"Good grief." I rose from the chair and headed to the kitchen for a napkin.

I pretended to be amused by the whole thing, but I caught Ida Belle's quick glance as I walked by and knew she'd zeroed in on my unease. The truth was, when I'd drunk the tea, I hadn't been contemplating the question I'd given Nora.

I'd been thinking about Carter.

CHAPTER NINE

By the time I spotted Blanchet, the party had technically crossed several legal lines—sketchy party favors, booming stereo system, teens had made off with one bottle of wine, that we knew of, and there had been some random nudity but mostly at the repaired hot tub, and none of it had been intentional. At least, I didn't think it had been. And since no one had elected to remain in their nude state, the party moved on as if it were just another afternoon stroll. You had to love Mardi Gras. It made everything unimportant and fun.

I'd just left Ida Belle and Walter in a corner of the yard where they'd started up a poker game. Since it wasn't going to be strip poker, Gertie and Jeb had headed for the hot tub. Wyatt had gotten sick at the last minute and had to beg off, which had disappointed both Wyatt and Nora, but then Ronald discovered a shared kinship with Nora for what they both called 'junk jewelry' and now they were in the dining room, gleefully digging through a box of her overseas bargains and eating stuff he would regret tomorrow. Since everyone was otherwise occupied and happy, I figured I'd go check in with Blanchet.

He stood on the corner of the porch, holding a cup of beer and staring out at the crowd, but I could tell his mind wasn't present even though his body was. I headed for the porch and walked up beside him.

"Parties not your thing?" I asked.

He shrugged. "I was never much of a partier, but on a different night, I could have had some fun with this. The drinks and food are good and plentiful, although I am carefully avoiding that section of home-baked stuff."

"Good call. After one of Nora's parties, I always worry that people will get popped with a random drug test. I guess it's hard for you to relax given everything going on."

He sighed. "I just wish I had answers. Even if Maya went back there of her own accord, if I just knew she was safe and that's what she chose, then I could let it go."

"Could you?"

"I think so. If the person you love tells you there's no chance, then that's where it all ends. But I never heard those words from her, and until I do, I can't help but hope."

I nodded. "You're a romantic soul, Blanchet. Don't let Gertie know. She might dump Jeb for you, especially given that your back is better."

He grimaced.

I laughed. "Too much information?"

"I think Gertie would be too much for me to handle today, much less if she was younger. That Nora is a piece of work, too. She totally grabbed my butt in the kitchen."

"Nora's harmless—as long as you don't eat or drink from her personal stuff. I wouldn't advise drinking tea here, either. Her cat, however, is another story. Yesterday wasn't his first run-in with the law." I told Blanchet about the cat and the pole-dancing event at Nora's New Year's party, and he laughed.

"I would have paid money to see that."

"Oh, there's video, much to Carter's dismay. I'll send you a link."

Blanchet was silent for a moment, then he turned slightly so that he could look at me more directly. "How are you doing with Carter going on this mission?"

I shrugged. "Since there's no choice in the matter, I'm good."

"Are you?"

"What do you want me to say? That I wish the Marines hadn't asked? I do. But there's no way I would have suggested he say no."

"And if the CIA called and asked the same of you?"

I thought for a minute then blew out a breath. "It would depend, of course, but if they called me back, then I'd have to assume it was due to similar circumstances as Carter—that the situation was critical, and they didn't think a mission would succeed without my help. Don't get me wrong, I hope that phone call never comes, but if we're talking big numbers of lives at stake, then I'd go without question."

He nodded. "You two are good for each other. I don't think many partners could accept that the way you do. I don't think I could. I respect the hell out of both of you, but I couldn't be in a relationship with either of you."

"Carter might be disappointed to hear that."

He laughed. "You're a good woman, Fortune Redding. I'm glad I met you, and I'm looking forward to seeing you in action."

"Remember, tomorrow we're going fishing, so dress the part. Don't worry about tackle. Ida Belle and Gertie have enough for the whole town."

He frowned. "Fishing?"

"Fishing with your buddies isn't illegal."

"Ah. But trying to find a cult that might be after that girl is interfering with a police investigation."

"You catch on quick."

"Fortune!" Ally called my name, and I turned to see her coming across the porch with Mannie right behind. They were both smiling.

I gave her a hug. "You're late."

"Blame it on this guy." She inclined her head toward Mannie.

"Work ran over," he said, and stuck out his hand. "Always good to see you, Fortune."

I nodded. "Andy, this is Ally, one of my best friends. She owns the local bakery and is responsible for the town's weight gain explosion. And this is Mannie. Her other half."

Blanchet shook hands with Mannie and smiled at Ally while I finished introductions.

"This is Andy Blanchet. He was supposed to be filling in for Carter but got overrun by that idiot Hermes. I'm sure you've both heard all about it by now."

Mannie scowled and Ally frowned. "That...well, I'm not saying it, came into the bakery this afternoon and hit on me. Right in front of customers. And it wasn't the usual older man, light-but-annoying flirty sort of thing. It wasn't even sugges-tive. He just flat out said he'd like to get me in bed."

I covered my mouth with one hand and looked up at Mannie, whose jaw flexed.

"You didn't tell me that part," he said.

Ally blushed. "It's not something I was interested in repeating, but when Fortune said his name, it just all came out."

"What did you do?" I asked.

"Not enough, as he's still walking around," Mannie said.

"I didn't do anything," she said. "I was so stunned that he just blurted out something like that. Aunt Celia was at the counter, and she turned around and told him to get out or she was calling the police. When he told her he *was* the police, then she said she'd be happy to call Mannie."

"Ha! Good for Celia. Finally on the right side of things. I bet that got him moving."

"Not as much as it would have if she'd actually called me," Mannie said, still fuming.

"I didn't want to get you in trouble," Ally said. "The man has connections, and you don't need the hassle. Besides, he made his retreat as soon as your name left her lips. Then the bakery crowd exploded with anger. I gave everyone a cookie to calm them down. I heard he was going to run for sheriff. Is that true?"

I nodded. "That's what he says."

"Well, he's not going to get any votes here the way he's rolling. It wasn't a pleasant experience, but if it helps get the word out to make sure people turn up and vote for Carter, then it was worth it."

My phone buzzed in my pocket and I pulled it out. Everyone I wanted to talk to—except Carter, of course—was at this party. I frowned when I saw a text from Myrtle, night dispatch at the sheriff's department.

Hermes is on his way to shut the party down.

I shook my head and texted back.

Of course he is. Thanks.

"Trouble?" Blanchet asked.

"Not for me, but there's something I need to take care of. Ally, why don't you grab something to eat. Mannie, I'm going to need you to play driver for me."

Blanchet raised one eyebrow and I motioned to a rocking chair. "I'll be back in a minute."

I sent a quick text to Myrtle to get her working, then headed across the back lawn and located Ida Belle, then Gertie, and explained the situation and what I had planned. Then I ran down Scooter, since I'd be needing mechanical services, and finally Dixon, a former resident who'd recently returned to Sinful.

"Did you ride your moped here?" I asked him.

"Yep. Scooter got me all fixed up."

"I need you to give Gertie a ride." I told him what I wanted and why, and he grinned.

"Happy to help."

All my accomplices took off, putting my plan into action, then I headed back to the porch and sat on the railing next to Blanchet.

"Is that the Mannie who's right hand to Big and Little Hebert?" he asked.

"That's the one."

Blanchet whistled. "And Herpes propositioned his lady. Wouldn't want to be him about now. You guys seem tight."

"Big and Little are friends, and big supporters of mine."

Blanchet grinned. "Layers upon layers of surprise. I bet Carter just loves them having your back."

"You have no idea. If you have to pee, go now. Otherwise, you're going to want to stay put for a bit."

"And I'm going to want to stay here because…"

"Alibi."

"An alibi for what?"

"Everything that's about to happen. Hermes is on his way to shut the party down."

"I see. And you're going to prevent that from happening."

"I'm certainly going to try. But neither you nor I can have

even a whiff of sketchy or Hermes will jump all over it. So we're going to stand here on the porch, and I'm going to take pictures and video of this very excellent party, with the occasional camera turn to you and me. So sit back and enjoy the show."

Blanchet smiled. "I can't wait to see your work."

––––––––

HERMES ARRIVED TEN MINUTES LATER AND STOMPED ONTO the porch. "Where's the homeowner?" he yelled.

I pointed to Nora, who was dancing with her cat in the middle of a broken sprinkler head. The cat was wearing Ronald's purple wig. Ronald, who was cheering on the two of them using branches from her rosebush as pom-poms, had replaced the wig with Nora's potted ivy plant. Clearly, he'd been sampling from Nora's end of the buffet.

"Shut this thing down!" Hermes yelled. "I want all of you out of here by the time I count to ten."

I shrugged. "It's not my house and I'm enjoying the free entertainment, the liquor, and the snacks. They are too. Guess you'll have to arrest all of us. Going to be a long night for you with all that paperwork. And you're a bit short on room down at the jail, but heck, we can just move the party. I mean, the judge will be thrilled to see us all in court when he's still nursing his own Mardi Gras hangover, right?"

Hermes's cell phone rang and he yelled, "What!"

I could hear Myrtle's voice booming out of the phone.

"Don't use that tone of voice with me. I'll still call your mother. Someone set the grass in front of the Catholic church on fire."

"It's grass! Who cares?"

"It's headed for the wooden cross they put up since Lent

starts tomorrow. Probably won't be a good look for you or the town."

"Then call the fire department."

"They're already on a call at the park. Somebody blew up two construction porta-johns. The toilet paper caught fire and launched into the construction bin, and they're having a time putting it out. As if that weren't enough, raccoons picked up some of the flaming debris and made off with it. They're going to be all night making sure the woods don't burn down. I suppose we should be thankful those toilets were emptied this morning and the crew had the day off."

"Where's Deputy Breaux?"

"At the big Walmart up the highway getting more cleaning supplies, like you told him to do. It's the nearest place open tonight. Maybe if you'd let him do his job instead of having him clean toilets, you wouldn't have to deal with this. But I've logged the issue and put that you'll be responding, since you made sure you're the only other one on duty here tonight. Or if you'd like, I can call the state police and let them know you can't handle things here and need backup."

Hermes turned fifty shades of red as he shoved his phone back in his pocket. "I'll be back, and I want this place cleared out by then."

I just laughed.

"I'm about two seconds from arresting you."

"No. You're about two seconds from becoming a viral internet sensation if that cross goes up in flames the night before Lent."

Hermes opened his mouth, then what I said must have finally registered because he whirled around and hurried off, faster than I'd thought him capable of. Blanchet, who'd been sitting quietly in the corner, stared at his retreating figure, then looked at me and grinned.

"Was all of that you?"

"Nope. I've been right here on the porch with you the entire time. Just give it ten minutes and he'll be back. While it's halftime, we should go grab a round of snacks."

Blanchet and I headed inside and picked through the ravaged table and countertop of food to find the non-Nora-doctored stuff. I took some pics and a short video of the scene, then with plates piled high and clutching a fresh pour of beer, we headed back out onto the porch and ate our snacks while we watched Ronald attempt to teach Nora and the cat how to ballroom dance.

"Is that cat still alive?" Blanchet asked.

I zoomed in on my video and squinted at the camera.

"You know cats—nine lives and all. He's probably just stoned. He stays that way most of the time. Nora's not so careful with storage of her wares."

At that exact moment, Nora ripped off her long black skirt that she'd been tripping over, exposing bright pink biking shorts and thighs that hadn't seen the sun since the prehistoric days.

Blanchet grimaced. "I see."

"Oh honey!" Ronald exclaimed. "We've got to get you some spray tan before you blind people with those. But not tonight. I think the cat wants to try cha-cha-cha."

I turned off video and took a couple more shots of people gathered on the lawn.

"Hermes is going to be back to arrest someone," Blanchet said.

"I'm counting on it. But I needed to buy some time for my stage II person to get some tools."

Blanchet raised one eyebrow. "Tools?"

I grinned. "Trust me."

My cell phone signaled an incoming text from Myrtle.

Idiot can't handle all the mayhem. He's headed back to arrest you three. Kept him going as long as I could.

Scooter stepped out of the house onto the porch and gave me a grin. I smiled and texted back.

No worries. We're good to go.

Then I texted Ida Belle and Gertie to hurry back and sat back to wait on Hermes.

"It's almost showtime," I said to Blanchet and clinked my beer against his.

A couple minutes later, Scooter ran by and told me Hermes had just pulled up. I glanced around, a little worried that I hadn't spotted Ida Belle or Gertie. I needed them back in place. Otherwise, Hermes was going to know they'd been the ones causing all the problems. Unfortunately, they'd been delayed, so it looked as though I would have to buy some time. I sent a couple more texts, then relaxed back in my chair and waited on Hermes to come blustering along.

I didn't have to wait long.

He barreled out onto the porch, huffing and puffing as if he'd just run a marathon. He immediately locked in on me and Blanchet sitting on the corner of the porch and made a beeline for us. He shoved a piece of wadded paper in my face, and I could actually see a vein in his forehead throbbing.

"I know you're behind this," he said.

I unfolded the paper and burst out laughing. It was a picture of Hermes and below it was the slogan *Stop the disease. Don't vote for Herpes.*

Blanchet leaned over to see and started laughing so hard tears came to his eyes.

"These were plastered on every storefront downtown," Hermes ranted. "That's defacing personal and government property. Not to mention slander."

"Libel," I said.

"What?"

"The correct term is libel. Slander is spoken words. Libel is written. But since I didn't write it or tape them downtown, I don't know how you plan to hang libel or defacing property on me. I've been right here on this porch since you left, except for the couple minutes I went inside to fix a plate."

"That's true," Blanchet said. "I've been right here with her."

"Like I believe anything that comes out of either of your mouths."

I pulled out my phone and showed him my screen. "You don't have to believe me. I've got a whole screen of proof right here."

"Then it was those other two under your orders. Where's that one who wears flannel? I don't see her playing cards anymore."

He looked over at Walter, who'd just stepped onto the porch.

"Bathroom," Walter said.

"All this time?"

He shrugged. "Too many cookies and expensive whiskey. I tried to tell her, but it's a celebration, after all. You're welcome to check, of course, but just so you know, I go stay at my own house for a couple days every time she overeats. It's either that or send her down to the gas station."

Blanchet let out a strangled cry and hunched over, his shoulders shaking.

Steam was practically coming out of Hermes's ears. "And the other one?"

"In the hot tub," I said. "Go ahead and talk to her. Fair warning, though, everyone in there is naked and over seventy."

He hesitated for a moment, then whirled around just as Jeb

stepped onto the porch, soaking wet and wearing a Mardi Gras mask over his most important parts.

"Somebody done run off with my clothes," he said. "Hopefully we'll find 'em before the night is over. Glad I wore my mask into the hot tub. Anyway, Gertie's wanting to know if we can used flavored oil in the hot tub or will it cause problems with the motor?"

"Probably ought to save the oil for home."

"I told her that. But there's this movie with these mechanics who fall in love that she's wanting to reenact. Motor oil looks like a hard cleanup, so I figured the flavored stuff might be a better pick. There's this scene where they're in the garage—"

"Nope," Ida Belle said as she stepped out onto the porch. "You have the same rules as Gertie. No details about sexy time."

Jeb grinned. "When you're as old as me and can still pee in under ten minutes, life is already exciting. Then I met Gertie and boy howdy. Well, better get back to it. My skin's not going to shrivel itself."

Since he was shriveled before he got into the tub, his statement was hilarious. Even more so when he turned around to leave and we got a full-on view of his wrinkly butt as he headed off.

"I should arrest that man for indecent exposure," Hermes said.

"You'd have to put him in your truck that way," I said. "And technically, a good attorney is going to argue he's wearing a G-string bikini since that mask elastic is up his butt."

Blanchet fell out of his chair.

Hermes glared at him, and I could tell he was attempting to come up with a reason he could arrest him for laughing when Nora and Ronald stumbled onto the porch, elbowing each other.

"What fine gentleman do we have here?" Nora asked, batting her eyes at Hermes. Since one of her fake eyelashes was currently resting on the end of her nose, it was an interesting visual.

"I saw him first!" Ronald said as he put one hand on his hip and kicked it out with a sexy smile.

"But it's my house," Nora said. "I'm calling dibs on the party favors. Come on, handsome. I just went to one of those sexy goods parties and have a round of stuff to try out."

Ronald gave her a horrified look. "You can't put cheap party goods on your unmentionables. They chafe!"

"I got some stuff that will numb that right up," Nora said, then frowned. "But I guess that defeats the purpose, right? I'm going to have to think on that one. In the meantime, just plain naked works."

She gave Hermes a sexy grin.

"If you're going to arrest us, you have to start with her," I said. "After all, this is her place and her party."

"This isn't over," Hermes said through gritted teeth.

I grinned. "Not by a long shot. I mean, it's not even midnight."

"Maybe I'll just take you in. I might not be able to charge you, but I can hold you overnight just because."

Mannie, who'd slipped back onto the porch next to Ally, rose and took a step toward us.

"You should stick around," he said to Hermes. "I'd like to discuss the proposition you made to my girlfriend, in her place of business, in front of a dozen people. Or we could leave and discuss it, because unlike you, I prefer to handle my personal business without witnesses."

Hermes's eyes widened and he took a quick step back into

Nora, who fell backward over the huddled Blanchet. As she fell, she tossed the cat, who'd been passed out in her arms, and he awakened on the drop back down and managed to turn himself feet down.

Right onto Hermes's head.

The cat did the usual cat thing and dug into Hermes's scalp as though his life depended on it. Hermes screamed and grabbed the cat, trying to tug him off, which only made the cat dig in harder. I grabbed Blanchet's beer and flung it at the howling animal. He immediately vaulted off Hermes's head, bounced off Ronald's chest, then vaulted into the house. I figured after the week he'd had, he was probably going to pack a suitcase and move.

With Mannie standing there, arms crossed, and not even a hint of a smile, Hermes must have decided that this wasn't the hill to die on. He glared at all of us before stomping into the house. Blanchet looked up from the floor, tears streaming down his face.

I extended my hand to him. "It's not over yet. Hurry."

Blanchet managed to crawl up from the floor, and we all ran through the house and made it to the front window just as Hermes stepped off the porch and got a good look at his truck.

Sitting on cinder blocks and missing all four wheels.

A man and woman I didn't recognize were in the back seat. The windows were down and the man was swinging a red bra out of it.

"Hey, Uber guy!" he yelled. "We've been waiting forever. She's got her bra off, man. Have a heart. Let's get this going!"

Gertie rushed into the living room—finally back from her reign of terror—and stared out the window.

"Who the heck is that?"

I started laughing so hard tears came to my eyes. "I have no idea. That one wasn't me, I swear."

"Looks like the Parkers' grandson," Ida Belle said. "Makes sense. He's had a couple DUIs."

Blanchet started laughing until he shook all over again. "How does it make sense? He's sitting in a truck with no wheels."

"It's Sinful," Ida Belle said, as if that explained everything.

And really, it kinda did.

Hermes looked back at the house, spotting us all looking out the window, and shook his fist. "You're all going to jail for this."

I opened the door and yelled out of it. "How the heck are you going to pin that one on us when you were standing right there with us when it happened? Sounds like the town is out of control. Stuff like this never happened on Carter's watch."

I closed the door and right as Hermes reached for his handcuffs and took a step toward the house, a huge bolt of lightning came down and struck the front of his truck so hard, the hood flew right off it. Hermes went sprawling onto the sidewalk. The couple in the back seat jumped out, half clothed, and scrambled across the yard and down the block.

Mannie, anticipating that Hermes had fallen off the ledge of sanity, stepped out the front door and just stood there, arms crossed. Hermes, who'd started up the walkway again, paused, gave Mannie a cautious look, then pulled out his phone.

"Breaux! I need you to pick me up right now!" he yelled as he started walking off.

We all collapsed in the living room, laughing so hard our ribs were certain to hurt the next day. Even Mannie worked up a laugh, although if I was Hermes, I'd try really hard to avoid him for basically the rest of my life.

Since most people were too drunk to notice Hermes had even been there, the party had never stopped. Once we picked ourselves up from the living room, we headed back out to resume Mardi Gras business. I ran down Scooter and Dixon and thanked them for their roles, and then spent the rest of the night chatting with friends, drinking beer, and eating cookies. I was seriously going to have to exercise for a month to get rid of the calories I'd consumed. Nora, who'd been on hostess overtime all night, finally passed out in a lawn chair along with Ronald and the cat, who'd apparently elected to keep living with her. All three of them were wearing more jewelry than Liberace.

When everyone had mostly trailed out, we did our best to restore a little order to her house. Then since everyone else was paired up and could head directly home, Blanchet offered to drop me off.

"So what exactly did you do with those wheels?" he asked as he drove.

"I didn't do anything with them. I was right there on the porch with you the whole time."

He laughed. "Touché."

"The unnamed party put them in Farmer Frank's pasture. He has llamas."

Blanchet raised one eyebrow.

"Ever been around llamas? They're more territorial than a Malinois. And they spit. Farmer Frank gives his llamas tobacco when he sees someone trespassing. He has crap night vision, but by the time I send an anonymous tip in about those wheels, it will be daylight, and the llamas will be locked and loaded."

Blanchet chuckled. "You know, your résumé is impressive enough, but watching you work is like seeing a magician perform. You've really made a place for yourself here. These people love you and, more importantly, they trust you to act without question. That's huge, especially in the South. People don't give that kind of respect lightly."

"And I don't take it lightly, which is why I'm always trying to do what's best for this town and its people."

He nodded as he pulled into my driveway. "It's a good fit for both of you. Guess I'll see you tomorrow for fishing."

"I'll send a text when we're on our way to pick you up."

I jumped out and gave him a wave from my porch as he drove off. I sighed as I let myself in the house. Blanchet was a nice guy. I really hoped we could get him some answers about Maya, but at the same time, I worried what those answers might be. If cults couldn't control members with threats, they tended to eliminate the problem. I really hoped Maya hadn't been subject to an elimination.

I grabbed a bottled water from the kitchen before heading upstairs for the shower. I spent a good amount of time under the stream of hot water, then dried my hair and headed to bed. It was close to 2:00 a.m. but I already knew sleep would be elusive. With everything going on here and worrying about Carter over there, it was really hard to quiet my mind enough to rest. But I needed to try. Operating at 100 percent capacity was more important now than ever.

I plumped up my pillows and hopped into bed. I was just reaching to turn out the lamp when my phone signaled an incoming text. It was Carter! I grabbed my phone and my heart dropped when I read the two words.

I'm sorry.

I let the phone go and it dropped onto the floor. He didn't have to explain. I knew exactly what those words meant. Carter wasn't going to be safe on an aircraft carrier. He was going to be on the ground, right in the middle of whatever Force Recon was doing.

I picked up my phone and saw a second message.

I love you.

I texted back.

Stay safe. I love you.

The message showed Delivered but didn't show Read. Ten minutes later, the status hadn't changed. Nor had it an hour later when I finally gave up and turned off the light.

The only thing I could do now was pray.

CHAPTER TEN

I WAS UP BEFORE DAWN THE NEXT MORNING, AFTER A NIGHT filled with awful dreams. I'd expected as much. Even Merlin seemed to clue in that I wasn't doing all that well and didn't give me his usual amount of grief over breakfast. Instead, he waited politely in his eating corner while I made coffee and even stuck to casual observation while I downed a cup standing in front of the pot and stared at the cabinets. Finally, I made up his breakfast. He ate it all without a single sound, then sat by the door and waited quietly until I let him out to do his business.

I shook my head as he walked out. If the cat had zoned in on my malaise, then Ida Belle and Gertie would be all over it. I knew I'd have to tell them, at least as much as I knew, which was basically nothing. I sat at the table wondering if Carter had said anything to Emmaline. When my phone rang twenty minutes later and I saw her name in the display, I had my answer.

"I got a text from Carter in the middle of the night," she said. "All it said was 'I love you.'"

"Yeah, I got one too."

"I texted back but he never answered. What does that mean?"

"That the mission started and he's no longer allowed outside contact."

I didn't go into details. There was no point in telling her that Carter was now in the field rather than safely tucked in a war room. I would worry enough for both of us, and it still wouldn't change anything.

"I hate this," she said.

"So do I."

"I should have asked him not to go."

"You didn't?"

She sighed. "I couldn't. Honor is like breathing with Carter."

"I know."

"I was hoping you would ask, but I should have known better. You're both cut from the same cloth."

"If it makes you feel any better, I'm just as conflicted as you."

"I'm worried, Fortune. Why did the Marines need *him*? Why is he the only person who could do whatever they're going to do?"

"I have to assume he's the only person left who was part of a prior mission in the same location."

"It's been years. Why don't they have a satellite or a drone or a damned magician who can conjure up that information for them?"

Since I'd never heard Emmaline cuss, it made my heart clench. I wished there was something I could say to make her feel better, but then, if I had such words, I'd tell them to myself as well.

"I wish they did," I said finally.

"I'm going to wear out my knees praying, but I guess that's our only option at this point."

"I'm afraid so, and trust me, I've tried to come up with another."

"Well, I'm going to start calling my prayer group ladies as soon as it's a decent hour. I'm sorry to call you so early."

"It's no problem. I was already up."

"I figured you might be. You let me know if there's anything I can do for you."

"You too. I'll swing by as soon as I can and take Tiny for a run."

"You might have to settle for a walk. That dog is so lazy."

"Then a walk it is."

"Take care, Fortune."

"You too."

I disconnected and sighed. I hated this for me and especially hated it for Emmaline. She was an awesome woman, and I knew how much she loved her son.

Enough to let him be who he is.

I sighed again. That was the bottom line for both of us.

Ida Belle and Gertie wandered in an hour later, and much earlier than I'd expected to see them. Ida Belle looked the same as always, but Gertie looked as if she'd spent a week at a fraternity party.

"Lord, that was a fantastic time!" she said. "Wyatt missed a good one. Jeb's still asleep. I tried to wake him up a couple times, but he just snored and kept going. At least the snoring lets me know I didn't kill him. After we got home—"

"No." Ida Belle held up one hand.

"You are no fun. What the heck are we supposed to talk about when we're pretending to fish? Guys talk about their conquests all the time."

"We're not guys."

"Blanchet is going. He's a guy. You and Fortune might as well be guys. God knows your romantic streaks are practically vapor."

I frowned a bit and glanced out the window. Ida Belle, who never missed anything, narrowed her eyes at me.

"What's wrong?"

I pulled my phone out and showed them the text. Ida Belle's eyes widened and Gertie sucked in a breath. They'd both been military spies. They knew the score.

"No," Gertie whispered, her face pale.

Ida Belle shook her head. "We all know Carter well enough to know he didn't feel there was another choice, but I hate seeing this."

I nodded. "Emmaline called me before dawn. He told her he loved her and didn't text back after she responded."

"She didn't understand the implications," Ida Belle said. "Did you tell her?"

"No. I didn't see the point. She's already worried sick and worrying more isn't going to change anything but her own health."

"This sucks," Gertie said. "More than anything has in forever. How are you doing?"

I shrugged. "I'm doing. It's not like I don't get it. If the situation were reversed, I have no doubt it would be Carter here worried about me. We are who we are. Neither of us is interested in changing ourselves or each other."

"The hallmark of true love and respect," Ida Belle said. "It took me a lot of years to realize that Walter would be that way for me."

"I don't think he could have been when you were younger," Gertie said.

"I agree. Everything has its season. This is ours." She looked at me. "And you and Carter will have yours."

"I thought we were already, but then this. Oh well, I guess I can't really expect people like us to have uncomplicated lives. If I wanted that, I would have settled for a nice, steady accountant, and Carter would have settled for one of the many local women who wanted a husband, a picket fence, two kids, and a golden retriever."

Ida Belle laughed. "I can't even picture that. Are we still on for finding the hermit?"

"Yep. Cassidy can't hold the girl at the hospital forever, so we need to make tracks on this as quickly as possible."

I sent a text to Blanchet, who surprised me by responding right away, but then, he hadn't really drunk much the night before, and with everything that was riding on this, I guessed it shouldn't be surprising that he wasn't able to sleep late.

He was waiting in the driveway when we pulled up and had dressed the part—jeans, tennis shoes, long-sleeved flannel shirt, and a ball cap. Ida Belle gave him an approving nod as he climbed in.

"You ladies are early risers," he said as we pulled away. "Not that I'm complaining. Didn't get a lot of sleep last night. Things keep rolling around in my mind, and I can't make sense of them but can't get them to stop either. Where are we going, anyway?"

"First, we're going by the café to pick up our lunch," Ida Belle said. "Then we're stopping at the General Store to get supplies, then we'll head back to Fortune's to launch."

"Well, good grief, I could have just driven myself over there. I didn't realize the boat was at Fortune's place."

"If you'd have driven yourself, we'd have had to carry the supplies," Ida Belle said.

He laughed. "Can I ask what we're having for lunch?"

"Meat loaf sandwiches, chips, and cookies," Gertie said. "But if you get hungry before then, I have two bananas, a protein bar, beef jerky, and a side salad in my purse. I tried to shove some MoonPies in there, but I would have had to take out the dynamite or the glitter, and I don't travel without either of those. I also have a dozen grapes in my bra."

Blanchet blinked. "Ah, I'll let you know."

We picked up our lunch and were headed into the General Store when we spotted Hermes leaving the sheriff's department. He took one look at us, scowled, and stalked over, pointing a finger at me.

"I know that situation last night was you. It cost me a fortune to get that truck lifted onto a flatbed. And as soon as I find those wheels, I'm going to run prints on them."

"I was sitting right there on the porch the entire time. And although I'm extremely good at what I do, even I can't summon lightning."

Blanchet shook his head. "Your cousin isn't going to back you on that one. There were at least fifty witnesses who put Fortune in the backyard the entire night."

"Fifty intoxicated, or worse, witnesses."

"And video," I said. "I have a good hour of video and pictures—all with me in them. So unless video can be intoxicated, and I've figured out how to bypass the incredible amount of security Apple has embedded, I'd say that gives me all the alibi I need, especially when you add that your wheels were stolen while you were staring right at me."

"You may not have done the actual deeds, but you were behind it."

"So let me get this straight. In the time it took for you to crash the party, threaten Nora and most of the guests, including me, I managed to coordinate strikes around the town and have your vehicle vandalized. All while being in prime view of the entire party and yourself. I only wish I had that much pull. Especially the psychic communication end of things I would have needed to have."

"You're grasping at straws," Ida Belle said. "Take your nonsense somewhere else. People here have things to do."

"I'm watching you," he said. "*All* of you. Why are you still here, Blanchet?"

He shrugged. "I told Carter I'd house-sit and unlike you, I like the people. Don't have a job to get to back home. No kids, wife, or houseplants. Besides, it's been fun watching you fail. Not that the opposite ever occurs, but I'm just usually not around to see your greatest hits."

Hermes stared hard at Blanchet, unspeaking. Finally, Blanchet smiled and Hermes whirled around and stomped off.

"If I want to make a complaint about that man, who would I complain to?" Celia's voice sounded behind us.

We all turned around and I looked over at Blanchet.

"It's hard to say, ma'am. Normally, I'd say the mayor, but obviously Hermes got appointed over your mayor's head, so she won't be able to help. What kind of complaint would you like to make?"

Celia straightened herself up and a flush ran up her face. "That...that *swine* propositioned my niece in her bakery yesterday. In front of customers and in lurid detail. Everyone is talking about it. There's even video."

"So he sexually harassed her?"

"Absolutely." She glanced at me, Ida Belle, and Gertie. "I know we don't always see eye to eye on things, and I haven't exactly been Carter's biggest supporter, but if that man is put in charge, this entire town will become hell and no woman will feel safe. He shouldn't even be allowed air, much less a badge."

"We agree," I said. "Unfortunately, we haven't figured out a way around him. But I do think a phone call to the ADA is a good idea, especially if you can get your hands on that video."

Celia frowned. "Why the ADA?"

"Because they're buddies, but the ADA is gunning for the DA position. If he finds out how Hermes talks to women, especially when he's wearing a badge, I don't think he'll keep backing that horse. And since the ADA isn't a big fan of mine and you're a longtime resident and relative of the victim, it will have a lot more weight coming from you."

Celia gave me a firm nod. "Then that's exactly what I'll do. I would say I'd make the same complaint to the governor, but that man has cheated more than professional card players. Why people keep voting for him, I have no idea. Thank you and good day."

"Who was that?" Blanchet asked as we climbed into the SUV.

"Our nemesis, Celia Arceneaux," I said.

Blanchet whistled. "Carter told me all about her. Leave it to Hermes to get sworn enemies on the same side. The man has a gift."

I nodded. "If I hear he's pulled that crap with Ally again, he's going to answer to me."

"If you can beat Mannie to him," Gertie said.

"He sure knows how to step in it." Blanchet grinned. "We can only hope he's dumb enough to do just that."

Gertie nodded. "The good thing is, no one will have to post bail because they'll never find the body."

"Probably true," I agreed. "But I'd prefer to keep Mannie and the Heberts from being the focus of an investigation. And I don't want Ally knowing that she was the cause of a man's demise, even though most people would be pleased about it."

"Let's just hope he hacks enough people off that even the governor can't help him with a run for sheriff," Gertie said.

"I'm sure there will be no shortage," I agreed. "But if we

can solve this case that he keeps ignoring in his quest to get something on me, it will put another nail in his coffin."

Blanchet nodded. "Then let's get to fishing."

———

It was still a little chilly, especially with Ida Belle going full throttle, but the sun was shining, which made it a beautiful day. Or it would have been if we'd actually been going fishing. And if Carter wasn't in the middle of whatever the heck he was in the middle of. But that was our reality, so we might as well roll with it.

Because he was our guest and client, I'd offered up my passenger seat in the boat to Blanchet, and I shared the bench cushion in the bottom with Gertie. Every time Ida Belle took a corner with the boat sliding over the water, Blanchet let out a whoop. I was glad he was enjoying himself, even if only for a short time. It took us about twenty minutes to cross the lake and enter the bayous that stretched into Mudbug, and then another twenty to maneuver around to the channel Lottie had indicated.

Ida Belle cut speed as soon as we rounded the corner into the narrow bayou, and we started scanning the banks for any sign of life. If he was still alive and still lived in the same place, I figured his actual home would be back in the trees, but if he was living off the land, then we would probably see crab pots or trout lines along the way. And sure enough, about twenty yards from the tree line, Ida Belle pointed to a line tied to a post just off the edge of the bayou.

"I can see a trail on the bank," she said.

"Pull closer and I'll get on the bank and follow it," I said. "The rest of you continue ahead and make sure I'm clear."

Hermits lived in remote places because they didn't like

people. They also tended toward an affinity for firearms and protecting their personal space. Since I had no idea where his space began or ended, I ran the risk of gunfire. Being on foot would be seen as threatening where being in the boat wouldn't be viewed the same because people often traversed the channels looking for the best fishing spots.

The trail was well worn, beaten down to nothing but dirt, which meant it was used often. Weeds in the bayou practically grew overnight, so whoever was using this trail wasn't setting the occasional crab pot for a boil. And he wasn't accessing it by boat. I was sure the hermit had one, but he probably only used it when he had to go into town to trade for supplies. Otherwise, walking was zero cost except for time, and if he was living alone out in the middle of the swamp, I figured he had plenty of that to spare.

As I approached the tree line, I looked ahead to the boat and Ida Belle glanced back and shook her head to let me know they hadn't spotted a structure yet. Of course, we were assuming he had one. It was a rare individual who chose to sleep rough, but I couldn't completely discount the possibility. A minimum of a tarp or some other material to keep him dry would be needed, but that could easily be camouflaged in the thick brush.

I eased into the trees, scanning the area for any sign of life and listening for movement other than the normal swamp sounds or the boat. If I was indeed tracking the hermit, then he'd been out here for a long time and had learned to move silently in order to hunt and to avoid being hunted. I didn't think for a minute that he could take me in a fair fight, but he could easily position himself with coverage and shoot me. I was in his Vietnam.

I was about fifty yards into the brush when I heard the faint rustling off to my left. Since there was no breeze, I knew it was something with a heartbeat causing the sound. I froze and crouched, trying to pinpoint the location of the noise, but then a man's voice boomed out.

"You ain't hiding. Best get out the same way you came. I got a 12-gauge pointed at you."

I stood, my hands over my head, and locked in on the hermit, tucked behind a cypress tree about fifteen yards away.

"Are you the man who lives out here? Sometimes buys stuff at the store in Mudbug?"

"Ain't no business of yours."

"No, sir, but I'm hoping you can help me."

"Ain't got no dealings with the outside unlessin' I need supplies."

"A young girl has been found in the swamp near Sinful. She's hurt and can't remember who she is. We think she might have been part of the Brethren. A lady in Mudbug said you might know where to find them."

"You a cop?"

"No, sir. I'm a private investigator, and I'd like to help the girl. If she was trying to escape the Brethren, I don't want to see her go back there. And she was too young to be out in the swamp on her own. I'm worried that her mother is still out there or that whoever they were running from caught up to her."

He stepped out from behind the tree but didn't lower his shotgun.

Seventy if he was a day but looked older. Six foot tall, even with the slight hunch in his spine. Probably arthritis and I imagine he dealt with quite a bit of pain. No threat hand to hand, but the shotgun had a wide blast radius.

"You think a woman was running from the Brethren with her daughter?" he asked.

"It's a theory, and right now, the only one we've got. No

one locally knows who she is, and no missing persons reports have been filed that match her description. But we think she might be related to a woman who went missing years ago, and the Mudbug lady who told me about you thought that woman was part of the Brethren. Lottie Pendarvis is the woman's name who told me about you. Do you know her?"

He frowned, then nodded. "Sounds familiar. I think one of her kinfolk used to help down at the store in Mudbug."

"Her nephew. Anyway, she said she'd seen you talking to some of the Brethren once when they came for supplies and since you probably know this swamp better than anyone, you might know where to find them."

I heard footsteps behind me, and then Ida Belle's voice called out. "Fortune? You all right? We've been calling."

Crap. I'd turned my phone on silent when I jumped onto the bank and had turned off vibrate as well.

"I'm good!" I yelled. "Go grab the supplies, will you?"

"Who's that?" the man asked, tightening his grip on the shotgun.

"Friends who are helping me. Ida Belle and Gertie from Sinful, and a male friend of mine. Retired. We brought some supplies with us in case we found you—some jugs of water, casting net, rope, tarps—thought it might help out a bit, especially if you were willing to talk to us."

"You tell them not to come close or I'll blast all of you."

"We'll stay over here, I promise. Do you have a name? Mine is Fortune."

"Hadn't had use for one in a while, but people used to call me Spinner."

"That has to do with fishing, right? I'm fairly new around here and just learning all the fishing jargon. Do you mind if I put my arms down?"

"Go ahead, but don't you move fast."

I heard footsteps behind me again and called out. "Approach slowly. I'm talking with Mr. Spinner, and he's armed and needs to be sure we're not here to make trouble."

A couple seconds later, the three of them emerged from the woods and into the small clearing near me, their arms full of goods.

"See," I said to Spinner, and pointed to the items. "I'm going to have them put everything down and then we'll talk. And I've got some money for you if you're willing to help."

Spinner didn't appear remotely concerned about Ida Belle and Gertie, but he locked in on Blanchet and studied him for a long time before nodding. If he hadn't been pointing a shotgun at me, I would have been amused that he considered the three women the less lethal of the group.

"Don't know for sure where they live at," he said. "But don't matter none. No womenfolk need to go messing with the Brethren. If a woman done run off from them with her kid, you should pay attention and leave them well enough alone."

"You think they're abusing women?"

"I think they abuse anyone who don't toe the line. And with religious folk, that line can be a murky mess. People ain't got limits when they sure God is behind 'em."

"That's true enough. But if this woman ran and they found her, we'd like to help her and her daughter. We're afraid the Brethren will come after her, and if the girl becomes a ward of the state, she'll be easy enough for the Brethren to take back."

He stared at us for a long time, and I could tell he was still confused by the entire situation but also tempted by the goods we'd brought. Finally, he nodded. "I'll tell you what I know, but don't say I didn't warn you. The Brethren ain't gonna tolerate people trespassing. They ain't gonna ask questions like me."

"I understand. But we have to take that chance...for the girl's sake."

"Can't tell you no exact names of places—probably ain't the same anymore since I stopped fishing that area—so you'll have to make note of the landmarks I give you. That will get you to a place where I seen them working trout lines. I figure they don't stray too far away from home for the gas savings, but I could be wrong. They stopped everything when I pulled by and stared at me until I drove off. I recognized one of them as the man I talked to at the store one day."

"What did you talk about, if you don't mind my asking?"

"He asked me about my bait. Brought a thirty-pound black drum to the store to trade and he was wanting to know how I caught 'em. I told him what I was using and he just turned around and left. Not so much as a nod."

"And that was the man you saw in the boat that day working trout lines."

He nodded. "It were him and a younger one. Not more than a boy, really. The boy looked scared but the man stared right through me. I lived in these swamps a long time and they ain't much I'm afraid of. But I wouldn't go messin' with the Brethren. Hadn't been back to that area since."

"And how long ago was that?"

"Don't have no use for keeping time out here, but I guess it's been three winters or better."

I was a little disappointed that it had been so long. Anything could have forced them away from their old hiding place—discovery, hurricanes, a shift in the bayous and land, or even the disappearance of the good fishing spots. But for that matter, him spotting them could have caused them to pull up stakes and move as well. At least it was a starting point, which was better than nothing.

"I'm going to take my phone out of my pocket so I can make notes, okay?"

He looked a bit confused at my comment, but then, he

probably had no idea what a smartphone was. I held one hand away from my side and eased my cell phone out of my front pocket.

"Okay, go ahead," I said.

Spinner started giving me directions, using where we were as a starting point, and I prayed Ida Belle could make sense of it all. Things like 'where the tide meets at noon' and 'the old tree that the raccoons used to live in' weren't exactly GPS coordinates. But it was the best we were going to get. When he finished, I thanked him.

"I'm going to put my phone up now and pull out the money. It's a hundred dollars."

His eyes widened. "Why you gonna give me that much money?"

"It doesn't go as far as it used to. And it's my way of thanking you for talking to me. Well, and not shooting me when you had the chance."

He shrugged. "Don't like to waste bullets on things I can't eat. And you a little skinny."

For a split second, I thought he was serious, then he gave me a partially toothless grin, and I smiled.

"Do you want us to haul these supplies somewhere for you?"

"Nope. They fine right there. I can get 'em."

"Okay. I'm going to tuck these bills under this jug of water, and we're going to leave. But if you ever need anything, Ida Belle's husband owns the General Store in Sinful. I know it's farther, but he'll help you and won't ask questions. He's good like that."

"'preciate it."

I stuck the bills under the water jug, and we all turned and walked slowly off. It wasn't until we were back in the boat that I felt some of the tension leave my shoulders.

"Holy crap!" Blanchet said as we pulled away. "I can't believe we found the guy."

"I can't believe he's still alive," Gertie said.

"I can't believe he didn't shoot you," Ida Belle said.

"I have to admit, it crossed my mind more than once," I said.

Given how long Spinner had been living outside of society, I was a bit surprised at how clear his mind appeared to be. Most people didn't do well with that level of isolation for even short periods of time, much less decades. I'd gotten really lucky. Especially since I'd probably come dangerously close to his living quarters.

When we reached the mouth of the bayou, I had Ida Belle stop and we looked over my notes. "Does any of this mean something to you?"

It was a mess of odd explanations, coupled with the occasional reference to direction and some hand waving, which I'd also made note of. Ida Belle read my notes and pulled up a satellite image of the area.

"When he was talking, I got the impression that the first landmark is around this area, but I won't be able to decide where to go afterward unless we can find the first one."

"Is that far from here?"

"About thirty minutes, assuming these channels haven't shifted since the satellite took this photo."

"Is that Mudbug?" I asked, pointing to an area not far from us that showed clearly defined structures.

"Yep. That big dock is behind the General Store. Like in Sinful, a lot of people pick up in their boats."

"Let's drop in there on our way. And after that, make that travel time forty-five minutes instead of thirty so we can take a hard look at the area as we go. Maybe talk to any fishermen if we see some out."

"You got it."

I was a little surprised that Spinner lived so close to Mudbug. I'd expected a hermit to be more secluded, but then, he didn't seem lacking in conversational skills and mentally, he seemed sound enough. Maybe he just didn't like people. And since the locals knew he was out there and didn't want to be bothered, they respected his choice and gave him a wide berth. My younger self would have been all over the solitude, but not necessarily the living arrangements. I'd done enough living rough with the CIA and wasn't interested in more.

CHAPTER ELEVEN

WE PULLED UP TO THE DOCK BEHIND THE GENERAL STORE and everyone went inside, figuring we'd grab a drink and maybe a snack while we were there. Ida Belle knew the store owner—an older man who looked about the same age as Walter. He had kind eyes and a nice smile, and I briefly wondered if it was a requirement for the job.

Late seventies. Six foot one. Two hundred ten pounds. Sill in excellent shape and forearms told me he was still moving his own stock around. No threat, directly, but that sign above his head advertising fresh boudin for sale might be my downfall.

"Otto, this is my friend Fortune Redding. Fortune, this is Otto Kraus. His family moved to the swamps from Germany more years ago than either of us is counting."

"But they don't hold it against me," Otto said, smiling as he extended his hand. "You're the one who found the skeleton in Mary Joseph's closet—or rose bed, as the case may be. The rest of my family headed for the city long ago, and they're always asking why I want to stay in such a small place. 'Sleepy little towns where nothing happens.' Well, that was something, all right."

"People can always surprise you," I said. "Did you hear about that girl found in the swamp over in Sinful?"

"Oh yeah. Had a deputy come around asking questions, but I didn't recognize the girl. Said he was going to check around town, but he took a phone call right after he spoke with me and drove off. I figured maybe they'd found her family."

More like that idiot Hermes had called him off the job and asked him to do something really relevant, like sort the Post-its by color.

"No. Her identity is still up in the air," I said. "I'm working on a theory—and it's more than a long shot—but do you know anything about the Brethren?"

He frowned. "You think she might have been one of them? That girl in the picture couldn't have been more than ten years old. Why would she be out in the swamp like that?"

"What if she was running away? Maybe with her mother? Her parents haven't stepped forward and there's no missing persons file on her."

He shook his head, his expression grave. "I don't like to hear that. A girl that young should be playing with stuffed animals and blowing bubbles like my grandkids."

"I agree, but if we can't come up with something soon, she'll become a ward of the state. If the Brethren are looking to get her back, it won't be hard to do once she's in the system. There's too many kids and not nearly enough oversight."

"That's a bad situation. I wish I could help but I haven't seen the Brethren in a lot of years. Was trying to think...maybe five, no, more like eight or better."

"They haven't come for supplies?"

"No. At least, not the men I dealt with before. If they got new ones, then they're not coming regular or buying big enough for me to guess who they are. But other stores have opened up along the bayous. They might be using someone else."

"Have fishermen seen them?"

"Not that anyone's said to me. At least, not in a lot of years. But then, people say they're deep in the swamp somewhere north of here. Locals aren't going to risk getting lost that far back when there's plenty of fish closer to home and they're using less gas. Plus, there's far less chance of being shot. A good bit of what they used to spend in here was on ammo, and they were armed every time they came in."

"Did they ever talk to you?"

"Nothing beyond what they wanted to buy, and it wasn't for my lack of trying. A shopkeep's job is more than just pushing merchandise. We're the hub of a town. Walter probably knows the genealogy of everyone in Sinful *and* what they bought for breakfast food this week."

"That's true," Ida Belle agreed.

"Thanks for the information," I said. "And I'm going to need a couple pounds of that boudin."

He grinned. "Best in the state."

We finished up our purchases and made our way back to the boat. As we were loading up, I heard a voice behind me. A voice I didn't want to hear.

"Just what do you think you're doing?" Hermes asked.

I turned around and saw him standing there, hands on hips and wearing a constipated look.

"Getting snacks and going fishing," I said. "Not that it's any of your business."

"Why is he with you?" Hermes pointed to Blanchet.

"Because he's Carter's friend and I'm a good host," I said.

Hermes glared at Blanchet, who was clearly enjoying his frustration at Blanchet's refusal to leave town.

"Don't you have better things to do than fish?" Hermes asked.

Blanchet grinned. "Not really. I'm retired, and even if I wasn't, few things beat fishing, especially with a boat of beautiful women."

Hermes huffed. "There's fishing in Sinful."

I nodded and held up my bag. "But we came here for the boudin. Best in the state."

Hermes pointed a finger at me. "I don't know what you're up to, but it better not be anything to do with my investigation."

"Does your investigation involve boudin or fishing?" I asked.

He glanced down at the boat, which was full of fishing tackle, then glared at me and stalked off.

"He's going to wear out his shoes with all that stomping," Gertie said.

Blanchet grinned. "I have to say, I am enjoying this so much it was almost worth being relieved from my duties. Except, of course, the part where everyone is screwed because Herpes is incompetent."

I nodded. I could appreciate his take as I was also enjoying rubbing it in. "Well, let's head out and do Hermes's job. Someone has to."

I untied the boat and jumped in, tucked my boudin away safely in the bench storage, and then we were off. Since Ida Belle was going slower this time, Gertie and I sat on the bench for a better view, and I pulled out my phone and attempted to follow the satellite image as we went. I'd scanned the satellite images for the general area around Mudbug the night before, looking for signs of structures in the swamp, but hadn't been able to spot any.

The swamps as you progressed away from Mudbug had

extremely dense areas, almost like everglades. You could easily have homes back in there that wouldn't show even in the winter because of the heavy moss clinging to the trees. And I was willing to bet that even if the Brethren lived in traditional structures, they were probably so well camouflaged that you wouldn't be able to spot them from overhead. They'd simply look like part of the natural landscape. I'd walked on top of entire compounds in the desert and had no idea of it because they'd been covered with sand. The Brethren's homes were probably cleverly positioned beneath heavy trees, vines, and other foliage that didn't die off in the winter.

The place that Ida Belle suspected was the first landmark was about twenty miles from the store dock, into the thickest area of the swamp. Bayous branched in all directions, making the satellite image look like an inside shot of the human body, with blood vessels spreading out in all directions. If they wanted to hide, they'd picked the right place for it. Some of the channels didn't even look passable, but that might simply be due to the timing of the tide. I'd seen some bayous that became land when the tide was out only for that land to disappear beneath the murky water when the tide came back in.

When we located what we believed to be the first marker, we considered the available channels and made comparisons with the satellite images, then headed deeper into the swamp. Every time we found a location that appeared to fit Spinner's description, we continued to the next. As the foliage got denser and the bayous narrower, I really hoped that we were on the right track. If we'd been off even once, then we were just cruising hopelessly around.

I was also worried about the Brethren.

So far, I'd spotted no signs that anyone was living off the land. If the group was still out here, they weren't working this area for food. When we reached the last landmark that

Spinner had given, Ida Belle stopped and I scanned our surroundings.

"Channels going in four directions," I said.

Ida Belle nodded. "And we don't even know that their place is one of those. It could be back up the one we just came down and on any one of those million offshoots we passed on the way here."

"We should have brought a drone," Gertie said.

"It crossed my mind, but if we got one close, they'd shoot it down."

"And then they'd know for sure we were coming," Blanchet said.

"Assuming they're still out here, we knew it wouldn't be easy to find them," I said. "Not if they've stayed hidden for as long as they have. Do you have any thoughts on direction? Put seclusion as the top priority with defense as second. Obviously, they have boats and could go anywhere to fish or run crab pots and the like, so I don't think that's a deciding factor when it comes to location."

"So you want me to find the castle in the swamp. Well, we've got the moat part, that's for sure."

She studied the four channels and pointed to the one in the middle. "See the way the water swirls just past the entry to that one? It's because there's something big enough down there to cause a shift in the current. Might be something submerged, but this far out, I'm going to guess it's the bank."

"It goes underwater when the tide's in and shows when it's out."

"Yep. And the best way to keep people from finding you would be to pick a place that they can't physically access half the time."

"Okay, then let's check it out, but we need to make it quick. Tide's going out."

Ida Belle raised one eyebrow. "That is not an issue for me."

She directed the boat into the channel, and when we got near the swirling water, I stuck my pole down into it and hit the muddy bottom about a foot under the boat. "It's embankment. Probably three feet wide."

"Bet it gets dry as a bone in the sunlight," Gertie said. "They'd be able to walk right across if they wanted to hunt or fish on the other side of the channel."

We continued down the bayou, the boat touching the embankment in some areas. A couple times, I wasn't certain we'd even fit through, but the foliage gave way, giving us the inches necessary to make the fit. I hoped the embankment beneath the tide line was as wide as the current one. If not, we were going to have a rough go getting back out.

The deeper we went into the swamp, the darker it became. The giant cypress trees on both sides leaned toward the tiny channel, their branches intertwined overhead. The thick moss blocked most of the sunlight, only allowing a dull glow and the occasional spotlight to seep through.

My senses were all on high alert. We were in a completely vulnerable position—entering enemy territory. The Brethren had every advantage, and we had exactly zero. All it would take was a couple good shots and we'd disappear. But one thing had become glaringly clear—if this was where the girl had come from, there was no way she'd gotten out alone.

As we approached a huge bend in the bayou, I felt the hair on the back of my neck stand up. Someone or something was watching us. Millions of insects and birds were, of course, but I didn't have a defensive response to those things. The only time my alert system went off was when I was being tracked by a predator.

I eased my pistol out and motioned to the others to do the same. The tension in the boat was as thick as the swamp brush. As Ida Belle slowly guided the boat around the corner, I held my breath and lifted my weapon, ready to fire if needed.

Then I stared in surprise when I saw that the bayou ended in a small cove.

I studied the entire area but couldn't lock in on where the eyes were coming from. But they were there. Of that, I was absolutely certain.

Ida Belle had the boat turning in a tight circle, keeping the engine on low, but not killing it. I scanned the bank, considering my options, then rose and leaned over to talk to her.

"Get me close to that log on the right side. It creates the perfect dock and that's a little too much of a coincidence for me, especially as there aren't other trees for at least thirty feet behind it. I'll take Blanchet. You and Gertie cover me."

She nodded and gave the boat a nudge, sending it right up next to the log. I motioned to Blanchet and jumped out of the boat and onto the log. It was wide and sturdy, and I easily walked across it to the bank. Blanchet jumped off the log next to me and we headed for the tree line. I paused just inside and studied the brush and the ground. Ida Belle was a better tracker than me, especially in the swamp, but she was also the most skilled at driving the boat. And if I needed a sniper shot for cover, she was the woman I wanted on the other end of the rifle.

"Here," Blanchet said, his voice low.

He fingered a tiny broken branch close to the ground. The break had been recent. Something big had passed by and that branch, which had been brittle because it was dying, had snapped. The rest of the bush had simply sprung back into place.

I nodded. "Impressive."

"I spent a decade into big game hunting. You have to be careful not to become dinner."

My hope ticked up a notch. Surely two first-rate trackers could find what we were looking for. We pushed past the bush and paused again to study the area. I found a leaf depressed into a patch of moss and we shifted right and paused again. We kept up this slow and deliberate process for another ten minutes and had only managed to cover twenty yards of swampland.

It was no wonder the group had never been found. If we continued at this rate, we might track down their location by sometime next year. I no longer felt the eyes on me, which was almost as troublesome as knowing I was being watched, so I prayed it had been an alligator or maybe a bear, assuming they were this deep in the swamp. But that niggling voice in the back of my mind didn't believe that.

Blanchet pointed to a split in tall weeds, where it was clear someone had passed recently. I was momentarily confused by the obvious sign of passage as it appeared whoever was living here had gone to great lengths to disguise their trail before now. But then, maybe they'd assumed no one would make it this far.

Blanchet stepped between the bushes, and I heard a tiny pop, like the snap of a string. I immediately grabbed his shoulder and pulled him backward as hard as I could. The blast sent us flying a good ten feet.

We crashed into a bush, and I felt the short, hard branches digging into my skin through my long-sleeved tee. But we'd have to assess the damage later. I jumped up, grabbed a stunned and confused Blanchet, and pulled him up.

"Run!" I said and took off back to the boat.

I heard Blanchet's footsteps behind me, so at least he wasn't so addled he couldn't follow directions. When I burst out of the trees and onto the bank, I saw Ida Belle and Gertie crouched in the boat, guns trained at me. I didn't even pause before running down the tree trunk and jumping into the boat. Ida Belle had scrambled into the driver's seat and was ready to fire the engine just as soon as Blanchet got in.

He had just emerged from the trees when I landed in the boat, and was now running across the trunk, looking a little unbalanced. I prayed he'd make it to the boat before he fell. He had two more steps to go when he appeared to lose his balance and pitched forward, tumbling off the trunk and into the bayou. I heard rustling in the marsh grass on the other bank.

"Gator!" Gertie yelled and fired off a round.

Blanchet's head popped up at the side of the boat, and Gertie and I leaned over to haul him in. We'd barely gotten him over the side before the gator surfaced at the side of the boat, obviously disappointed that his snack had gotten away. Gertie and I dropped on the bottom of the boat as Ida Belle fired up the engine and gunned it.

Blanchet struggled a bit to get turned over and in a sitting position, but I couldn't tell if that was because he'd been injured from the blast or his fall or if it was simply because of the harsh, speedy turns Ida Belle was making to get us out of the danger zone. I waited for a decent straight stretch, then launched up into the passenger seat next to her. As we approached the end of the channel, I wondered just how much of the embankment had been exposed.

She made the last turn before the mouth of the bayou, and I could see the rutted edges of the bayou mud forming a line from one side of the bank to the other. I glanced over at Ida Belle, who nodded. She'd seen it too.

"Hold on!" she yelled.

I was relieved to see that she was wearing her seat belt, and I snapped mine on just in time for her to crank up the speed on the boat to the limit. Blanchet glanced back at us, his eyes wide, and I motioned for him to stay low.

A couple seconds later, we flew up the exposed earth and the boat launched out of the bayou and into the air. Gertie let out a loud whoop as we went, then seemed to levitate out of the boat and went flying over the side as we landed. Ida Belle spun the boat around so quickly we almost lost Blanchet, but he wisely flattened himself on the bottom of the boat and only got thrown into the side.

Gertie stood on the edge of the bank, covered in mud and laughing as we pulled up. "Lord, that was a ride! Better than those roller coasters at Six Flags. I'm in mud up to my knees though."

Ida Belle edged up to the bank and I jumped out of my seat to help her into the boat, effectively covering both of us with the slimy mud. She dropped into the bottom of the boat next to Blanchet, who still appeared somewhat dazed by it all. I scrambled back into my seat and motioned for Ida Belle to continue. We were still too close to the Brethren to have a stop-and-chat.

Ida Belle made quick work of the channels and finally slowed when we reached the large bayou that bordered Mudbug.

"What the heck was that?" she asked.

"There was a trip wire," I said.

"Is that what happened?" Blanchet asked. "I didn't even feel anything, but there was this tiny noise. I had barely even registered it when Fortune grabbed my shoulder and pulled me backward. If she hadn't, I wouldn't be sitting here right now."

Ida Belle frowned. "Trip wire?"

I nodded. "Someone was watching us when we got to the cove, but they never made a move. Now I know why."

"They didn't have to," Ida Belle said grimly. "They've rigged the perimeter."

"That sounds more David Koresh than Billy Graham," Gertie said. "Why would a bunch of religious nuts who are mostly nonexistent to the rest of the world need that kind of security?"

"Good question," I said. "My guess is the usual answer."

"Something illegal," Blanchet said, his expression dark. "You think they're trafficking women?"

"I don't know what they're up to, but it seems highly likely they're holding people there against their will."

"There's no way that girl got through that minefield and all the way to Sinful without help," Ida Belle said.

"I know. I wish we could talk to her."

"If she doesn't remember anything, how can she help?" Gertie asked.

"Maybe she doesn't remember because people aren't asking the right questions," I said.

Blanchet nodded. "You think if you prompt her with questions about the Brethren, it might get her mind to firing again."

"I've seen it before."

"You managed to access her in the hospital once already," Gertie said.

I shook my head. "They'll be keeping a close watch because of that, and if Hermes is doing his job correctly, he'll have a deputy stationed there."

"I wouldn't bet on that one," Blanchet said.

"I hate to say it, but your best chance might be when the hospital releases her and she's placed in a home," Ida Belle said.

"The problem being I'm not the only one who can get to her then." I looked down at Blanchet. "You all right?"

He nodded. "Probably going to be feeling my age tomorrow, but my ears have stopped ringing."

"Let's head home. Gertie, Blanchet, and I need a shower, and I need to give Emmaline a call and make sure she's not climbing the walls. Maybe Harrison will have some news for us."

"Or Myrtle," Ida Belle said. "She's keeping tabs on Hermes...best she can anyway."

Blanchet raised one eyebrow. "The sheriff department's dispatcher is a spy?"

"Who do you think tipped me off last night?" I asked. "And made up those flyers and hung them downtown?"

He laughed. "Hermes has no idea what he's up against."

CHAPTER TWELVE

WE MADE A SWING BY GERTIE'S CAMP TO GET SOME FISH from her live box and tossed them in the cooler. Then we headed for my house. I wasn't remotely surprised to see Hermes walking across my backyard as we docked.

"That was a long fishing trip," he said. "Must have been hitting well. Why are you muddy?"

"I fell out of the boat," Gertie said. "It happens. Fortune helped me back in."

"Why are you on my property?" I asked.

"I'm the law. I can be wherever I want to be."

"I think you need to review the lawbooks again."

"I'll be happy to leave if you can produce some fish. Otherwise, I might decide you were out there interfering with my investigation."

"How, exactly? The girl was found in Sinful bayous, not Mudbug, but I'm fairly certain she didn't grow there among the cattails. And since I didn't see you out in the bayous searching for clues, I have to assume there aren't any there. Unless, of course, you're admitting to not doing your job. In which case, we wouldn't be interfering with anything because you're not doing anything."

Hermes's face turned red, and I knew he was trying to come up with any reason to arrest me, but he didn't have anything that he could make stick. He was walking a fine line antagonizing me, but I knew he was just dying to kick the line to the side and go for my jugular.

"I've about had it with you. Show me the fish, or I'm taking you in for impeding my investigation."

I had already leaned over and opened the bench where the built-in cooler was. I grabbed the biggest trout I could find, turned around, and chucked it at him. Hermes had the reaction speed of a tortoise, and when the fish smacked him right in the chest, he yelped like a child. The fish then slid down his shirt to the ground, leaving a slimy trail on its way down. Then after a couple seconds of warm air, it started flopping around on his shoes.

"I've got more," I said. "How many would you like to wear?"

"I should arrest you for assaulting an officer of the law."

"Prove it."

"What?"

"Prove it. I have three people here who will state that I was minding my own business on my private property and unloading my fish when you trespassed and stepped into the path of a toss that was already in motion."

"Four people." Ronald's voice sounded from the side yard, and I looked over to see him step in between the bushes that bordered our properties.

Hermes glanced over, and his dismay was so comical that I wished I had it on video. Ronald had outdone himself. He was dressed as Dorothy from *The Wizard of Oz*, complete with the braids and the shiny red shoes. He had a basket on one arm and a stuffed terrier on the other.

"Looks like I found the Wizard," Ronald said. "And he's just as fake as the movie one."

"I don't know what kind of tomfoolery you people are up to," Hermes said, "but you best get back to where you came from."

"That would be somewhere over the rainbow," Blanchet said, and started laughing.

Ronald winked at Blanchet. "I like you."

He took a step closer to Hermes and gave him a once-over. "But I also like a challenge. I could work with you. Bring out that sexy-cop look that I love so much."

Hermes's eyes widened, and so much blood rushed into his face that I thought his head might explode. Blanchet collapsed on the side of the boat.

"I'm free tonight," Ronald said.

Hermes spun around so fast he probably twisted an ankle, then retreated at a half jog. We all burst into laughter and Blanchet looked up at Ronald, tears streaming down his face.

"You're a genius."

Ronald shrugged. "Macho bullies like Hermes never know how to handle another man hitting on them. At Nora's last night, I heard about what he did to Ally at the bakery. I figured I'd give him a taste of his own medicine."

"What's with the outfit?" I asked. "You usually don't dress up this much midweek."

"Oh, just a bunch of us girls are getting together for a Judy Garland night in New Orleans, and I'm trying to pin down my outfit."

"Are there prizes?" Gertie asked. "Because I bet you win."

"There are, but I heard that hussy Caspien got a real

terrier. Well, I must run. Good day, ladies, and very handsome gentleman."

Ronald flicked his hand over his head in a wave and disappeared through the bushes again.

Blanchet wiped his eyes. "I might have to move here. Seriously, nothing interesting ever happens in my town."

"We're definitely not short on interesting," I said. "But we have another problem. Hermes is keeping tabs on us. I mean, he didn't follow us into the bayou, but my yard makes the third place he's accosted us today. I had my suspicions when we ran into him in Mudbug."

Blanchet sobered a bit. "I thought you stopped for the fish because you wanted them for dinner, but I get it now. You figured he might show up here and wanted them for cover."

"The one advantage to people like Hermes is they're predictable," Ida Belle said.

"Let's just hope he doesn't evolve before we solve this case," I said.

Blanchet frowned. "He might be predictable, but he's not psychic."

I nodded. "He's got spies."

———

I'D JUST STEPPED OUT OF THE SHOWER WHEN MY PHONE started ringing. I grabbed it from the counter and checked the display. Harrison.

"The bas—he did it!"

"Did what?"

"He got the girl released from the hospital. Cassidy called me fit to be tied, but her boss said he didn't have a choice. Apparently, Hermes ran it up the pole and someone with enough juice to sway him made a call. He's not happy about it either, but the test results don't give them enough to insist she stay."

"Where is she now?"

"A social worker took her and said she'll be placed in a temporary foster home until her parents are found or they decide they need a long-term plan."

"Do you know where the foster home is?"

"No. The social worker won't share that kind of information, of course, even though the foster parents are required to bring her back to the hospital for follow-up in two days."

"What do you want to bet Hermes will do everything he can to get her pulled from the hospital."

"Bet on it. Cassidy got the social worker's name, but I don't know that it will do us any good. Not like she's taking the girl home with her."

"Crap. We need to know where she is. We ran into a problem today looking for the Brethren." I described our hunt to Harrison and the subsequent explosion.

"That sounds more like a cartel than a religious group."

"Yeah. That's what I was thinking, but I haven't floated that idea yet. I mean, they're buried out in the swamp, It's not the right conditions for cannabis. Too wet."

"Meth?"

"Definitely a possibility. Not like anyone blinks at explosions around here. Could be an illegal still or someone lazy fishing."

"Or Gertie's purse."

"That's a given. But you need a lot of supplies for cooking meth, and no one in Mudbug has seen the Brethren in years."

"They wouldn't shop local for that kind of supplies. Might have moved all their shopping to the city. Less likely someone will pay attention."

"That's what I was thinking. They started local and small

but as they made more money, they could afford to take their business to NOLA. That would be the most likely hub for distribution as well."

"That and all those boats roaming the Gulf," he said.

"True. Crap, there's too many possibilities here to attack them from another angle."

"I wish Hermes hadn't zeroed in on you. Then you could try to track them from the supplier end. But if he's accosted you that many times today, then he's got people watching."

"This whole thing has been like going down a rabbit hole."

"You made good progress today, though. You got a general location for the group, and we know they're worshipping something besides Jesus, or they wouldn't need all that firepower."

"And they have some people trained in explosives. Blanchet didn't even realize what had happened. Only someone with a high level of military training or experience with this on the ground would have reacted the way I did."

"You thinking they got military in there?"

"Not everyone goes in to serve their country. Some are running from prosecution to begin with. When they get out, they're just more dangerous criminals with a larger knowledge base."

Harrison sighed. "I'll let you know if I get anything else on the girl. Cassidy knows people with social services back in DC. They might not have any insight to things down here, but she's going to make some calls anyway."

"I get it, but tell her I said there's nothing she could do to prevent this one. Hermes is on a mission."

"His mission is going to get that girl killed or sent back to some kind of hell on earth."

"We're just going to have to see that it doesn't."

I disconnected and got dressed. By the time I'd made it

downstairs, Ida Belle, Gertie, and Blanchet were pulling up. Blanchet was moving a little stiffly. Gertie, who'd had her own tumble, appeared right as rain. I gave her a suspicious look as she skipped into the kitchen.

"You've been taking meds from Nora again, haven't you?" I asked.

She grinned. "It's like I never even fell out of the boat. That woman could make a fortune selling this stuff."

"She's already got a fortune," Ida Belle said. "And way too much time on her hands."

"What did you take?" Blanchet asked, easing himself into a chair.

"Nora's recently started using her foreign country finds to mix up her own drugs," I said. "God only knows what's in those pills Gertie's taking."

"Something awesome," Gertie said. "Look at me and look at Blanchet."

"To be fair, Blanchet was hit by an explosive blast," I said. "That's a far cry from falling out of the boat."

"You got any more of those pills?" Blanchet asked.

Ida Belle and I stared at him in dismay.

"Really? You're going to hop on that train?" I asked. "You don't even know if the stuff in those is legal, much less safe."

He shrugged. "Retired, remember? Don't have to drug test, and I'm closer to death than further away. My whole body aches, and I'm pretty sure you tore my rotator cuff when you pulled me. Not that I'm complaining, mind you. Besides, I ate a piece of cake at her party and haven't felt my knees ever since. I wouldn't mind my shoulders going the same direction."

Gertie sat her purse on the table and opened it up. She pulled out a bag of sunflower seeds, a plastic container with grapes, a bag of glitter, a sandwich, two sticks of dynamite, a knife, two pistols, and a set of fuzzy pink handcuffs before locating the bottle of Nora's pills.

Blanchet stared at the bounty on my kitchen table. "I don't know whether to be impressed or scared."

"Scared."

Ida Belle and I both spoke at once.

"This is my small bag," Gertie said as she poured a pill out into Blanchet's hand. "You should see what I can fit in my larger one. One time, I took an entire lasagna to church. I didn't have time for breakfast that morning."

Blanchet tossed the pill in his mouth, downed it with water, and we all watched him. When several seconds had passed and he didn't keel over in the seat and his pupils remained normal, we figured we might as well move on.

First, I filled them in on Harrison's phone call.

"There's got to be a way to track the girl down," Blanchet said. "We have to get to her before that explosive-loving cult does."

"I agree, but we don't have anything to go on. Social services isn't going to give out that information and neither is Hermes."

My phone signaled an incoming text and I glanced at the display.

Scooter.

Curious about what Scooter might need me for, I accessed the text messages and saw he'd attached a video.

Hermes versus the llamas...guess who wins?

"Everyone huddle," I said. "Scooter filmed Hermes trying to get his wheels."

Gertie jumped up clapping her hands. "This ought to be good."

I pressed Play and everyone leaned in, watching as Hermes pulled up in a sheriff's department vehicle and jumped out, stomping and cussing at the sight of his wheels stacked in the middle of the pasture. For a minute, it looked as if he was going to leave and send someone else to retrieve them, but then he caught sight of a gate about twenty feet away and must have figured he could just roll them out himself.

He headed for the gate and started across the field to the wheels. I watched in the distance for the llamas, which I was certain had been dispatched as soon as Farmer Frank had seen Hermes enter his pasture.

We didn't have to wait long.

"There's the llamas!" Gertie said.

We all locked in on the black and brown specks moving across the pasture at a good clip toward Hermes. He'd gotten one wheel out of the gate and was headed back for the second, and in keeping with being the biggest fool in the parish, he'd left the gate open. He wrangled the second wheel down from the heap, then leaned over to upright it. When he rose, he found himself face-to-face with the llamas.

The brown one, Mocha, was the worst spitter. Hermes didn't even have a chance to register shock before he caught a wad of spit and Copenhagen right in the face. Espresso, the black one, doubled down, not wanting to be outdone by his partner.

Hermes yelled and pulled out his gun, but before he could get off a shot, a bullet tore through the wheel he'd just lifted and he straightened up and we saw Farmer Frank yelling and running across the field toward him. Scooter must have been filming from some distance away, but we could still make out the word 'trespassing.' And there was no guess about Frank's feelings on the matter when he sent a second round into another one of the tires.

Hermes yelled something that sounded like 'sheriff,' but Frank's hearing was about as good as his night vision. His answer was another shot in the last remaining wheel. Hermes took off running for the open gate, the llamas hot on his heels and spitting the entire way. By the time he reached his vehicle, the entire back of his white T-shirt was stained brown and the llamas sent a couple parting shots onto his window before he tore out of there.

The one wheel that he'd managed to acquire—and the only one without a bullet in it—rolled out of the back of the truck and off down the road. The llamas chased it for a while, then Frank made it to the gate and called them back in. They came running into the pasture and he stroked their heads and necks while they preened, looking superbly pleased with themselves.

By the time the video ended, we were all laughing so hard it took us a good five minutes to recover. I finally managed to lift my phone up again and sent Scooter a text.

Absolutely brilliant. Are you posting it on YouTube?

Already done. Look up Sheriff Herpes and the Llama Showdown.

I owe you. Big time.

Nah. It was fun. And no one deserves it more.

I shook my head. "Hermes is going to be out for blood after that."

"He still can't pin it on you though," Blanchet said. "You were right there in front of him when it happened. And he can't pin anything on Farmer Frank either. He has every right to protect his pasture and his llamas."

"I'm pretty sure those llamas don't need protecting," Gertie said. "They're better than guard dogs."

Ida Belle's phone rang, interrupting our glee, and she frowned as she checked the display. "It's Lottie."

As soon as she answered, I could hear the excitement in Lottie's voice.

"She's here!" Lottie said.

"Who's there?" Ida Belle asked as she put her phone on speaker.

"The girl! The one you showed me a picture of."

My pulse quickened.

"You saw the girl in Mudbug?" I asked.

"Yes. I was making my daily walk to the church to work on the flower beds and saw her in a car with an older woman. I was so flabbergasted that I stepped in a mudhole and tore a brand-new pair of knee-highs. Then I thought—what would those girls do? So I followed them."

"You ran after a car with torn hose?" Gertie asked, her voice encouraging. "That's hard-core."

"Thanks! I have to admit, I almost passed out—both from the jogging and the fear—but thankfully, they weren't going far. Would have been easier if I could have cut through Old Man Nesbitt's yard but he's got that blind, angry dog and I didn't want to risk it. Not without food on me."

"That's why I always carry food," Gertie said.

"See how much I'm learning from you? Anyway, the car turned a couple blocks ahead and I sneaked into Milly Scranton's bushes to watch. The woman and the girl got out of the car and went inside June Nelson's house. The woman came out about ten minutes later and left without the girl. Is the girl related to June?"

"I don't think so. But social services took her from the hospital and were going to place her in a temporary foster home."

"Oh! That makes sense. June fostered kids for years. She was widowed fairly young and never had any of her own. She was one of those transitionary homes, so none of them stayed for long. Had a lot of kids in her house over the years, but I thought she'd stopped fostering a good while back."

"They might have called in a favor, wanting to keep the girl in the area until her memory returns or her parents show up."

"If they do."

"Yeah. If they do. I really need to talk to the girl, but the police aren't going to allow that. Do you know June well?"

"As well as you know anyone, I suppose. We're not close, but we go to the same church. She has a great garden and makes some of the best preserves I've ever had. Has a sister in Mississippi who's got some chronic issues and sometimes she has to head off and see to her for weeks at a time. My guess is that's why she had to stop fostering."

"Do you think she'd let us talk to the girl?"

"Hmmm. That's a tough one. June's nice but she's always been a stickler for the rules. Had a row with one of the judges at the local fair over preserves that didn't exactly align with the rulebook. First time anyone had ever seen her raise her voice, so it was a bit of a surprise. So if she's been told to keep the girl from talking to anyone except social services or the police, then I imagine that's what she's going to do."

"Do you think she would talk to me?"

"I don't see why not. Except for that judge thing, she's always been nice. And I guess everyone is due at least one hissy fit in the thirty years they've lived here."

"Okay. Thanks so much, Lottie. If you see anything else, let us know, but don't get caught watching them. The guy who replaced Andy as the temporary sheriff is a real piece of work."

"Hhmmmpf. Already got an earful about that fool at my ladies' high tea today at lunch. He's hit on a couple of the women's granddaughters, and they're not amused."

"High tea? I didn't think that was a big thing in these parts."

"Well, instead of cream and sugar, we spike ours with

whiskey. Maude said that's why we should call it 'high' tea. She's a real joker."

I laughed. "Sounds fun. Thanks again, Lottie."

"You're welcome, and please keep me in the loop. I hate thinking about what happened to that poor girl and what might happen again if you can't get her some help. And I'm worried about her mother."

"I'm worried too."

I disconnected. "Do you guys know this June Nelson?"

Ida Belle frowned and shrugged, and Gertie gave me a somewhat hesitant nod.

"A little," Gertie said. "We've crossed paths on some charity stuff. And Lottie's right about her preserves. But nothing stands out. She's your typical small-town widow—has a good house that's paid for, has a garden and roses, goes to church."

Ida Belle nodded. "All of which makes her ideally suited to be a temporary foster home. She projects stable and safe to most people."

"But not to you?"

"I think she's a bore," Gertie said.

I laughed. "You probably thought the same about Lottie and here we find out she's been boozing it up in the middle of the day with the ladies and calling it 'tea.'"

"That's true. I might have to up her rating, especially given that she chased that car, torn hose and all."

"Lottie said June's been here for thirty years—how old is she? And where was she before?"

"I'd put her at midsixties," Ida Belle said. "Keeps in shape though. Not sure where she lived before moving to Sinful, but I want to think someone said Gretna. Her house belonged to her uncle, maybe, but he'd passed some years before, and it had been rented out by the lawyers. I know because I looked into buying it for a rental, but she wasn't interested in selling."

"I think her husband had been gone about a year when she moved here," Gertie said. "He was a lot older, and I heard he'd been sick for a while. I assumed she'd held the house in case she wanted a change after he was gone."

Ida Belle nodded. "A year is about the time you fish or cut bait on a major loss. So she uprooted and moved to a new town. Got her credentials to foster. Starting winning every contest for preserves in the parish."

"No kids of her own?"

Gertie shook her head. "Probably couldn't have them, but that's not the kind of thing people discuss much at charity events. She was always doing things for the kids, though, crafts and stuff. One of the church ladies over there said a lot of the kids she fostered still keep in touch, even though they were only with her for a short time."

"That says a lot," I said. "Sounds like she couldn't do it longer-term because of her sister. What's wrong with her?"

They both shrugged.

"Don't know that anyone has ever said," Ida Belle said. "But I'd assume something chronic and progressive as she's been absent from events more and more the past couple years."

I nodded. The good news was June sounded like a solid choice for leaving a scared young girl with. The downside, of course, was that being a great preserve maker didn't prepare her in any way to deal with the trouble that was probably headed right to her doorstep. No way Hermes was going to give the girl police protection, and to be fair, I wasn't sure Carter could have swung it either. Not officially. But Carter would have sat there himself on his off time and tapped his friends to fill in the others. I was fairly certain Hermes didn't have actual friends. Just people he owed and who owed him.

"Okay, we'll try to talk to June tomorrow."

"What's on the agenda for tonight?" Gertie asked.

"Dinner," I said. "I'm starving, and it's moving past sunset and into dark. There's nothing else we can do tonight. So who's up for the café? The special tonight is pot roast."

Ida Belle and Gertie nodded.

"Blanchet?" I asked.

"Heck yeah. I figured that went without saying—bachelor, home-cooked meal. They're probably going to get tired of seeing me down there."

He jumped up from his chair and reached back to grab his cell phone, then winced, anticipating the jolt of pain that was coming from his shoulder. He paused, his hand perched midair, and smiled, then grabbed his phone and did big loops with his arm.

"Look at this! It worked. Nora is a genius!"

Good. God.

CHAPTER THIRTEEN

DINNER WAS FANTASTIC, AS USUAL, AND WE WERE ALL stuffed and happy—at least about the food—as we exited the café. Blanchet had driven over himself and gave us a wave as he set off. I'd ridden over with Ida Belle and Gertie but was considering a walk home, just to burn off the calories.

As soon as we exited the café, I noticed a young Black woman on a bench farther down the sidewalk watching us. Since people-watching was a hobby in most small towns, I didn't dwell on it, until more people exited after us and her gaze never shifted. I stepped to the outside of Ida Belle and Gertie as we walked toward the SUV—and the woman—and talked cheerily about the meal. Being on the end meant I had to look toward the sidewalk to see either of them, which gave me plenty of opportunity to study the woman without her knowing.

Late twenties. Five foot five. A hundred fifteen pounds. Excellent muscle tone. I couldn't see a weapon on her, but her back wasn't exposed, and a purse sat on the bench next to her. Threat level undetermined.

As we got closer to the SUV, Ida Belle glanced over and

gave me a lifted eyebrow. She'd spotted the woman as well. Ida Belle pulled out her keys and unlocked the SUV and as the doors beeped, the woman rose and walked our way. I slipped my hand behind my back and saw her glance at it and hesitate so slightly most wouldn't have noticed, then she kept walking toward us.

"Excuse me, but are you Fortune Redding?" she asked.

"Who's asking?"

She stuck her hand out. "My name is Blair Johnson. I'm with the Department of Children and Family Services oversight division."

"So Internal Affairs?"

She forced a smile. "Something like that. I'd like to speak to you about the girl you found."

"I didn't find her. That was a local fisherman."

"Yes, let me rephrase. I'd like to speak to you about the girl to whom you administered CPR."

I frowned. "Is something wrong?"

"Obviously, the circumstances surrounding her are less than ideal, so I've been asked to step in and monitor the situation."

"Monitor it for what?"

"Ms. Redding, I'm sure you didn't fail to notice the unusual manner and location in which the girl was found. And the fact that no one has come forward to claim her or even reported her missing is of great concern to our department. Most children we process have known histories, and that information allows us to make better choices about their care and placement. But given the lack of information in this case and the girl's loss of memory, we're left with a bit of a dilemma regarding long-term care, assuming her parents never materialize."

I frowned. Although everything she'd said rang true, someone about her bothered me.

"Pardon me for saying so, Ms. Johnson, but you look kinda young to be supervising a bunch of social workers who've probably been at the job longer than you've been an adult."

She stiffened a bit. "And you, Ms. Redding, look too young to have been one of the CIA's top agents, but I have it on good authority that is absolutely the case. If you need to know my résumé in order to speak with me, I hold a PhD in psychology from Stanford University."

"Impressive. So why in the world would you take an expensive and hard-to-obtain degree into the bayous of Louisiana to rake in less than minimum wage when you factor in work hours?"

"Because I grew up in southeast Louisiana, Ms. Redding. And my family has more money than God, so I don't have to worry about making a living. I have the luxury of indulging my own interests, which happens to be helping children."

"Good enough. But I don't know what I can tell you."

"None of you had ever seen the girl before that night?"

We all shook our heads.

"And no one from the area has recognized her or suggested she might belong to a certain family?"

"No," I said. "Everyone is at a loss, and Ida Belle and Gertie know everyone in this town."

"There's been some suggestion that a religious group took up around here decades back. Do you know anything about them?"

I shook my head. "Only what everyone else knows. They're supposed to live somewhere out in the swamp beyond Mudbug, but people rarely see them."

"And no one has ever found their dwellings?"

I looked at Ida Belle and Gertie, who both shook their heads.

"People have tried over the years," Ida Belle said. "High school kids, mostly. Out on a kick, you know? But no one has ever come up with anything."

"Why are you asking about some Bible thumpers?" I asked. "Do you think that's where the girl came from? If so, how the heck did she get to Sinful? Why was she in the middle of the swamp—no camp or boat in sight?"

"Those questions are exactly why I'm here," she said. "Children who've been raised in those stringent religious organizations often have special issues to work through."

"You can call it a cult. Everyone else does."

"However you'd like to label it, we want to make sure we can address those issues should her memory return."

"And make sure she wasn't being abused in case someone from the cult comes to claim her."

"Yes. Obviously."

"Well, I'm sorry I can't give you more information. I really would like to help the girl. She's far too young to be on her own and it scares me to think about what she's probably already been through to have arrived at the place she did. I heard a social worker removed her from the hospital."

"Yes, well, they can't keep her there without medical reason. She's been temporarily placed until we can sort her case better."

"And you're overseeing that sorting?"

"That's correct." She pulled a wallet out of her purse and handed me a card with her name and phone number on it. "If you think of anything else, please give me a call."

We stood next to the SUV and watched her walk away. She climbed into a brand-new BMW sedan and drove off.

"What the heck was that?" Ida Belle asked.

I shook my head. "I don't know. But I don't like it."

"She kinda gave me the willies," Gertie said. "Isn't a social worker supposed to be more warm and fuzzy?"

"Technically, she's monitoring social workers, not working as one," Ida Belle said. "So I'd assume a lack of warm fuzzies is required if you're sitting in the judgment seat. But the whole thing felt off."

"Definitely," I agreed. "But she's on the same train of thought we are, and I have to wonder how she got there. The people who might have ideas about what we're up to aren't talking about it."

"No," Ida Belle agreed. "It's certainly not impossible for two people to come up with the same idea, but considering she's not local, someone would have had to send her off in that direction."

"It wasn't Hermes," Gertie said. "He can't find his butt with both hands. And even if he got a clue, no way would he make it known."

Ida Belle nodded. "Might have to share the glory."

I looked at the card again and the receding taillights headed out of Sinful and toward the highway. "Let's try to speak to June first thing tomorrow morning. If this woman is legit, she would have talked to June, right? Tried to talk to the girl?"

"You would think," Ida Belle said.

But something made me unsure.

———

My cell phone sent me jolting out of a dead sleep and I leaped out of bed, grabbing my pistol as I went. By the time my feet hit the floor, I'd zeroed in on the reason for the sound, and Merlin, who was used to, but still disapproving of, my antics, glared at me with one eye, then promptly tucked his head under my pillow and went back to sleep.

I grabbed the phone. Harrison. Three o'clock a.m.

This couldn't be good.

"A call came in tonight in Mudbug from June Nelson," he said as soon as I answered. "A prowler around her house. Dispatch sent out a unit, but they didn't find anything."

"Crap! I was hoping we'd have a couple days to work with before they tracked the girl down."

"So was I, but looks like no luck on that one."

"How do you know about the call? I thought you were traffic only."

"The night unit is two rookies. It's a stupid setup, and not the one Carter structured for Mudbug, I can assure you. But that idiot Hermes has been shifting everyone around. Honestly, I think he's doing it just to hack us all off. No one wants him here."

"So if he can get people to quit, he stands a better chance at the sheriff run and putting his own lackeys in place."

"Which is exactly why two second-year deputies with little training were put together. Fortunately, they're both bright and eager to have long careers, so they called me and asked how to handle the situation. I walked them through it. Now I'm praying Hermes doesn't check our phone logs, because he'll use it as a reason to write everyone up."

"Did they find anything at all? What did June say?"

"She said the girl awakened her crying out in her sleep. She went in to check on her, but she was only dreaming. She put a hand on her to calm her and that's when she saw a shadow move by the window. The blinds were closed, so it was just the movement in between that registered, but that's a pier and beam house, and the bottom of that window is a good four feet off the ground, so it had to be something tall enough and wide enough to register through the slats at that height."

"So not a stray cat."

"Definitely not a stray cat. They covered the flower bed with a tarp and will get CSU out there, but it's a mulched bed. I doubt they're going to find anything."

"Probably not. I don't like it."

"I don't either, which is why I'm calling you from my truck on the way to Mudbug."

"You're going to stake out her house."

"Someone has to. God knows Hermes isn't going to take care of this."

"Be careful."

He snorted. "You think a sloppy intruder can get the best of me?"

"Of course not. I meant Hermes. If he catches you doing anything surrounding this case, he'll push for you to be dismissed. If he can make that happen before Carter gets back, it might be hard for him to get you reinstated."

"I was a spook, remember? Hermes will never know I was there."

I dropped the cell phone on my nightstand and flopped back on the bed. I knew it would take forever to get back to sleep if I could manage it at all. But I did feel better knowing Harrison was going to stake out June's house. Unfortunately, my emotions warred between hoping the intruder was foolish enough to return so he could catch them and hoping he'd stay away so Harrison wouldn't get caught dipping into Hermes's business.

I closed my eyes and counted center mass shots, hoping to drift back off, but gave up after I'd killed at least twenty terrorists. It was useless. Until I calmed my mind, sleep wouldn't happen, so I headed downstairs for my recliner, hot chocolate, and boring TV. The last time I looked, it was closing in on 5:00 a.m.

My front door opened, and I jumped out of my recliner, grabbed my pistol and aimed it at the door. Then I blinked and saw Ida Belle and Gertie standing there, Blanchet behind them.

"That was impressive," Blanchet said.

Gertie nodded. "We haven't seen it in a while, but I'm always amazed at the speed, especially since she's asleep when she reacts. That CIA training must be something."

Ida Belle gave me and the room a critical look. "Couldn't sleep?"

I waved my gun toward the kitchen. "No. Harrison called me at 3:00 a.m. and I couldn't get back to sleep, so I came downstairs to try here. What time is it?"

"A little after seven," Gertie said. "You and Ida Belle must share the same disease because she had me out of bed at the butt crack of dawn. And this guy was out jogging. Before sunrise! I don't know what's wrong with you people."

Ida Belle motioned for me to sit and went about making coffee. "So tell us about the call—because no way Harrison called for no reason, especially at that time of night."

I filled them in on the situation at June's while the coffee brewed and finally started to feel somewhat human after my first cup.

"It's too early to hit up June just yet," I said. "But that's the first thing on my list today. Blanchet, you'll have to sit this one out."

"Why?" he asked.

"Because old Southern women who have been widowed for a coon's age have no use for men," Gertie said.

"It's true," I said. "She won't talk around you."

"I get it," he said. "So...breakfast?"

"Where do you put all that food you consume?" Gertie asked.

"Running before dawn," I said.

"If that's what it takes, I'll just work on eating less," Gertie said.

"It's Thursday," Ida Belle said.

"What does that mean?" Blanchet asked.

"Free blueberry muffin with the chicken fried steak breakfast," I said.

Gertie grinned. "I'll work on eating less tomorrow."

CHAPTER FOURTEEN

WE LINGERED OVER BREAKFAST, TAKING UP SOME TIME BY chatting with the locals. Everyone wanted to know about Carter and when he was coming back. Most had heard about Hermes or experienced him firsthand and weren't impressed. All had seen the video and wished Farmer Frank would have taken a few shots and saved us all some hassle. They all wanted to know what they could do about the situation. I appreciated the support Carter was getting and wished I had answers for them. Heck, I wished I had answers for me.

Finally, we'd delayed long enough and left the café. Blanchet crossed the street to the General Store, figuring he'd ask Walter if there was anything he could help him with because he didn't feel like sitting in Carter's quiet house all day. Ida Belle, Gertie, and I headed for Mudbug.

June's house was one of the small quaint cottage types in a pretty neighborhood with large lots and humongous oak trees. Huge azaleas grew everywhere, so there were plenty of ways for someone to traverse the area and go unseen. Ida Belle did a pass down the street first, and I spotted a woman in the front yard pulling weeds out of a flower bed. We'd already decided to park on the next street, just in case Hermes pulled a drive-by, so we made a leisurely stroll back around the block to June's.

She straightened up and frowned slightly as she caught sight of us heading up her walkway. Then she must have recognized Ida Belle and Gertie because her expression softened and she nodded.

"Good morning, ladies. It's been a while."

"We've missed you at the last couple of events," Gertie said.

June smiled. "You mean you've missed my preserves."

"*Everyone* has missed your preserves," Ida Belle said. "But we've missed you as well."

June looked pleased.

"How is your sister doing?" Gertie asked.

She gave us a sad look. "Not so good, I'm afraid. Her husband does his best, but he's not a caretaker and he still works...has to with all the bills. Medicare doesn't cover everything actually needed, and older bodies can't do things the way we used to. So he hires out more, which costs money. I've had to spend a lot more time there this past year, especially as she's been declining faster. I've told him he has to start thinking about a facility. Neither one of us can keep doing this forever."

"What does your sister say?" Gertie asked.

June shrugged and shook her head. "She's so hopped up on pain meds, you can't get a clear thought out of her most days. I don't know that she'd even realize she was somewhere different. Doesn't know me most of the time."

"I'm so sorry," Gertie said. "That's hard."

"The Lord doesn't give us more than we can handle, right?" June said, and looked over at me.

"I'm sorry," I said. "We've never met. I'm Fortune Redding, a friend of Ida Belle and Gertie's."

June's face brightened. "You're the lady who saved the girl."

She reached out and grabbed my hand and squeezed it. "I'm so glad to meet you and thank you personally. Lord, that poor child. When I think of what she must have been through."

"We heard that you're fostering the girl until her situation is resolved," I said.

"I guess I should have expected that would get around quickly," June said. "It's big news around here, after all. I can't let you talk to her, though."

"I understand," I said. "But I was hoping we could talk to you."

"Don't know as I'd have anything relevant to say, but I'm happy to take a break and say nothing important. I put a fresh pitcher of sweet tea in the refrigerator before I came outside to tackle those beds. Head on up to the porch and I'll bring us out some."

We stepped onto the large screened porch on the front of the house and June went inside. There was a big patio set with thick cushions on one end, so we took seats there. Her drapes were flapping out of the open windows and I tucked them behind the chair so they wouldn't blow in my face. June came back out as I was tucking, carrying a tray with glasses and a pitcher of sweet tea.

"Sorry about the drapes," she said as she poured. "I forgot to tie them off inside when I opened the windows. I love to get that cross-breeze through the house to air it out. Then I know it's spring."

"Me too," Gertie agreed.

"How do you ladies like my new porch?" June asked. "Just had it screened in. Keeps the bugs off in the evening so I can sit out here with my book."

"It's really nice," I said, actually meaning it.

I preferred being outside when the weather was nice but didn't have a large sitting area like this. Not that it was required, as I mostly sat alone or with Carter, but maybe I should consider an addition to my small back porch area and enclose it.

"Walter keeps wanting to add a big front porch to my house because that's where all the breeze is in the evening," Ida Belle said. "Don't get me wrong, it would improve the looks, but if you sit on the front porch, then people stop and talk to you. That doesn't sound relaxing to me."

June waved her hands. "See those screens? You can see out of them but not in."

I nodded. "I noticed that coming up the walk."

"Hmmm," Ida Belle said. "I might consider a porch if I can sit out there without having to talk to random people."

"Your neighbors aren't 'random,'" Gertie said.

"When I'm trying to relax on my porch, everyone's random but Walter. Sometimes even him."

We all laughed.

"Fortunately, the breeze is in my backyard," I said. "I might have to consider adding something like this. It would be nice to read outside without fighting off the mosquitoes."

"Maybe enclose the hot tub too so people don't keep coming by and deciding they want to get in with us," Gertie said. "They never bring their own booze, either, and we always have to share the good stuff."

June smiled. "I suppose those are called first-world problems, since most don't get to sit in a hot tub drinking good booze or relax on their porch with a cup of tea and a book. But I can see where it might get crowded if too many catch on."

"So how is the girl doing?" I asked, figuring I should get to the real purpose of our visit.

"She's finally asleep again, poor thing," June said. "I know she can't remember what happened, but she's obviously been through it. Wakes up all night thrashing about and hollering in her sleep. Looked pale as a ghost with huge dark circles under her eyes at breakfast. Barely ate a thing, but I managed to get a little in her, then sent her back to bed. I put a television in there, hoping it would take her mind off things."

"I guess you can't really let her leave the house," I said.

"Given the circumstances, the caseworker thought it would be better if she wasn't seen outdoors. I told her everyone in the parish would know the girl was here within a day, but I don't think she believed me. She's from the city."

Ida Belle nodded. "They don't understand how small towns work."

"Well, we're definitely not here to make things worse for her," I said. "I just wanted to check and see how she was doing. It was kind of dicey, getting her breathing again, and the hospital can't give me information, and well, I couldn't let it go until I knew for sure she was all right."

June reached over and squeezed my hand. "You're a good woman, Ms. Redding. And that girl is lucky you were there, and that fisherman. When she's got a placement or they locate her family, I need to track him down and thank him as well."

"He was pretty stressed about the whole thing," Gertie said. "But then I guess I would be too. I'm glad she seems all right—physically at least."

June sighed. "I suppose she's as good as she can be, given all that she must have gone through. She's bruised, of course, and looks a tad bit malnourished to me, but everything's working right except her mind."

"Is she verbal?" Ida Belle asked.

"She can talk. She just doesn't choose to often. Mostly, I get nods or head shakes. It's fairly common, though. All of the kids I took in were older and had been through trauma or they wouldn't have been with me in the first place. I was emergency placement, you see. Her behavior is similar to what I've seen before."

"I find it interesting that she still exhibits the signs of trauma even though she can't remember what happened to her," I said.

June nodded. "I studied some child psychology years ago, hoping to do a better job with these kids, and Lord knows, I've spoken to a therapist or two. They told me that the subconscious mind acts to protect them even if their consciousness isn't aware of the danger."

"Which is probably why she has nightmares. Her subconscious is trying to warn her."

"I think so. And that's probably part of the reason she's so cautious when she's awake. Well, that and she doesn't know anyone around her, including herself. I can only imagine how unnerving that is."

"Well, I'm glad she's with you, June. I've been worried about her ever since the paramedics put her in that ambulance. I'm glad she's all right physically, but I really wish her parents would turn up. I have to say, it concerns me a lot that they haven't reported her missing."

June gave me a grave nod. "The implications of that aren't lost on me, but so far, I've not heard anything about recent accidents or homicides. Of course, assuming it happened out in those bayous, they might not ever find anything."

"And we may never know what happened unless she remembers."

"I'm afraid that's the case. I waver between hoping she does so that all this can be answered, and we can make a plan for her to move forward, and hoping she never remembers because how she was found lends itself to circumstances no child should have to deal with."

"Probably better for her to never remember," Gertie said.

"If her family is gone—no matter the reason—and she's going to have to start over in a new place anyway, might as well do it with no bad memories."

June nodded. "You might just be right on that one."

Suddenly June stiffened and her face flashed with anger as she stared past me at the street.

"Oh no, he doesn't," June said, and jumped up from her chair as a sheriff's department truck pulled up to the curb.

She stomped off the porch and met Hermes halfway down her walk.

"This whole screen situation is awesome," Gertie said.

"Sssshhhhh," Ida Belle shushed her. "He can't see us, but he can still hear us."

"I need to talk to the kid," Hermes said.

"Well, that's just too bad," June said. "You frightened that girl enough yesterday. Unless her caseworker says I have no choice, you won't be doing it again."

"The kid is a key element to my case."

"That *child* is a victim, and you'd do well to start treating her like one instead of acting like she's a fingerprint you found somewhere."

"And she's probably a witness to a crime."

"She's not a witness if she can't remember, and you're not going to harass her. If you want to do some police work so badly, why don't you figure out who was lurking around my property last night."

"The forensic team didn't find anything. There's nothing I can do."

June snorted. "Of course not. Well, unless you have a warrant that gives you rights to enter my property, I'm going to ask you to step off it and go do your job instead of harassing little girls. And unless you have permission from her case-worker to speak to her—which I'm going to imagine would only be allowed in the presence of said caseworker given how much you upset her yesterday—then I don't think we have anything else to say to each other."

Hermes turned five shades of red and I could tell he was mad as hell but also knew he didn't have a leg to stand on. Not legally.

"Have you spoken to a woman named Fortune Redding?" Hermes asked.

"You mean the woman who saved the girl's life? No. Why do you ask?"

"She's been caught interfering with police business before, and I think she is again. Her *boyfriend* seemed to think that's okay, but I don't run things that way."

June straightened up and put her hands on her hips. "Even if Ms. Redding does contact me, someone inquiring about the health of a child they literally brought back to life is not *interfering* with crap. It's called acting like a human being. You should try it sometime."

June whirled around and came back onto the porch. Hermes stared after her for a couple seconds, then finally accepting defeat, he turned around and headed back to his truck, stomping, of course. June was still scowling when she plopped back down in her chair.

"That man makes me mad enough to spit," she said. "And that's just something ladies don't do."

"I couldn't help but overhear," I said. "Did you say you had an intruder last night?"

She nodded. "The girl was having a nightmare and I went in to check on her. I saw a shadow at the window—way too big to be an animal, which is what that idiot suggested. I called the cops, and two nice deputies had a look around the outside of the house and drove around the neighborhood, but they couldn't find anything."

"Have you ever had trouble like that before?"

"Not really, but crime's been on the upswing everywhere, right?" She sighed. "It used to be these tiny, tucked-away towns were the perfect haven from the stuff on the five o'clock news, but now... Well, sometimes I just don't know what to think."

Gertie nodded. "It does seem like the simple life is no longer simple."

"Speaking of not simple," I said, "has a woman named Blair Johnson spoken with you?"

"No. I don't think I've ever heard that name before. Who is she?"

"Some kind of oversight person with Children and Family Services. She accosted us downtown in Sinful last night, asking questions about the girl. I figured she'd be talking to you at some point."

"No one has contacted me yet, but I suppose if she's talked to you then she'll be around eventually. Hopefully she'll do a better job speaking with the girl than that fool sheriff did."

I rose from my seat. "I really appreciate you talking with us, Ms. Nelson."

"Please, call me June. Ms. Nelson was my mother-in-law, and I don't want to be confused with that woman, God rest her soul."

I smiled. "Thank you for letting us know the girl is okay, in the major ways anyway. And I'm glad she has a safe place to stay with someone who'll take good care of her. I'm sure she needs it."

I gave her my card. "If you think of anything we can do to help, please let me know."

June took the card and tucked it in her pocket. "I'll do that. You've got quite the reputation around here after all those shocking revelations about Mary Joseph that you brought to light. No one would have ever known."

"Stay safe, and if you suspect anyone is lurking around again, don't be afraid to call the police as often as you need to," I said. "And you might want to mention it to the caseworker."

June bit her lower lip. "You think it might have something to do with the girl?"

I shrugged. "No way to know, but I'm sure you've dealt with enough kids coming from abusive situations to know that the parents don't always make rational choices when it comes to trying to get them back."

She gave me a grave nod. "That's a fact, and me and my 12-guage will take it under advisement."

"I hope we see you at the Mudbug fair this spring," Gertie said.

"I'm planning on it," June said, and smiled. "I need some more blue ribbons for my wall."

Gertie laughed. "As long as you don't take up knitting. I have to win somewhere."

We headed out and June scanned the street. "Where's your car?"

"We stopped at the General Store on our way over and left it downtown," Ida Belle said. "It was such a pretty day we figured we'd walk, especially since we had the breakfast special at Francine's."

June chuckled. "I've had that special. You probably should have walked all the way here from Sinful."

June waved as she turned around and we headed off.

"At least the trees are so plentiful she won't be able to see us rounding the corner at the end of the block," Gertie said.

"So what do you think?" Ida Belle asked.

"I think we need to pick up some more of that boudin before we leave Mudbug," Gertie said.

"I meant about the girl."

"I think we need to figure out a way to get the girl protection," I said. "Harrison can't sit out here every night."

"But we can," Ida Belle said.

I nodded. That's exactly what I'd been thinking.

───────

I SCANNED THE STREETS AS IDA BELLE PULLED AWAY, HOPING we didn't run into Hermes. I'd half expected him to pop up when we were getting into Ida Belle's SUV, but she'd parked it behind a huge tree with limbs covering the sidewalk and dropping into the road. He probably hadn't made the effort to drive up and down every street. But I suspected that his visit to June's was more about us than questioning the girl again.

Which made me think of another thing that was bothering me.

I pulled out my cell phone and dialed Mannie and asked if he could run a plate for me, then hung up and located the number for the Department of Children and Family Services and dialed the headquarters.

"Yes, hello, I have information on a case and need to speak to Blair Johnson."

"I'm sorry, ma'am, but we don't have anyone by that name working here."

"Um, she said she was in the oversight division for the caseworkers. I'm looking at her card." I read out the number.

"That's not a number I have in my system. Did this woman attempt to gain information from you about a child in protective custody?"

"Yes. But I don't know anything that would compromise the child in any way. I was just in the area when the child was found. I don't even know her name."

"Sometimes the parents or other abusers pull stunts like

this to try to get the children back. If you see this woman again, please contact the police. Given her behavior, it's likely she's already wanted."

"Thank you. That's exactly what I'll do."

I disconnected and looked at Ida Belle and Gertie.

"I knew her story sounded off," Ida Belle said.

"Then who is she?" Gertie asked. "Clearly, she's not the kid's mother."

"Do you think she's with the Brethren?" Ida Belle asked.

"Before yesterday, I would have said not likely. Hard to make the leap from living rough deep in the bayous for decades to driving a brand-new BMW, but now that we know they're protecting something other than the gospel out there, I can't give you a definite no."

"Maybe Mannie will come up with something on the plate," Gertie said.

My phone signaled an incoming text and I saw Mannie's name in the display.

"That was quick." I opened the text and read it out loud. "Car is registered to Johnson Trust. The only available address is to the law firm who handles the trust. They're located in NOLA."

I sent him a quick 'thanks,' then shook my head. "Well, the rich part of her story checks out, but also muddies the waters. Why would a rich girl be after information on our victim? And why masquerade as child services?"

"The answer to the second question is because then more people will talk to her, but I've got nothing on the first," Ida Belle said.

"Without knowing who the woman actually is, we have no idea what she's after."

"We know it can't be good," Ida Belle said.

I nodded and stared out the window. Blair Johnson bothered me on several levels. One, she was rigid and borderline rude, which the whole trust thing played into, assuming it was true. But then there was her ego associated with being assumed too young to be qualified. She'd spit out her credentials awfully fast, and she appeared to be telling the truth when she'd done so. So was Blair Johnson a very well-educated, rich woman who had gotten foolishly involved with a cult? Or was she the outside face of a criminal organization and that's where the BMW money really came from? Or did she have some other agenda that I hadn't clued in on?

"Life was a lot easier when everyone wasn't so good at lying," I said.

Ida Belle laughed. "People have always been good at lying. You just weren't paying attention because the lies didn't matter."

"Maybe. But every day, I feel more and more like that hermit has the right idea."

"I'm not going to argue with you on that one," Ida Belle said. "At least, not philosophically. But I like my creature comforts too much to live that stark every day."

Gertie nodded. "I don't even like staying at the camp for extended periods of time, and my camp is super nice. But it's still far away from people, and I don't hate all of them yet like you two."

"Hey, I like plenty of people," I argued.

"Name twenty," Gertie challenged me.

I thought for a second. "Can we make it ten?"

My cell phone rang again, and I frowned when I saw Whiskey's name in the display. We were what I'd loosely call friends, but he didn't make a habit of calling me. In fact, we usually never spoke unless I was in the bar or happened to see him downtown.

As soon as I answered, he started talking and I could tell

from the first words that he was highly agitated and upset, so I put him on speakerphone.

"They arrested him," Whiskey said. "Deputy Breaux and some guy that looked like a rat came right into the bar ten minutes ago and made him lie down on the floor while they cuffed him."

"Arrested who?" I asked, my heart sinking.

"Nickel. I tried to talk to them, but the rat guy said they didn't have to tell me nothing. Just told him he was being arrested on suspicion of murder and Hermes had ordered them to take him in. Deputy Breaux dropped back just a bit as the other guy walked out and told me to call you and said he was sorry."

"You didn't know the other deputy?"

"I've never seen him before, and pretty much everyone in local law enforcement has been in this bar for one reason or another."

"Hermes probably brought one of his own guys over from his old department."

"What the hell are they talking about, Fortune? Murder? You know Nickel. Even the old Nickel wouldn't have killed anyone, much less the man he is now."

"I know. I have absolutely no idea what they're talking about. I haven't heard anything about a body being found. But I have to tell you, this could be a huge problem. Remember that girl that Kenny found?"

"How could I forget?"

"Well, before she wound up in the bayou, she'd been hiding out in Nickel's camp. I found evidence of it the other day. We did a sweep of the area to remove anything that might indicate she was there, but we don't have the equipment to do a full forensic clean."

"Jesus. You've got to be kidding me. Nickel hasn't even been to that camp in months."

"I know, but Hermes isn't going to believe him. Let me make some calls and see if I can get some information on that body. And once Nickel is processed, I'll get him a lawyer."

"I can't believe this. What the hell am I supposed to say to my dad when Nickel doesn't show up tonight to make his dinner?"

"Don't worry about your dad," Ida Belle said. "I'll round up the Sinful Ladies and make sure he's covered until we get this situation resolved."

"Thank you. I really appreciate that. Jesus. I can't believe... You'll let me know as soon as you know something, right?"

"You'll be the first person I call, but it's more likely you'll hear from Nickel first. So same goes."

I looked over at Ida Belle and Gertie, who were clearly just as shocked and confused as I was. The wheels had officially come off the bus.

CHAPTER FIFTEEN

I CALLED HARRISON AND TOLD HIM ABOUT NICKEL'S ARREST. He put out some feelers and discovered that Hermes had found a body in the swamp early this morning—like at dawn early. That in itself sounded suspicious enough, but the deputy who filled him in said Hermes had claimed he was going out to track where the girl came from. All of which left me even more confused. Maybe I'd underestimated Hermes's ability. Maybe he actually *did* have some skills and had managed to find Nickel's camp and pin it as her hideaway, even without the benefit of the shoe or a prize bloodhound.

But no way in hell had a body been there when we were, because Rambo would have clued in on that before anything else. Ida Belle had been training him as a cadaver dog, and he'd taken to the smells of human decomposition with zero training. Even more impressive, he ignored other decomp, like birds, animals, and fish, and went straight for the human every time. Scooter had produced some impressive puppies, although I was a little worried about what might happen if we just turned Rambo loose in the swamps. It might send Carter's caseload through the roof.

Assuming he still has a caseload when he gets back.

I shook my head, not wanting to think about that. As soon as we hit Sinful, we headed to my house to wait. At the moment, the situation with Nickel was critical and I figured as soon as he was allowed to make a call, Whiskey would call me. It only took an hour. Nickel was no fool. He knew better than to talk without a lawyer and most certainly knew the law better than Hermes did.

"He's asked for a lawyer and refuses to speak," Whiskey said. "They haven't told him anything except a body was found at his camp."

"No time of death? No ID?"

"Nada."

"So they arrested him for owning the property that a body happened to wash up on? No inquiries into motive or opportunity? Good Lord, we're all potentially doomed."

"Yeah, but the bigger problem is Hermes got a warrant and they're sending a forensic team to search his camp. They're going to find evidence the girl was there. Like you said, you couldn't do a real clean on it. If they tie him up in all of this—with his record—I just don't see him getting a fair shake."

"I agree. But I need you to worry about your dad and your business and let me handle the legal end of things. I'll call my attorney right now, and trust me, he's the best you can get anywhere in the US. Hermes won't know what hit him."

"Thank you. It helps knowing you're backing him. And tell Ida Belle and Gertie thanks for me. Two of the Sinful Ladies showed up at dad's thirty minutes ago, fixed him breakfast, and now they're cleaning the house and doing laundry. He says they've promised him they'll play poker as soon as they're done. I can't tell you how much it means to know someone's there with him."

"What did you tell him about Nickel?"

"I said he went to Baton Rouge for some sort of certification. Pop doesn't know any better, and I can extend the requirements for that as I need to."

"Sounds good. I'll let you know as soon as the attorney speaks to him."

I immediately dialed a fan from my CIA days—retired federal prosecutor Alexander Framingham III., aka the Grim Reaper. There wasn't an attorney in the country who signed up to sit on the opposite side of Alexander unless he wanted to be made a fool. The man was the quickest I'd ever seen to process things, and his ability to turn people inside out was amazing to watch. He'd retired to New Orleans but still took on cases that interested him. He'd represented me once before—well, for the minimal amount of time it took him to get charges dropped—and I knew he wouldn't hesitate to dive in if I asked.

He answered on the first ring. I gave him a rundown of the situation, starting from finding the girl, then explained a bit more about Carter's absence and the issues with Hermes and his reputation.

"Okay," he said when I finished. "I started driving that way as soon as you said you needed an attorney in Sinful. Give me an hour and meet me at the sheriff's department."

"Hermes isn't going to let me anywhere near Nickel. He probably won't even let me in the front door."

"He will if you're my consultant."

"I have no problem with that, but can I ask why you want me there?"

"I figured you'd want to see me take this idiot down."

He disconnected and I looked at Ida Belle and Gertie and smiled. "I love him."

Gertie nodded. "If he wasn't so scary, I would have totally made a pass at him. All those smarts and so hot."

"I hate to be the one agreeing with Gertie, especially about men," Ida Belle said, "but I don't hate looking at him. I just like his acerbic wit even more."

"Smart is sexy," Gertie said. "Well, we have an hour to wait. Is there anything else we can do? I hate just sitting here."

"Me too," I said. "But I have to admit, I don't know which direction to go at the moment. We have a lot of information that doesn't fit together in any way I can see."

"I wish the girl could remember," Ida Belle said. "I have a feeling that what's buried in her mind is the key to all of this."

"Definitely," I said. "And I have to tell you, this new body worries me a lot. Who does it belong to? We all know it wasn't anywhere near that camp when we were there, so when did it turn up and why?"

"Maybe it was an accident and Hermes is just using it to hassle Nickel and get access to his camp to pin things on him," Gertie suggested.

"I can absolutely see Hermes pulling something like that, but since he's already yelling homicide, when that body just came out of the water, then death must have been something super obvious, like a gunshot wound."

"Maybe he was looking for the girl," Ida Belle said.

"But how did he die and where was he the night the girl was found? Or the day we were at Nickel's camp?"

"Assuming he didn't kill himself, which is a safe bet at this point, that means he wasn't alone," Ida Belle said. "So maybe two different men—different sides? Same side and a fallout?"

"Exactly. We need more information."

"Maybe we'll be able to ascertain more when the identity is released."

"Assuming they can identify him."

"You don't think the girl killed him, do you?" Gertie asked.

"I don't think so. I mean, if she did, then where's his body been this whole time?"

But I wasn't thrilled with the thought, and it was one that had already crossed my mind.

"Maybe he was injured and left," Gertie said. "He could have died farther up the bayou and fallen in, then drifted down to the dock."

"I don't think he would have been wandering around the swamp for three days with a life-threatening injury."

"Not by choice," Ida Belle said. "There's another option here—whoever got the girl out could have been the one who killed him. Maybe they both ran and she got away. Maybe she came back for the girl and ran into one of the Brethren."

"Too many options," I agreed.

"I have to say I'm not a fan of some of them," Ida Belle said.

I nodded. "Me either."

———

ALEXANDER WAS WAITING FOR ME ON THE SIDEWALK outside the sheriff's department. Ida Belle and Gertie had come with me, claiming they were going to sit on the bench outside and just wait for the explosion that was certain to happen. Alexander looked every bit the famous federal prosecutor in his custom suit with his perfect haircut and magazine-quality teeth. He gave us all a big smile as we walked up.

"I have to thank you for calling me," he said. "I've been so bored lately. I'm not sure retirement is going to work. I took up golf. Have you ever played golf? I'm surprised there's not more violence on golf courses."

I laughed. "I really appreciate you coming, and I am certain that if you wanted to go back to work, there would be no shortage of places looking to hire you."

"I think you should consider politics," Gertie said.

He blanched. "Yuck. No. There are more criminals in politics than in Angola."

Ida Belle nodded.

"Are you ready to do this?" he asked.

"Absolutely!"

We headed inside and Gavin, the day dispatcher, looked up at me, clearly panicked. "Uh, can I help you?"

"Yes, I'm Mr. Doucet's attorney."

Gavin jumped up from the desk. "Oh, right. Let me just get Hermes—sorry, Sheriff Hermes—for you."

He hurried off and Alexander raised one eyebrow. "Looks like your friend has the employees running scared."

"I'm going to guess he's threatened all their jobs. I know he did Harrison."

"Harrison? Ben Harrison? Your counterpart at the CIA?"

"Yes. He and his fiancée fled the city, and he took a job as a deputy here back last year. But Hermes knows about our past, so he's been relegated to traffic duty."

Alexander stared. "He's got one of the CIA's top agents writing tickets? Are you kidding me?"

"I couldn't make this stuff up. You'll see. There's no laws of science or sense that explain Hermes."

And speaking of the devil, he exited Carter's office and headed our way, hitching his pants as he walked and puffing his chest. Good Lord, I wish I had video, because this was going to be awesome.

"I'm Sheriff Hermes," he said, casting a dirty look in my direction. "What can I do for you?"

"I'm Alexander Framingham III, Mr. Doucet's attorney. I'm here to speak to my client."

"Yeah, all right, but she's not welcome in here."

Alexander stared. "You're saying a taxpaying citizen of this town is not welcome inside the sheriff's department? Has there been a change to state law that I'm uninformed on?"

Hermes flushed a bit. "It's not about no law. This woman has been interfering in my investigation."

"Then why haven't you arrested her?"

"There's this thing called proof," I said.

Alexander nodded. "I see. So what you're saying is supposition. Well, until you have enough evidence to arrest her, I suggest you refrain from statements that imply the citizens of this town aren't welcome to engage with law enforcement."

"Fine, she's welcome to stand right there for the next ten years, but she's not talking to your client."

"Well, then I'm afraid we have a problem, because Ms. Redding is a consultant for my practice. I require her for note-taking. I'd prefer to speak to you first, so that we can go over the charges and the evidence before I speak to my client."

"Look, Mr. Fancy Suit, I don't care whose attorney you are. You'll speak to your client and me when I say so, and if I don't want her there, she won't be."

"Is that a fact?" Alexander smiled and pulled out his cell phone.

Hermes eyed him. "Who are you calling?"

"The ADA," Alexander said. "I'll get this cleared right up. Hello. This is Alex, can I please speak to the ADA? It's urgent. Yes, Ryan, Alex here. Doing good, how about you? A quick word, I'm in Sinful trying to speak to a client who's requested me, and the acting sheriff here has informed me that he's unwilling to explain the charges or the evidence surrounding my client's arrest and seems to think I shouldn't be permitted to speak to my client either. That's correct. Certainly."

Alexander handed his phone to Hermes. "He'd like to talk to you."

I could only make out a few words of what was being said, but I could tell by the way the color washed out of Hermes's face that the ADA had informed him of exactly who Alexander was. Then I caught the words 'Grim Reaper' and 'colossal idiot' and was certain the ADA wasn't referring to Alexander with that second one. The last thing I caught was 'apologize' before the phone went silent.

Hermes, who hadn't spoken the entire call, handed the phone back to Alexander. "I apologize for my behavior. I was out of line. If you'd like me to go over the facts of the case, I can do that now."

"That would be perfect." Alexander gave him a huge fake smile and he turned around and headed down the hall for the conference room.

"Such a child," Alexander said. "All that stomping."

"I know. He does it every time he loses a battle of the wits."

"Then he's going to need better shoes and new knees."

We headed into the conference room and took seats at the table across from Hermes. He grabbed a folder from the table and opened it up. The first thing he tossed our way was a photo of a body partially hidden under the dock at Nickel's camp. I could tell it hadn't been in the water long. Mainly because it was still largely intact, and things didn't last long in the water here.

"Pulled that body out of the water at your client's camp around six this morning," Hermes said. "Bullet right through his chest. Sent a forensics team there and they pulled a recent victim's print from inside. A young girl who was found nearby two nights ago, half drowned."

"Who is the man?" Alexander asked, and handed me a pad of paper and pen from his briefcase.

"He hasn't been identified."

"Okay. Who is the girl?"

Hermes shifted in his chair. "We don't know who she is either. She was unconscious when she was found. She's awake now but has no memory."

"So let me get this straight, three days ago you found a girl, whom you haven't identified, and evidence that at some point she'd been inside my client's camp. Then early this morning, you found a body under the dock of my client's camp, and you don't know who he is either. You didn't mention finding the man's prints inside my client's camp, so I'm going to assume you didn't, which means you can't even connect the two of them to each other, much less to my client."

"So you think it's a coincidence that girl was hiding in your client's camp and then this dead guy turns up there with a single round through his heart?"

Alexander smiled. "Sheriff Hermes, I thought I'd made it clear earlier that I don't deal in supposition. I'm a facts guy. That's what I present to juries. So let's change things up a bit—does my client have an alibi for last night between the hours of say..."

He looked over at me.

"No earlier than 4:00 a.m.," I said. "Assuming he was in the water the entire time."

"Okay, so let's just back it up a bit," Alexander said. "Does my client have an alibi between the hours of midnight and 4:00 a.m.?"

Hermes frowned. "He said he was at his father's house."

"And is that where he resides?"

Hermes shrugged. "Don't know. His living situation isn't any of my business."

"His father is terminal," I said. "Nickel takes care of him the majority of the time and his brother runs their bar. He has his own place, although he hasn't been staying there much lately."

"What's your point?" Hermes asked. "Even if he was there all night, there's no witnesses other than the old man, and he's hopped up on painkillers."

Alexander frowned. "I would think you could show more respect to a man who sounds like he exists in less-than-ideal circumstances. And likely served as most Southern men of his age did."

I nodded. "Army."

Alexander gave Hermes a stern look. "My respect comment goes double for men who've served this country."

"Fine, whatever! He's a saint. But that doesn't change what I said. He's not a reliable alibi. Not with the drugs he's on."

"Who else had access to my client's camp?"

Hermes frowned. "I don't know."

Alexander sighed and gave him a look as though he was a child who'd disappointed a teacher. "So you didn't even bother to ask my client who else had access to his camp?"

"I can answer that," I said. "Nickel left a key there because he was always forgetting his. So half the fishermen in Sinful have used it at some point to escape a bad storm. I could probably trot fifty people through a courtroom who knew about that key."

Hermes threw his hands in the air. "Who the hell leaves a key to their camp like that?"

"In my experience, people who don't have anything to hide," Alexander said. "So let me get this straight, you have questionable opportunity, zero motive, and a whole town of people representing reasonable doubt. So what grounds are you holding my client on?"

"It's *his* camp." Hermes crossed his arms across his chest and set his mouth into a pout.

"Your takeaway being what? That murderers always commit the crime on their own property? Are you completely ignorant of this country's legal processes, or do you just not want to play by the rules set forth by our federal and state supreme courts?"

Hermes puffed up and turned so red that I wondered if he was going to pop. Maybe a heart attack brought on by high blood pressure was a way to get rid of him.

"Sheriff, are you going to charge my client?" Alexander asked. "Because I'll need to talk this over with the ADA."

"I have the right to hold him."

"Sure, keep him for a few days. But when you have to release him because there's no more evidence against him then than there is now, I'm going to pursue a harassment suit against the department and you personally to cover the costs of his father's care while he was detained without cause."

"Do you even know why they call him Nickel? You act like he's a pillar of the community. He's a felon."

"Because *I* take the time to acquire the facts in all my cases, I am well aware of my client's past. And he served his time. He's also a local business owner along with his brother, with whom he is close, and he is the primary caretaker for his father, who is terminal. He's never even been issued a passport. There isn't a judge alive who would consider him a flight risk. So again, are you going to charge my client?"

Hermes grabbed the folder and threw it against the wall and stalked out. I looked longingly at the scattered papers, but Alexander shook his head.

"Not worth it," he said. "And my guess is they don't contain anything more relevant than what's coming out of that fool's mouth."

"You think he's going to release Nickel?"

"He better. Good Lord, when you told me this guy was an idiot who was trying to railroad your friend, I hoped you had a tiny bit of it wrong, but his entire case is a farce. He can't even identify the victim, much less connect him to Nickel. Every day, I wonder how some people made it to adulthood."

I nodded. "Hermes has friends in high places—starting with your buddy the ADA, and he's some distant cousin to our illustrious governor. I'm convinced he's got something on the governor because they're definitely not friends in real life. Hermes has zero class. I can't see our head of state inviting him to a black-tie event."

He shook his head. "The likes of him would eat caviar with his fingers and break wind in the punch bowl."

I heard Hermes mumbling down the hall, and we looked up to see Nickel walk in the room ahead of a very disgruntled Hermes. Nickel looked happy to see me, but also confused. One glance at his hands and I understood the confusion. He wasn't wearing cuffs.

"You're free to go," Hermes said. "But don't leave town."

"I haven't left town since the day I got out of Angola," Nickel said. "You think I'd bounce when my dad is dying? What kind of man are you?"

"Loaded question," I said.

"And presumes he's a man," Alexander said.

Hermes glared at all of us, then whirled around so fast he ran right into the doorjamb with his face. He cursed, then did his usual stomp away.

"Well, looks like my work here is done," Alexander said and extended his hand to Nickel. "Alexander Framingham III. It's a pleasure to meet you. Now let's get out of here before that moron tries to rewrite some more legal code to suit himself."

As we headed out, Gavin gave me a huge smile and a

thumbs-up and I nodded. I felt sorry for everyone having to deal with Hermes. The only person in the room who didn't look happy was a deputy I didn't recognize. He stood at the back of the room, arms crossed, and glared at us. Based on the thin, pointed face, I assumed he was the second deputy that Whiskey had told me about.

Five foot eight. A hundred forty pounds. Far more attitude than muscle tone. Absolutely zero threat except for the obvious Hermes connection.

When we hit the sidewalk, Ida Belle and Gertie jumped up, clearly surprised. Then Gertie rushed over to hug Nickel, who looked a bit embarrassed by all the attention but was probably too relieved to care.

"You're out?" Ida Belle said.

Alexander grinned. "Did you doubt my superpowers?"

"Not for a minute, but I have no doubts about Hermes's stupidity and stubbornness."

"Well, it took a bit for him to accept that he had nothing the ADA would risk taking to trial—and an actual call from me to the ADA to point out the respect the ADA has for me and his lack of desire for facing me in a court-room. But finally, common sense and the actual law prevailed."

I laughed. "Hermes doesn't have any common sense. You backed him into the corner of no return. He can't afford to alienate the people who put him in the position to begin with. Thanks, Alexander. I can't tell you how much I appreciate this."

"Me too," Nickel said. "Man, I don't know you or even understand what you did, but if you ever need anything, I'm your guy. And drinks for life at the Swamp Bar."

Alexander gave him a broad smile. "It's charming, I'm sure, but I have to run. I got a call from another friend on the way over here. He's been arrested for stealing his maid's underwear."

We all stared.

"Was he having an affair with her or is it a creepy stalker thing?" I finally asked.

"Neither. He was wearing them. But we can't have that kind of thing getting out about state representatives, now can we? Call me if this circles back around and I'll be here in a flash. And Fortune, give me a ring when you've wrapped all this up and we'll do lunch, because what little I know is fascinating. Ladies, always good seeing you."

And with that and a wave, he climbed into his Bentley and left.

"Who *is* that guy?" Nickel asked.

"Alexander is a retired federal prosecutor—a famous one. He's known as the Grim Reaper."

Nickel's eyes widened. "Holy crap! When I was in, cons would talk about the big cases sometimes. The Reaper took out the biggest and best—arms dealers, drug cartels, human trafficking rings. He always won and didn't care who he implicated in the process. 'The truth is all that matters,' he used to say. The man is legendary. I can't believe I just shook hands with a legend. Do I even want to know how you're friends with him?"

I smiled. "He *is* impressive. And let's just say he's a fan of my former work."

Nickel nodded in understanding. "You got him the goods on the bad guys. Makes sense."

"Come on, we'll give you a ride to the bar. Whiskey's blood pressure is probably through the roof, and he's not going to calm down unless he lays eyes on you. That way I can tell you all what happened with Alexander at the same time."

"I want to see Whiskey, and need to pick up my truck, but I've got to get back to my dad."

"Don't worry about him," Ida Belle said and motioned to her SUV. "The Sinful Ladies are rotating in pairs. He's had plenty to eat and good company. And Whiskey came up with a reason for your absence, so he won't think anything of you being gone for a few more hours."

Nickel looked relieved. "Man, I appreciate everything you guys have done. Taking care of my dad and getting me out— the Grim Reaper... No one is going to believe it. You've got some interesting friends, Fortune."

"I hear that a lot."

CHAPTER SIXTEEN

As we made the drive to the Swamp Bar, Nickel recounted his arrest and jail visit.

"That Hermes isn't right," he said. "There was talk about him when I was inside. Rumor is he's the kind that will take money to look the other way."

"I totally believe that," Ida Belle said.

"But it makes no sense that he'd want the sheriff's job," Nickel said. "His jurisdiction would be a bunch of small towns. What's the big draw? Can't be a lot of money to be gained around here."

"Control, for one," I said. "Men like Hermes are power hungry, and since fear is the only way they can get that power, that's what they focus on."

Nickel nodded. "He's certainly not going to get it through respect. He spoke to the other deputies and the dispatcher like they were dogs. Made me mad. Except for that one guy— the guy who arrested me with Deputy Breaux. I've never seen him before, and I make it a point to know the local law enforcement."

"I'm pretty sure Hermes imported some dedicated backup."

Nickel shook his head. "What kind of loser gets off on pushing around a bunch of regular folk?"

"There's a lot of money buried in these small towns," Ida Belle said. "And people have secrets to go along with it. Look at Nora. We know she's loaded but outsiders wouldn't. But men like Hermes can find that out easily enough. Pair that with her penchant for illegal substances and she's an easy target for payoffs."

Nickel's face flashed with anger. "I hadn't even thought about that. I'm smart enough not to take anything that woman is mixing up, but she's harmless in the big scheme of things."

I nodded. "Which is exactly why Carter prefers to avoid her in person and walk away if anyone is talking about her."

"I get it. If he doesn't know, he can't be accused of not doing anything. Carter's a good man. I know the Marines needed him badly or he wouldn't have gone, but selfishly, I wish he'd turned them down."

"We all do," Gertie said.

Ida Belle pulled up in front of the bar and as we were walking up the steps, the door flew open and Whiskey ran out and grabbed Nickel, squeezing him so hard that Nickel grunted. When Whiskey let him go, he reached for me, and I got an equally hard squeeze. When he was done passing out hugs, he waved us inside, a huge grin plastered on his face.

"Well, heck, get inside. I'll pour a round and you can tell me what happened."

We all took a seat at a table and Whiskey put his most expensive brandy and whiskey on the table along with coffee and a couple other choices for mixing. Everyone selected their drink, we clinked them together to celebrate Nickel's release, and then I told them about the exchange between Hermes and Alexander. Everyone had a good chuckle at Hermes's expense but when the laughing was over, everyone sobered a bit.

"This could all still be a problem for me, right?" Nickel asked.

"If Hermes can convince the ADA to push the issue, then yes," I said. "I don't think he has enough to get an indictment, much less a conviction, though. And the ADA is bucking for a promotion. He's not going to want to attach his flag to a sinking ship."

Gertie nodded. "Besides, Fortune's going to solve the whole thing and then Hermes will have to go pound sand."

"Anything I can do to help, you know I'm there for it," Nickel said.

"Did Hermes show you a picture of the dead guy?" I asked.

Nickel nodded. "I didn't recognize him."

"Are you sure? The body was rough."

"Yeah, death and the water will do that to you, but I'm pretty sure I've never seen him before. Just a sec."

He went behind the bar and came back with a pad of paper and a pencil and started sketching. A couple minutes later, he turned the pad around and showed us a sketch of the dead guy —except this one was alive and without bloat and decomp.

"This is excellent," I said. "You've got all bone structure perfect—the brow ridge, the nasal cavity. Even the tissue depth looks like a perfect fit. Where did you learn to do this?"

Nickel shrugged. "I was always good at drawing. All that stuff you said—brow ridge and tissue depth—I don't know nothing about that. I just draw what I see or in this case, what I should see. But that guy, I ain't ever seen before."

The others studied the drawing and shook their heads as well.

"He's never been in the bar," Whiskey said. "I don't know everyone in the parish, but if I've seen a face even once, I'll remember that I've done so. Might not recall when and where, but I get that flash of recognition, if that makes sense."

"It does," I said. "Your memory for faces is one of the many reasons you're a great bar owner. You can address everyone as if they're personal friends. Then they stay and drink longer and come more often."

He grinned. "Don't tell people my secrets."

"So he's not from around here," Ida Belle said, "but he wound up dead under Nickel's dock, right after the girl was hiding there. There's no way that's a coincidence, regardless of the obvious lack of connection."

"Absolutely not," I agreed. "I wish we had time of death."

"He hadn't been in the water for long," Nickel said, "or there wouldn't have been much of him left."

I nodded. "But he could have been killed somewhere else and dumped there later. And the water is still cold enough to skew things. I guarantee you, though, there was no body within miles of your camp when we were there, or Rambo would have locked in on it."

"So was the man looking for the girl and the mother got into a scuffle with him and managed to shoot him?" Gertie asked.

When Whiskey and Nickel gave her blank looks, she explained. "We've been leaning toward the girl's mother being the one who got them out of there given that it sounds like the women might be living in less-than-ideal circumstances."

"Got them out of where?" Whiskey asked.

"We might need to backtrack a little," I said. "But I need you to keep this absolutely silent. Other women and children could be at risk."

I gave them our base thoughts on the Brethren, leaving out

the explosives and the hard indication that they were a criminal organization rather than religious. When I finished, they both nodded, their expressions grave.

"I don't like to think about women and kids being held by a bunch of religious nuts," Whiskey said.

"What the heck is going on here?" Nickel asked.

I shook my head. "I wish I knew."

————

Since we had nothing else on our agenda, we headed over to the General Store to find Blanchet and bring him up to speed. Walter had several ladies in the store and pointed to the back of the shop. We scanned the storeroom but didn't see him anywhere, then I heard a metal clang outside. On the cement pad behind the store, we found Blanchet working on a lawn mower.

"You take up a new career?" I asked.

He looked up at us and smiled. "More like revisiting an old one. My old man was a heck of a mechanic. He had me fixing small engines in grade school. Scooter was overrun on repairs, especially with spring coming and everyone getting back to lawn stuff, so I told him I'd help out. I've already finished two so far."

He reached down and pulled the crank and the engine fired right up.

"Three," he said, looking pleased. "Please tell me you've had as much success as I have."

"I'm afraid not, but it's been very interesting."

We all sat at the picnic table, and I brought Blanchet up to speed on everything that had happened since breakfast. When I was done, he shook his head.

"That's a heck of a lot packed into three-quarters of a day."

I showed him the sketch Nickel had done and he shook his head. "Doesn't ring a bell. But is anyone else surprised that Hermes found a body? That he even knew which direction to start looking?"

Ida Belle shrugged. "For all we know, he might have been combing the area around where the girl was found. He would have headed up that bayou sooner or later. And a body stuck against the side of the dock would be hard to miss. Even for Hermes."

"Him finding that body was just timing and luck," Gertie said.

"I'm surprised he was out there at all, especially that early."

"My guess is he's doing those things when he assumes we'll still be at home so that he's free to spend his day checking up on us," I said.

"So what are your thoughts on the Johnson woman?" Blanchet asked.

"She confuses me. The woman appears to have access to the money she claims, and I don't doubt she's highly educated, although I'm certain a call to Stanford would yield the same results my call to family services did."

"Fake name, maybe? Rich girl taken in by the cult?"

"She wouldn't be the first or the last, but we all know that's no cult. Something illegal is going on out there."

"They could have roped her in with the New Age religion thing though, especially if they wanted access to her cash and help with regular people-facing things," Blanchet said. "Or all that money could have come from whatever they're doing out in the swamp and not from inheritance."

"The only thing I know for certain is she's not the girl's mother. But I don't trust her or her motives."

Blanchet nodded. "You think the girl is all right with June?"

"I think so. June seems to have a good handle on the

psychological challenges that foster kids have, especially those in emergency placement. And she doesn't like Hermes. I think she'll protect the girl."

"At least there's that. So what's on the agenda now?"

I shook my head. "I'm stumped. I think I need to sit on things for a bit and see what I come up with."

My cell phone rang and I saw Harrison's number in the display.

"Someone attacked June Nelson in her home. She got off a shot, but only took out a lamp and her drapes. He backhanded her hard enough to black her eye and put her out. When she came to, her attacker was gone. So was the girl."

I jumped up from the table and cursed. "You've got to be kidding me. In broad daylight? How did the guy get in?"

"I'm getting the story thirdhand at this point but sounds like he jimmied the back door. She was on the porch reading and heard a noise. Thinking the girl woke up, she headed inside and saw the guy cross the hallway. She yelled at him to get out and grabbed her shotgun that she'd left propped on the outside of the door, and when he rushed her, she fired but missed. He clocked her, and she went down for the count."

"Is she all right?"

"I think so. The paramedic who passed it on got the story from the deputy. He said her face is going to hurt for a while, but she seemed more upset about the girl than anything. Hermes has finally decided to kinda do his job and has everyone he can spare looking for this guy. I'm on my way to Mudbug now."

"Did anyone tell you Hermes pulled a guy with a slug through his heart out of the bayou at Nickel's camp early this morning?"

"What? No!"

"There's too much crazy crap going on. We have to find that girl, Harrison."

"I'll call if I hear anything."

"We're going to head out and look ourselves."

"Kinda figured you would."

I disconnected and we all stared at one another. This was the worst possible turn things could have taken. And it wouldn't have happened if Hermes had taken his job seriously instead of fixating on us. The girl should have had police protection or been left in the hospital where more eyes were on her.

"What's the plan?" Ida Belle asked.

I lifted my phone again and dialed June. It took several rings, but she finally answered, her voice somewhat slurred.

"June, it's Fortune Redding. We just heard about what happened. Are you all right?"

"Oh, Fortune! It's awful. That man was there, in my house, and I tried to shoot him, but I must have jerked at the last minute. I missed and gave him time to attack me. And now the girl is gone."

She started sobbing and I felt my heart clench. I couldn't imagine how bad she felt.

"We're going to go help look for the girl. Can you give me a description of the man?"

She coughed and then I heard her blow her nose. "Tall and stringy. Probably a good six inches taller than me. Dark brown hair and eyes. Hair was cut short, like a military guy. He was wearing jeans and a black T-shirt."

"Had you ever seen him before?"

"No. Go find her! The police won't let me leave my house. *Now* they decide to put a cop here. That poor girl. I was supposed to protect her."

"You did everything you could. I'll let you know if we find something. Stay safe."

I rose from the table. "There will be a ton of coverage on land. I think we should take my boat and head toward the Brethren's camp."

"If they're behind enemy lines again, we won't be able to breach," Blanchet said. "Not without considerable risk."

"I know, but maybe we can find a fisherman who saw them —maybe talk to the hermit again. If we can prove someone took her that way, we might be able to convince the state police to move on their location with an air strike. But we're going to have to have something good enough to launch that kind of rescue."

"Maybe we'll get really lucky and run across this guy on the way," Ida Belle said.

"If we do, I'm putting a bullet in him," Blanchet said.

"Only if I don't beat you to it."

We loaded up some supplies and quickly headed out. I'd been mulling something over ever since I'd hung up my phone and finally reached a conclusion. I signaled to Ida Belle to cut speed so I could make a phone call and dialed Blair Johnson.

"Ms. Johnson, this is Fortune Redding. I heard about the attack on June Nelson and the girl's abduction and wanted to offer my help. Is there anything I can do?"

"What? Oh, Ms. Redding. Yes, it's a horrible situation, but the police have assured me they're doing everything they can."

"So you've alerted the state police? Because they have far more resources than the sheriff's department. A child abduction would rate their help."

"Of course. And yes, every option is being utilized. I know you'd like to help, but the more citizens we have moving around, it will only inhibit the police from doing their job. So we're asking everyone to stay alert and please call me if you see something that you think warrants my attention."

"Call you? And not the police?"

"Well, both, of course, but I'd like to be kept in the loop early on. Sometimes the police aren't as prompt as I'd like in that regard."

"Of course. I hope they find the girl soon."

I hung up and shook my head. "She didn't know the girl was gone."

"Are you sure?" Blanchet asked.

"One hundred percent. She got back into role quickly, but not quick enough. That uptick of volume and pitch when she first responded was a dead giveaway."

Blanchet looked confused. "But if you thought she didn't know, then why did you tell her?"

"Because I wanted to see if she was the one who had the girl."

"I wish we knew where to find her," Ida Belle said. "If she's in cahoots with the Brethren, then she might lead us right to the girl—in a way that wouldn't get anyone blown up."

I nodded. "Which is why you're going to haul butt to that last channel before it splits and we're going to hide under one of those cypress trees with moss and wait for a boat to drive by. There was no engine noise when I talked to her, so she wasn't in a boat or a car. If she thinks the Brethren got the girl, and she's in with them, then she might head out there to check and see for herself."

She fired up the engine again and gunned it. Blanchet, who'd been sitting on the bench, despite being warned by Gertie that he should share her cushion, fell over backward and crashed into the bottom. He scrambled up, crawled over the bench, and sat next to Gertie, giving Ida Belle a backward glance. I couldn't help laughing.

Hours later, we sat itchy and sweaty in the boat, our water half depleted and interesting conversation completely gone. Nothing had stirred on the bayou but mosquitoes, who'd hatched out from the current warming spell. And my patience had disappeared along with the cool breeze.

"Did I get this wrong?" I asked.

"If you did, it would be a first," Gertie said.

Ida Belle nodded. "That Johnson woman is definitely shady, and it's hard to get explosives wrong, considering Blanchet almost got blasted by them. Something is going on out there in the swamp, and we have every reason to believe that girl is somehow tied to all of it."

"Then where is she? If the Brethren got the girl from June, then why haven't we seen any movement? There isn't another way in and out, is there?"

"Not by water," Ida Belle said. "This channel is the only one that feeds all the others in the area. If we assume their compound is in that extra dense set of swamp not far from the explosives, then this is the only way in. They *could* hide boats on another bayou and trek across the swamp to them, but that would be a good two miles minimum, walking through dangerous territory. I can't imagine that being their chosen route."

"No. Probably not."

"They still might have something set up as an escape route," Blanchet said. "For if someone managed to get by the explosives. Two miles isn't so far that someone wouldn't use it to avoid arrest."

"True." I blew out a breath. "So, what now? Maybe the girl wasn't taken there, and that's why there's no movement."

"Not even from the fishermen," Ida Belle said. "We haven't seen a boat since we left the main bayou."

My cell phone buzzed in my pocket and I pulled it out. Harrison.

"Hey, that Johnson woman just cruised June Nelson's house," he said.

Crap! I'd been wrong. "You're sure it was her?"

He described the car and told me the license plate.

I sighed. "That's her. What the hell is she doing cruising June's?"

"I don't know. Not like the guy June shot at is going to pop by for coffee. But what I find most interesting is she was slow driving until she spotted Hermes in the sheriff's department truck. Then she sped up and drove past."

"Did Hermes say anything?"

"Hermes wouldn't even see the girl if she was standing in front of him, much less notice some shady woman cruising by. He just barked orders at me and sent me off again on Mission Futile. He's got us searching Mudbug like the kidnapper grabbed the girl and stuck around. You spot anything in the bayou?"

"Nothing but mosquitoes. Maybe I got this all wrong."

"I don't think so—at least not the key points. But that Johnson woman is a wild card."

"Yeah. That one still has me stumped."

"What are you guys going to do?"

"I don't think there's anything we can do but head back. We can't risk trying to enter Brethren territory again. They've probably doubled security since we set off that charge."

"Especially if they have the girl. You think they laid eyes on you last time?"

"Yeah. Someone was watching, which means they know who we are. But we have to find that girl. The Brethren have already proven they'll kill people."

"I know, but going in blind is stupid and you're not stupid.

We have to believe they're not going to hurt her. At least not right away. She doesn't even remember anything, so it's not like she could cause them trouble. And if they have her back, then they'll probably lie low."

"Or pull up stakes and leave the area."

"Maybe. But either way, they didn't go to the trouble of taking her just to kill her. They could have done that right there in June's house."

I felt a bit of the tension leave my back at his words. "You're right. She's probably okay for the moment. But we have to move fast, which means I need a good plan to infiltrate."

"Let me know what I can do. Meanwhile, I'll keep my eyes and ears open."

"Tell me if you see Blair Johnson again."

I disconnected and motioned to Ida Belle. "Let's head back. I know it's disappointing, but there's nothing else we can do right now. Not out here, and it will be dark soon. The Brethren already have a huge advantage in the light. We don't need to make it even easier on them."

Just as she reached to start the boat, I heard a motor in the distance. "Wait!"

The way sound carried over the water, I couldn't tell at first which direction the noise came from except that I didn't think it was on the channel behind us. We were hidden fairly well where we'd stopped and with the sun starting to set, it made spotting us even harder. The engine noise grew louder, and I finally locked in one direction and pointed to the channel that led to the Brethren. I lifted my binoculars and locked in on the mouth of the channel just seconds before the small aluminum boat exited into the larger bayou.

It was Spinner.

So either he'd lied when he said he didn't traverse this area any longer or he'd made an exception after our conversation. But why? I watched as he pulled past our hiding place, then he cut his engine down to an idle and pulled something from his pocket.

It was a cell phone.

Which made no sense at all.

Unless Spinner was one of them.

CHAPTER SEVENTEEN

Spinner being one of the Brethren would explain a lot. Like why eyes were on us as soon as we'd hit their territory. Had Spinner tipped them off? Had they hoped to take us out in the explosion? It certainly reeked of a setup when viewed from this lens.

"What's he doing?" Ida Belle asked, squinting.

"He's looking at a cell phone," I said.

"What?"

They all spoke at once and then slowly, the same thoughts I'd had must have crept into their minds because everyone's expressions shifted.

Spinner cranked up his engine again and set off, and I motioned to Ida Belle. "Follow him as best you can without him noticing."

"And if he does?" she asked.

"Then we'll claim we're out looking for the girl," I said. "Given that we were asking about the Brethren in regard to the girl, it would make sense we'd check this area now that she's been abducted."

Ida Belle nodded and fired up the boat, keeping far enough

back that Spinner wouldn't see us unless he turned all the way around. When we reached the lake that Mudbug bordered, Spinner didn't head for downtown as I assumed he would. Instead he turned left and drove toward a bayou that I knew contained several camps owned by locals.

"What do you want me to do?" Ida Belle asked.

"Head for the edge of that peninsula and see if we can position behind that grove of cypress trees."

"You won't be able to see very far down that channel from that position."

"Not from the boat."

Ida Belle nodded and set out for the location I'd indicated. When the boat was secured as close to the bank as possible, I jumped onto the bank.

"I'm going with you," Blanchet said.

I shook my head. "I'll move faster alone. Stay here and keep watch. If he exits or anyone else comes through this pass, text me. And be ready to create a diversion or initiate an extraction."

Before he could argue, I spun around and sprinted into the brush, praying that the ground remained solid because I couldn't afford to move deliberately if I wanted to catch up to Spinner's boat. This area of the swamp was thick with trees, moss clinging to the tops of them, extinguishing what little was left of the setting sun. As soon as my eyes adjusted to the darkness, I picked up my pace, making sure I stayed within view of the bayou as I went. I could still hear Spinner's boat in the distance. The sound wasn't getting farther away, so I knew I was at least maintaining the gap, but I needed to close it.

I burst through bushes and onto a trail and increased pace. About ten seconds later, I heard the engine cut out and I hurried to the bank and lifted my binoculars. I spotted Spinner about a hundred yards down on the other side of the bayou.

He was tying off to a dock and I could see the faint outline of a camp farther back in the trees.

Crap!

I had no way to get across the bayou except swim and no way I was taking that risk at alligator dinnertime. Plus, the tide was going out and it would be a hard swim at that distance. I was just about to call Ida Belle when I saw figure with a ball cap exit the woods and head down the dock, pulling a flat cart behind him. I couldn't make out his face in the dim light, but his general shape looked familiar. I kept my binoculars trained on them as the man climbed into the boat with Spinner and helped him lift two ice chests onto the dock.

They both climbed onto the dock, but I still couldn't get a good look at the other man because his back was to me. They loaded the chests onto the cart, then Spinner pulled the cell phone out of his pocket and passed it to the other man. The man set it on top of the ice chests, then reached for his back pocket. I clenched, because the two options were wallet or firearm, but he pulled out a wallet and handed Spinner a wad of money. Spinner shoved the money deep in his pocket and jumped back in the boat without a word. He untied his boat and set off as the other man lifted the cart handle to haul it off.

I was cursing the distance between us when a light—probably on a timer—clicked on at the end of the dock. The man turned around and I finally got a good look at his face.

It was Otto Kraus.

———

I GAVE THE OTHERS A RUNDOWN OF WHAT I'D SEEN AS SOON as I got back to the boat and Ida Belle headed for Sinful. It was already dark, so we couldn't traverse the channels at her usual warp speed, but given her knowledge of the area, she still managed to get us safely there at a decent clip. Conversation in an airboat, even at less than full speed, wasn't really possible, but somehow, I knew that even if we had the ability to talk, the silence would have been deafening.

All the implications of what I'd seen that evening, combined with the girl, the trip wire, the dead guy, and the Brethren, painted a dark picture. The gloom was still everpresent when we climbed out of the boat at my house and made our way into the kitchen. I opened the refrigerator to get us some cold drinks and froze.

Someone had been here. The items in my refrigerator were fewer and not where I'd left them.

I spun around, pulling my gun at the same time. The three of them stared at me and their eyes widened as I put my finger over my lips. Ida Belle nodded, cluing in on what was happening, and motioned to Blanchet to cover the laundry room while I headed down the hall. Gertie fell in behind Blanchet and Ida Belle behind me as I crept toward the living room. I peered around the opening and saw a soda can on my coffee table, along with a napkin with crumbs on it.

I slipped around the corner, indicating the coffee table to Ida Belle as I headed to my office. I paused at the doorway, listening for any sounds inside, and heard a faint rustle, but nothing else. I peered around and Merlin gave me a one-eye-open stare from his perch on the back of the couch on the far wall. I stuck my pistol back in my waistband and headed over to the couch and peered behind.

And there was the girl. Fast asleep.

Relief flooded through me as I considered the best way to wake her without startling the life out of her when her eyes fluttered. She sat up, obviously scared, and I crouched down by the side of the couch, hoping that would be more reassuring.

"My name is Fortune Redding. We've been out looking for you. Are you all right?"

The girl relaxed a little and nodded.

"Do you want to come out? Are you still hungry?"

She nodded again, so I rose and backed away from the couch. Ida Belle had disappeared, and I figured had gone to warn Blanchet and Gertie to put their weapons away. When the girl emerged from behind the couch, I gave her a good once-over. She was rumpled and a little dirty, and the bruises she'd had in the hospital were still visible and starting to yellow, but she didn't appear to have collected any new injuries.

"My friends are here with me," I said as we walked. "They're good people. You're safe with them."

I stepped into the kitchen, pleased to see that someone had grabbed an extra chair from the dining room and Gertie was putting iced tea and a plate of cookies on the table.

"Do you want something more substantial to eat, dear?" Gertie asked.

The girl shook her head as she slipped onto a chair. "I had a sandwich. I'm sorry I took your food, but I was hungry."

"You're welcome to anything you want," I said. "We've all been really worried about you."

She gave me a hesitant look. "You're the lady who saved me, right?"

"A local fisherman pulled you out of the bayou, but I'm the one who gave you CPR. Do you know what that is?"

She nodded. "We all know CPR. They start teaching us basic medical stuff when we're around five."

Which made perfect sense if the Brethren wanted to ensure minimal contact with the outside, and then it hit me— her memory had returned.

"You remember where you're from?"

She looked panicked for a moment, and I wondered why. Then realization dawned.

"You never lost your memory, did you?"

She cast a nervous glance around the table, then shook her head. "My mom said if we got separated to pretend I didn't remember. She said no one could take me without proof, so I'd be safe until she could find me."

"What is your name?"

"Mariela. My mom is Lara."

I glanced at the others. We'd all known this was likely the case, but it was still a jolt to hear her say it. Blanchet stared at her, clutching the table, and I knew he was itching to throw a million questions out but was holding back because we couldn't afford to overwhelm her.

"Where is your mother?" I asked.

Tears sprang into her eyes. "I don't know. She said she was going to talk to the police and get help for everyone. She was supposed to come back for me, but it got dark and she still hadn't come back. Then I heard a boat and thought it was her, but two of the bad men were coming."

"The Brethren, you mean? You lived with them, right?"

She shrugged. "I've never heard that name, but I live in the swamp with other people. The moms and kids are nice, but the men are mean. They hurt the women. They think we don't know because they lock all the kids up together in one big room at night, but we can hear them screaming. My mom said we had to get away before I was grown, so I wouldn't have to live the way she and the other women do."

My jaw flexed and I clenched my fists under the table. I could tell the others were struggling to control their anger as much as I was.

"So when the men came to the camp, you ran?"

She nodded. "There was this secret door in the floor in the bathroom. I went down that and got out before the men came in."

"Did the bad men use the key hidden at the sink?"

"No. The door only locked from the outside, so my mom locked it when she left and slid the key under the door to me. I put it back when I ran 'cause it didn't belong to me."

I glanced at the others. That meant the Brethren had their own key. I wondered just how many keys to Nickel's camp were floating around the parish.

"Mom wasn't supposed to be gone long. Only an hour maybe."

"And when the bad men went upstairs, you ran."

"It was dark and I lost my shoe, but I was afraid to stop and get it. The moon was out sometimes but then it disappeared for a long time, and I fell into the water. I hit my head on something and I don't remember anything after that. Not until I woke up in the hospital."

"What happened today at June's?"

"I was in my room, and I heard Ms. Nelson yell, then I heard a gun. I tried the window but couldn't get it open, so I grabbed a lamp from the nightstand and stood on the chair next to the door. When he came into the room, I hit him in the head as hard as I could and ran out the back door and into the trees. There was a FedEx truck on the next street, and I climbed inside and hid behind some packages."

"That was very smart."

"I got lucky because he was going to Sinful. When he stopped to deliver a big box, he found me and started to call the cops. But I didn't want the cops. I wanted you. So I told him if he did that, I'd tell the cops he kidnapped me. He said he had a baby and a new bass boat and couldn't afford to lose either one and told me to scram."

"You're a really smart girl, Mariela."

She shrugged. "I guess. I made him look up your address on his phone so I knew where to find you, then I ran into the woods and worked my way around the neighborhood until I was able to sneak into your house. I broke a window in your utility room. I'm really sorry about that."

"Don't worry about it. But why did you want to find me?"

"I listened when Ms. Nelson talked to you. I peeked out the window. I saw you in the hospital, too, and heard the nice doctor talking about you. She said if anyone could help me, it was you. Ms. Nelson left your card on the kitchen counter, and I saw your name, and I remembered you guys saying you were from Sinful."

I stared at her for a moment, utterly and truly confused.

"How is it you know about things like FedEx and searching for people on cell phones when you live in the middle of a swamp without electricity? Are the people you live with religious?"

She frowned. "I don't think so. No one has ever prayed or anything and I've never seen a Bible. But we have class every day to teach about the outside world. They show us stuff on iPads and we have a TV in the schoolroom. They said it runs on satellite. We have generators for electricity, but we only run them when we're learning. When we're old enough, we have to go out and do stuff, so we have to blend."

"What kind of stuff?"

She shrugged. "My mom wouldn't say. Just that she didn't want me to have to do it, so she was going to get us out of there."

"What other kind of things do you learn?"

"We learn about how to travel—like in airports. And about cell phones and iPads and things like Uber and hotels. And we have Spanish lessons every day."

I glanced at the others and frowned. Just as we'd suspected, the Brethren wasn't a cult. It was a front for traffickers. The question was, what were they selling? I prayed it wasn't women and children, although breeding and raising them to be soldiers in their own little army wasn't any better.

"Has your mom always lived in the swamp?"

She nodded. "She said her mother had her there, just like she had me there."

I pulled out my phone and showed her the photo that Blanchet had given me. "Do you recognize this woman?"

She studied the picture and frowned. "She kinda looks like my mom, but I've never seen my mom wear that dress. And that girl looks like me, but it can't be."

"We think the girl in the picture is your mom, and the older woman is *her* mom."

Her eyes widened. "Really? I've never seen my grandma. She was gone before I could remember."

"Gone where?" Blanchet asked, his voice tense.

"I don't know. Mom wouldn't tell. I asked if she'd ever come back so I could meet her and mom said no."

Blanchet's expression twisted in pain, and he jumped up from the table, startling Mariela, and walked off down the hall.

"Did I make the man angry?" Mariela asked, and my heart broke all over again.

"No. He's just upset. He knew your grandmother and cared about her. He was hoping to find her again."

"I wish he could. If I had my mom and my grandma and we could get away from the bad men, then we could live like those people on TV, right? I could go to real school, and we could have a dog, and no one would lock me in a room every night while they hurt my mom."

She looked down at the table. "Did the man hurt Ms. Nelson because I got away?"

"He hit her but she's going to be fine."

She looked relieved. "That's good. She was nice. She fixed me good food and made that angry man leave when he upset me."

"The sheriff?"

"I guess so. He kept asking me questions about where I lived and where I'd been hiding. I just shook my head and looked scared and confused, like I'd practiced with my mom, but it just made him madder. What happened to my mom? She should have come for me by now."

"I don't know, but your mom is very smart. Look how she trained you and she got you both out of there. How many kids and mothers live there?"

She looked down at her hands and moved her fingers, counting. "Six kids, if you include me and the teenagers. They swear they're not kids, but the mothers say they are. And four mothers, including mine."

How many bad men are there?"

She frowned. "I'm not sure. I've never seen more than two at once, but there's at least five different ones."

"And do all the bad men carry guns?"

"Lots of guns. And mom said to never run away from the camp because there's explosives everywhere. She's been working on a way out for two years now. Finally, she said she was ready, and we had to wait for our turn to cook dinner. That was the only time we were both together and not locked inside. It took us a long time to go through the swamp. Sometimes we'd stop while she stared at the ground. We finally got to a place with a boat. Mom said that boat was hidden there in case the bad guys ever needed to get away."

My heart clenched at the woman's bravery and the care she'd taken trying to get her and her daughter out of a horrific situation. It sounded as if Blanchet had been right and the

Brethren had left a boat at a location deeper in the swamp, probably in the opposite direction of the cove we'd found. I wanted to believe the girl's mother had been delayed somewhere and hadn't fallen back into the hands of her captors, but I knew the chances of that were razor thin.

"Can you help me find her?" the girl asked, her lower lip trembling.

"I'm going to try."

"I don't have to go back to Ms. Nelson, do I? Can I stay here?"

"You definitely don't have to go back to Ms. Nelson. The bad men might look for you again, but the sheriff is looking for you, too. I'd get in trouble if he found you here, but I'll hide you here tonight. Tomorrow, I'm going to have you stay with a friend—somewhere that the bad guys and the sheriff will never look. Then I can go out and find your mom."

She didn't look convinced, but she nodded. "There was a man in a car. He parked down the street, but he was looking at your house."

"What kind of car?"

"A blue one."

"Would you recognize him if you saw him again?"

"Yeah. He was skinny, with a pointy face, and he looked angry."

Probably Hermes's flunky.

Mariela yawned and I took that as my cue.

"Okay, then let's get you to bed. You're exhausted."

"Will I be safe upstairs?"

"I'm going to have you stay in my bedroom. There's a secret hiding place in the closet. So if anyone comes tonight, you just hide in there and no one can find you."

Her eyes widened. "Have you had to hide from bad guys?"

"Before I moved here, yes. So I like to have a place I can

count on."

She smiled. "You're smart like my mom."

We headed upstairs and I showed her the secret panel in my closet, which seemed to excite her. Then I got her an old T-shirt of mine to sleep in and brought her clothes down to wash since they were all she had. She was already dropping off by the time I exited the room.

The others were collected at the kitchen table, drinking coffee and wearing grave expressions.

"You think Lara is back at the compound?" Blanchet asked.

"I'm afraid so. There's only two reasons I can think of that she hasn't come back for her daughter. I'm sticking with the first one, which is she's back at the compound, because that's the one that has her still breathing."

"Do you think she killed that guy Hermes found at Nickel's camp?" Ida Belle asked.

I blew out a breath. "Maybe, but the timing doesn't work. If she wasn't caught Monday night, then why didn't she come back for Mariela? And if she was caught Monday night, and she's the one who shot the guy, then where has the body been all this time?"

"If we assume it was the same two men who came into Nickel's camp, then maybe she managed to shoot one and the other one captured her and brought the injured one back to the camp to see if they could help him. Then they dumped the body at Nickel's camp later on."

I shook my head. "There's no way he survived a shot straight through the heart for more than a couple minutes."

"True," Blanchet agreed. "So the timing doesn't work at all."

"So what do we do?" Ida Belle asked. "If we tell the cops, they'll insist on taking Mariela and making her talk before they do anything. And if they plan a raid, I'm afraid of what will happen to the women and children in there, especially now that we know they're locked up like caged animals."

I already knew the most likely course of action if the men were threatened—they'd eliminate anyone who could identify them or testify against them at a trial.

"You think Spinner's working with them?" Ida Belle asked.

Blanchet nodded. "Viewed backward through the current lens, it *does* look like a setup. Spinner claimed he never went in that area anymore and then a day later we see him leaving it with a cell phone. Then he meets Otto somewhere other than the store dock to give him ice chests in exchange for money and that cell phone, probably because he has no way to keep it charged. That spells middleman at the least, active member at worst."

"It would make sense to have people set up as go-betweens," I said. "People who were otherwise assumed to be good community members."

Ida Belle shook her head. "I hate to think that Otto is into something illegal, especially involving those women and girls. He's been here a long time."

"So have the Brethren," I said.

"I wish we knew what they were trafficking," Blanchet said.

"I don't think it's people," I said. "I think those women are definitely being abused, but with Mariela's comment about learning how to travel and speak Spanish, my guess is they're using them as drug mules."

Blanchet's face flashed with anger. "No wonder Maya ran. I just wish she'd run farther than Mudbug."

"I wonder why she didn't," Gertie said.

"Probably no funds to do so," Ida Belle said, "and having a young child along didn't make that any easier. My guess is she picked up work as soon as possible to put some money together to get farther away."

"But she could have done that in a couple weeks' time," Gertie said. "At least enough to get them to the next place. Her staying doesn't make sense. Unless we assume she didn't leave because of Andy."

He sighed. "I hope that's not true. Because if she had a chance to get away and lost it over me, I'd feel horrible."

"I think that could have been part of it," Ida Belle said. "But I also think she might have stayed because she liked her situation. She'd found a nice town to live in, and a good place to live with a sympathetic landlord. She must have felt safe enough to take the risk of staying."

"And I'm sure she didn't have the appropriate documents to move easily in the regular world," I said. "She might have been trying to find someone who could create those for her and Lara and ran out of time."

"That's true," Blanchet said, "but it still makes my heart ache to think about it all. We have to find a way into that compound to get those women and kids out."

"Yeah. I'm going to have to dwell on that one for a while. I'll come up with something by tomorrow."

"I can stay here tonight," Blanchet said.

"So can we," Ida Belle said.

I shook my head. "That guy watching my house is the deputy Blanchet brought in, so we can't afford to do anything out of the ordinary."

"But Ida Belle and I stay here all the time," Gertie argued.

"Yes, but Hermes doesn't know that and neither does his flunky. So to them, it might look odd."

"Where are you going to stash Mariela tomorrow?" Gertie asked.

I grinned. "The one place Hermes is certain not to look. With Ronald."

CHAPTER EIGHTEEN

THE NEXT MORNING, I WAS UP EARLY AND HEADED INTO THE kitchen to put coffee on. Ida Belle had already texted that she and Gertie were on their way and Gertie was bringing fixings for pancakes. She wanted to make something good for Mariela. I had slept light as a cat the entire night, waking every time Mariela made a noise. And I'd kept getting up to check outside and sure enough, I'd spotted a dark blue Honda Accord cruising my block several times, which could potentially make getting Mariela next door to Ronald's somewhat difficult, especially since I didn't think taking a ten-year-old across my roof escape route was a good call.

By the time Gertie had a stack of pancakes going, Mariela came into the kitchen. I'd washed her clothes the night before and left them at the foot of the bed, so she was wearing the same thing, but she'd had a shower and her face had more color in it, which was a good sign. She saw the stack of pancakes on the table and smiled.

"I love pancakes, but we almost never get them."

"Well, you are welcome to as many as you want to eat,"

Gertie said. "I'm making enough for an army. And there's bacon too."

I grabbed the bacon from the microwave where it had been keeping warm and put it on the table. Ida Belle got us all plates and silverware and we all dug in. I'd texted Ronald to come over when he was up and mostly awake, and we were almost done with breakfast when he waltzed in the back door. Apparently, 'mostly awake' didn't imply dressed for outside because he was wearing a bright purple robe with a matching sequined sash and feather boa. His feet were clad in furry silver boots.

Mariela took one look at him and was enthralled. "That's the fanciest outfit I've ever seen in person."

Ronald, who'd stopped short in the middle of the kitchen at the sight of the girl, gave her a big smile. "Oh honey, this old thing? It's so last season that Gertie was a girl when they released it."

I was pretty sure Mariela didn't have a clue what he was talking about, but the theatrics made her giggle.

"Mariela, this is my friend and next-door neighbor, Ronald." I looked over at Ronald. "Mariela got away from the bad man yesterday, and I need to make sure that neither the man nor the sheriff finds her until all the bad men are caught. I was hoping she could stay with you."

"Of course! I love having pretty girls stay with me. I just got a whole batch of makeup in that I need to test."

"Why do you wear makeup? You're a boy."

"Well, girls shouldn't get to have all the fun. And sometimes I'm an actor and play different people." He gave her a critical eye. "I'm also collecting donations for the school clothes drive. I bet I have a couple things that would look great on you."

"That's it!" I said. "The clothes drive. That's how we get Mariela over to your house without anyone seeing her."

Mariela nodded. "The man in the blue car was there this morning when I woke up."

"And I saw the sheriff's boat cruise by when I walked over," Ronald said. "That idiot Hermes was in it."

"You'd think he'd be out doing his job," Gertie said. "A woman was attacked in her own home and as far as he knows, this girl has been kidnapped. Yet he's wasting time shadowing you."

"Surely he doesn't think June's attacker was working with us," Ida Belle said.

I shook my head. "I doubt it. More likely, he thinks we're going to figure out everything before he does, and he wants to be on hand to swoop in and claim the glory."

"That sounds about right," Gertie said.

I had some more colorful thoughts on the matter, but I didn't want to say them in front of Mariela, nor did I want to discuss our course of action for the day until she was safely tucked away at Ronald's house.

"Well, if everyone's done with breakfast, let's get Mariela over to Ronald's." I looked at the girl. "You'll be safe with Ronald. And because you're safe, we'll be able to look for your mom."

She gave me a grave nod and I cursed everyone who'd forced this girl into dealing with things she had no business dealing with at her age.

Fifteen minutes later, Ronald came up my front driveway, pulling a collapsible cart with empty laundry bags toward my garage.

"I figure this is easier than toting all those clothes a little at a time," he said, loud enough for his voice to carry to the man crouched down in the blue Accord parked across the street.

"Perfect," I said. "I'll stuff the donations in the bags, and you can add them to your sorting pile. How's the drive going?"

"Oh, fantastic," he said as we headed inside the garage and then into the house.

Ida Belle and Gertie stuffed two bags full of towels and linens and we carried them into the garage, where Mariela and the cart were positioned behind my Jeep. I put one of the empty laundry bags in the cart and Mariela climbed inside. Ronald had already cut some slits in the top of the bag, so I placed one of the other filled bags in next to her then tossed some loose clothes on top of the bags.

I gave Ronald a wave as he headed out of the garage with his cart of very precious cargo. He'd made it to the sidewalk when Hermes pulled up to the curb in the sheriff's department truck.

Crap!

"Sheriff Hermes," Ronald said and fluttered his eyes. "It's so nice to see a big strong man first thing in the morning. I'm sorting clothes for the charity drive. Would you like to help? I saw some pink taffeta that would look simply divine on you."

Hermes stepped backward, shaking his head, and practically jogged into my garage. Gertie popped up from the freezer with a package of fish and closed the lid.

"You only have one bag of catfish left," she said. "We'll have to pick up some more at my house to have enough for a fry."

She pretended that she'd just caught sight of Hermes and gave him a dirty look. "What do you want?"

"Just making sure you're not trying to do my job."

I blinked. "Well, as you can see, we're busy. But I probably should be doing your job since clearly, you're not. Why aren't you out looking for that girl?"

"How do you know about the girl?"

"Because I talked to June. She's not exactly impressed with you."

Hermes flushed. "You think I care what that old bat thinks?"

"If the color of your face is any indication, yes. And you should. June is your voting public. If anything happens to that girl—the one you insisted on removing from the hospital, where she had better security—and it gets out that you didn't provide police protection to a known victim, I don't think Carter has anything to worry about."

"We'll just see about that."

He stalked off and I closed the garage door so I didn't have to see his retreating backside, which was no improvement over the front. Gertie opened the freezer and hauled my bag of towels out.

"I hope you showered already, because otherwise, you're in for a chilly dry-off," she said.

"Quick thinking on hiding that extra bag." I shook my head. "I'm sure his flunky saw us carry two bags out of the house and saw two in the cart."

"So Hermes was in his boat earlier and cruised by, then shifted to the car," Ida Belle said. "If we didn't have serious business elsewhere, I swear I'd sit right here and make his life impossible."

"Why not do both?" Gertie asked. "We could easily get every woman over forty on the phone to the sheriff's department, demanding he do something about seniors being attacked in their homes and little girls being carted off. Most everyone has grandchildren, and there's no sense you wasting time doing things that a bunch of our friends would be glad to handle."

"Do it," I said. "Might as well heap on the misery and further ensure Carter has no opposition when this election comes around. Hermes already has the political connection advantage. I need to negate that."

Ida Belle made the call as we headed back inside. Ronald sent me a text letting me know that Mariela was safely inside his house and they were getting ready to try all his new makeup samples. It sounded like a horror story to me, but Mariela had seemed excited about it all.

Blanchet drove up a couple minutes later, and Ida Belle brought him up to speed on the morning.

"I made a few calls this morning," Blanchet said, "and finally ran down an old-timer in a nursing home in NOLA who used to live in Mudbug back when I was a deputy there. He said Spinner was former military. Want to guess what he did?"

"Explosives," I said.

"You got it."

"Did you ask the old-timer about Otto?" Ida Belle asked.

"Yeah. He said his son was Otto's accountant for a couple years here recently and he never could reconcile Otto's life-style with his bottom line."

"Maybe he inherited," Gertie said.

"But there was no interest earned on investments or other accounts that was significant in any way. He said Otto's house had everything top-of-the-line—Viking appliances, Sub-Zero refrigerator, and he bought a new truck every year, top-of-the-line there as well, and you know what a good truck costs these days."

"I suppose he could have saved for the appliances and bought them one at a time," Ida Belle said, "but you're right on the truck thing. Of course, plenty of people have no problem running up as much debt as places will give them, so there's always that possibility."

"True," Blanchet said, "but there's also the possibility that he's making money off the books that covers those luxuries."

"Well, hopefully when we overturn the apple cart, we'll be able to connect everyone that needs connecting," I said. "I'm not interested in people who've been involved with this getting away with it."

"So did you come up with a plan?" Gertie asked.

"I think so," I said. "We need to get Mariela's mother and the other women and children out of that compound, but I don't want to give the men time to kill them and get away, which means calling in the state police to storm them is out of the question. They'd know we were coming before the cops launched their boats. And with all their security measures, I don't give the state police much chance to penetrate. That's not the kind of training they received."

"We could infiltrate," Blanchet said, "but we don't know what the health or age of the women and children are, so they might not be able to leave without assistance."

"I think the best way to go at this is a direct and obvious attack," I said. "But with only the four of us because I don't want to bring anyone else in on the front line."

"Really?" Blanchet asked.

"If we catch them by surprise, then the men are more likely to immediately flee to avoid being caught rather than stick around to clean up the evidence."

Ida Belle nodded. "They'll scramble to save themselves, leaving the women and children behind. Then we can take our time with extraction. That's smart."

"I like it except for the part where the bad guys get away," Gertie said.

"I have a plan for that too. Ida Belle and I are going to head into the swamp and approach the compound."

"Why does Ida Belle always get to do the fun stuff?" Gertie griped.

"Because she can make that boat fly and knows the bayous

like the back of her hand. And I need a sharpshooter with me in case we have to pick people off. Besides, I need you and Blanchet to cover the second part of this."

"What second part?" Gertie asked.

I told her.

———

THIRTY MINUTES LATER, IDA BELLE AND I WERE IN MY BOAT, flying across the water toward Mudbug. When we reached the big lake that bordered the town, I motioned for her to stop, and we studied the satellite maps.

"We have to assume that Lara and Mariela went north, away from the cove we found, crossing the swamp area until they reached one of these channels. The Brethren probably keep several boats on tap in different locations in case they need to leave by an alternate route, but they would all be accessible by land."

"We don't know how many people are in there," Ida Belle said. "But I doubt they have enough boats to get everyone in the camp out at the same time, which plays into your theory that the men will flee."

I nodded. "But no matter how far north I go, all of the channels eventually dump into this one. As long as they stay in the water, they have to pass here."

Ida Belle studied the satellite image and nodded. "Agreed."

"Then let me make a phone call and we'll get this under way."

A couple minutes later, we were cruising up the channel and I scanned the bayou as we went, periodically using my binoculars to ensure the way ahead was clear. We passed a couple fishermen, but I saw nothing out of the ordinary. No sign at all of Spinner.

When we got to the branch-off that went to the cove, we passed it and kept going north until we located a small channel that ran about half a mile north of where we suspected their camp was located. Ida Belle slowed and we idled along, looking for any sign of passage, then I spotted something covered by brush. We inched closer and were able to make out the small boat tucked in a dug-out slot underneath a huge cypress branch with hanging moss.

"Pull farther up to where that big branch hangs over the channel. We can hide my boat behind it, and it shouldn't be visible from the land or from where their boat is stashed."

We secured the boat, then pulled on gloves and hats. We were already wearing long sleeves, so we had protection from the brush. Then we walked back down to where the Brethren's boat was and located a visible trail. I looked around for any sign of cameras but didn't spot anything. More likely, they trusted explosives to warn them if anyone was incoming. And their spies to tip them off that someone was headed their way.

Our progress was slow because I had to make sure we didn't wind up blown to bits and become lunch for the wildlife, and occasionally, I stopped to estimate our position in relation to where I thought their camp was. When we were about a hundred yards out from that location, I sent a text to Gertie.

You're up.

I got back at least ten emojis of grinning and clapping and assumed that meant they were ready to go. I motioned to Ida Belle and we continued down the path. The farther we went, the denser and darker it became, but so far, this path had been free from trip wires. My theory on secondary and escape routes seemed to be holding.

We'd progressed about half a mile from the boat when Ida Belle tapped me on the shoulder and pointed off to our left. I looked over and saw a small puff of smoke disappear into the trees, then another. Since there was no sound, I assumed it was a fire.

We'd found them!

I texted Gertie to make sure they were in position, then Harrison to let him know we were about to launch. Ida Belle and I crept toward the smoke, weapons ready. It didn't take us long to locate the source of the smoke—a firepit with a cast-iron pot on top of it—and a man with a pistol at his side, sitting in a chair in front of it.

I heard the plane overhead long before I caught a glimpse of it through the trees. We skirted the firepit and slowly crept around the perimeter, attempting to spot any other armed men. A bit away from the firepit, I saw green formations that didn't look natural. I pointed at them, and Ida Belle nodded. As we crept closer, I saw the windows and doors on the front of the structures. The roofs were flat and had turf growing on top of them. From the air, no one would be able to tell where they were.

I pulled the flare gun from my waist and gave Ida Belle a nod. We both pulled on goggles.

It was showtime.

I knew that as soon as I fired the gun, the men would immediately scramble, but we had the advantage because by the time they spotted the flare above the trees, we could be anywhere, and unless they were looking up when I fired, they'd have no idea what direction the shot had been fired from.

But our old buddy Bomber Bruce would know exactly where to fly, and Gertie and Blanchet would know exactly where to target.

I fired the flare up and then Ida Belle and I hurried behind a thick set of brush that offered a decent view of the doors on two of the structures. The man who had been watching the fire ran into view and yelled for someone he called Captain. A second man came out of one of the structures and looked up at the flare.

He cursed. "What the hell is that? We don't have flare guns."

"Maybe someone got lost nearby."

"This is trouble we don't need. We've got enough to worry about with that girl still on the loose."

A second later, the prop plane roared overhead, barely clearing the trees, and then bright oval objects began to fall from it. The first balloon hit the captain right on top of the head and exploded, sending bright pink paint all over him and the fire guy. They both pulled their guns and pointed up, but the plane had already disappeared.

I lifted my hand and crossed my fingers and Ida Belle nodded. This is where I hoped cowardice won out. When the roar of the plane signaled a second pass, I got my wish. The two men took off into the woods, yelling as they went that they were under attack. A third man came out of one of the structures and ran after them, and I saw another come from between structures and head the opposite direction. The second round of balloons fell, and it was a deluge of paint. I heard yelling and then more gunfire and I wondered if they were shooting at each other.

Then I looked up and saw a sight that took my breath away.

Ida Belle followed my gaze and gasped. "She's fallen out!"

CHAPTER NINETEEN

My heart clutched as I watched the silver-haired figure falling from the plane, and then a second came out after her.

"They jumped!" Ida Belle said. "Is she wearing a cape?"

"They were supposed to throw balloons out of the airplane, not themselves!"

A couple seconds later, they pulled parachutes and relief flooded through me, until a gust of wind took them off course. Then I heard more rounds.

And kids screaming.

I tore through the brush at a dead run toward the sound and slid to a stop in front of one of the structures. There was a padlock on the outside door. I tried to look inside, but it was too dark to make out anything.

"Everyone stand back!" I yelled and prayed they were listening and there was no bad guy locked up in there with them.

Then I squeezed off a round and blew the lock off the door.

I burst into the structure, saying a second prayer that

everyone inside was unharmed, and found myself looking at a group of women and children huddled in the corner.

"Any of the bad men in here?" I asked, and they shook their heads, but I could tell they weren't sure what side I was on. I didn't blame them. I wouldn't trust me either.

Ida Belle ran in beside me and the women's eyes widened, and they glanced at one another, now completely and utterly confused. I imagined when they dreamed of a rescue, this wasn't what it looked like at all.

"Is anyone hurt?" I asked.

Again, more head shaking, but no one spoke. Then a little girl pointed at the window and screamed.

I whirled around and saw a man lighting a stick of dynamite. I had zero doubt what he intended to do with it. Without even a second's hesitation, I aimed and fired. The bullet caught him right in between the eyes and he dropped, but the stick had already been lit.

"Duck!" I yelled, and everyone dropped to the floor as the blast shook the ground and blew out the windows.

Glass and pieces of split wood pelted my arms, which were covering my head, and I felt a couple of shards tear through the material and into my skin. I jumped up and immediately hurried over to the women and children. The small ones were crying and some of the women were as well. The rest looked shell-shocked. I could see nicks on them from the flying debris, but no one looked seriously injured.

"You're all safe now," I said. "But I need you to stay right here while I look for my friends. Is there someone who can take charge?"

A woman rose up, and it only took a second for me to recognize her as Lara Delgado. "I will."

"How many men were here?"

"I saw four before they locked us in, but I think there was

one more who was new. I heard him calling the others fools. I didn't recognize his voice."

"How many come to this camp?"

"Five different ones for the past several years."

"Great. You guys stay put and I'll be back."

Ida Belle and I rushed out and headed into the trees in the direction we'd seen Gertie and Blanchet drifting. Relief coursed through me when I heard them both yelling. I burst into a small clearing and almost ran into the back of Blanchet. I glanced around but didn't see Gertie.

"Up here!"

I looked up and saw Gertie, hanging about thirty feet up, her parachute tangled in tree branches.

"She looks like a giant tea bag," Ida Belle said.

"A tea bag with a Supergirl cape," I said. "What the hell were you thinking?"

"We were thinking you could use backup on the ground," he said. "And I was thinking I had to see this. Had to be here in case Lara was here."

"She's here and she's fine. The men fled, just like we thought they would. Well, except one, but he's in pieces so no longer a threat."

"This is all great, but can you get me down?"

"One sec!" I pulled out my phone and sent Harrison a text, telling him to be ready to apprehend, then motioned toward Blanchet's spent chute.

"Is that still intact?"

He nodded. "I manage to direct straight down into the clearing. According to Gertie, she 'fluked.'"

Ida Belle looked up and shook her head. "Odd how many of those random chance occurrences happen to Gertie."

"Grab that chute and let's stretch it out underneath her," I directed. "Gertie, do you have a knife?"

She frowned. "I'm not sure. Hold on."

She dug into her bra and tossed down a stick of dynamite, a half-eaten sandwich, and ten grapes.

"All that's left is my gun."

"Grab the edge and stretch it out, Blanchet," I said. "Ida Belle, shoot her down."

Ida Belle grabbed the parachute with her left hand so she'd be ready for the switch, then raised her pistol at the straps holding Gertie upright. She fired one shot and the strap snapped in two, leaving Gertie dangling sideways. She fired again and another snap went. Now she was hanging on by two opposite each other and kicking and flapping to keep her balance.

"She looks like a baby duck trying to lift off the water for the first time," Ida Belle said.

"Will you hurry up!" Gertie yelled. "I don't have much arms left and I threw down all my food. I can't be up here all day."

Ida Belle fired two rounds, one after the other, and the last two straps let go. As soon as Gertie dropped, Ida Belle holstered her pistol and grabbed the chute with both hands. Gertie landed in the middle of the chute and bounced up a good three feet in the air, whooping as she went. On the second fall, we all stepped forward when she hit the chute and she fell to the ground.

"Ouch!" she complained as she slowly rose. "You didn't have to drop me so hard."

"Since you're supposed to be in a plane halfway back to Sinful, I think the words you're looking for are 'thank you,'" Ida Belle said.

"We can talk about it later," I said, and hurried back to the camp. Lara must have been watching for our return because she stepped cautiously out the door as we approached, then her gaze locked on Blanchet and her eyes widened.

"Andy? Is that you?"

"Lara," he said, his voice catching.

Lara ran forward and threw her arms around him, laughing and crying at the same time. Blanchet joined in with her, and I felt my eyes water. Even Ida Belle sniffed. Gertie was laughing and crying along with them.

The other women and children inched out, and I assured them that they were safe and that people with boats would be here soon to get them out. They were obviously still in shock, and I could tell they were too scared to believe this horror of a life was over. These women and their children would need some serious help getting over what had happened to them, but I had some ideas on how that could happen.

"Andy, you have to help me," Lara said when she broke the hug. "My daughter is missing. I escaped with her, but they caught me and brought me back. She's out there somewhere alone."

"She's safe," I said. "With a good friend of mine."

Lara looked scared to believe what I'd said but Andy smiled and nodded.

"Mariela is safe," I said. "She's an extraordinary girl."

At the sound of her daughter's name, Lara knew we were telling the truth and let out a huge sigh of relief.

Blanchet stared at her, his expression somber. "Your mother... Mariela said she'd never met her."

Lara shook her head. "They keep us here to bring in drugs. We're expendable. If we get caught, then they leave us in Mexican prisons. The police there are corrupt. They don't make deals like this country does to get people out. Mama left for a trip ten years ago and she never returned."

My heart clenched. Maya had been held captive for another ten years in this place after she disappeared from Mudbug, only to wind up in a Mexican prison.

"Do you think she's still there?" he asked.

"I don't know if she's even still alive. I don't know why she brought us back here. I asked but she never explained."

Tears streamed down Blanchet's face, and he hugged Lara again.

"We'll do everything we can to find out what happened," I said.

My phone signaled an incoming text and I smiled. "The state police picked up three of the four guys that ran. They're still looking for the last one. And Hermes showed up, raising hell about someone calling the state police in over his head, so he went out there in the sheriff's boat trying to take over. Harrison says the state police weren't having it and sent him on his way."

"The governor can't fire the whole state just to prop Hermes up," Ida Belle said.

"There are three transport boats on the way to the cove to pick up the women and children," I said. "I'll lead and we'll get them all out of here."

"You can't go that way," Lara said. "There's explosives along the path. The men know where to walk to avoid them."

"Don't worry. I know how to find them."

She didn't look convinced, but the desire to get out of this hellhole was greater than her fear of the path to the cove. The other women and children had been clutching each other during our exchange and now some had collapsed on the ground, weeping as they realized their nightmare was finally over.

"Ida Belle, I want you and Gertie to head back and get my boat. Meet us at the cove. Blanchet and I will get these women and children down there for pickup. Remember, there's one missing guy still out there, so be on the lookout."

As Ida Belle and Blanchet headed off, I turned to the

women. "If there are things you'd like to bring with you, then please gather what you can easily carry. You've probably all been this way before, so you know how long the walk is. Only load up what you can carry, anything personal and maybe a change of clothes."

They all nodded and headed back inside to grab what they wanted. It only took them a couple minutes and what they held wasn't much, but then I didn't figure they had much.

"Okay, I want you to follow me single file. Put a child in between two adults so that they can keep watch. Blanchet will bring up the rear. If you see anything suspicious, yell. If anyone yells, including me or Blanchet, I want everyone to stop in place. Do you all understand?"

They all nodded, and I could see their excitement starting to build as they realized this was really going to happen. The youngest of the children was probably six, so that was a plus, and only one of the women appeared to be pregnant, but she didn't look far along. This wasn't going to be a fast trip, but I had every confidence that it would be a successful one.

It took us thirty minutes to make it to the cove, and Harrison was already there with the three rescue boats. The state police with him appeared slightly stunned at the collection of women and children, and their expressions shifted from sympathy to anger as they processed everything the group must have been through.

We got them all loaded about the time Ida Belle and Gertie pulled up.

"Thank you so much for getting the state police on board," I said to Harrison. "Where's Hermes?"

"When they made it clear he wasn't allowed to insert himself in any of this since it was going on right under his nose, he cut out. But not before he fired me."

"We'll see about that."

"That's what the state police said. I'm not worried about it. I'm just glad we rescued these women." He grinned. "It was nice partnering up again. That paint in the balloons was a stroke of genius. They tried to blend among the fisherman, but it wasn't possible. And that pink glitter isn't going to play well for them in prison."

"I'm sure you have Gertie to thank for that one."

"Everything is better with glitter," she said.

"What about the fourth man?" I asked. "What if he didn't get paint on him?"

"No sign of him, but there's still two boats sweeping the area, and the police have put out an alert. We'll get him, Fortune. If not today, then we'll track him down. At least one of those guys will make a deal. We'll get everything we need."

I nodded, but I didn't want some random bad guy hanging over my head.

He gave me a wave and shoved off with the state police. I motioned to Ida Belle. "Let's make a sweep and see if we can spot that last guy. I want to check near Spinner's camp first."

"He was moving awfully fast to be Spinner," Ida Belle said.

"Even Gertie moves fast when she needs to."

"Hey!" Gertie protested.

We climbed into the boat and set out, all scouting the bayou and channels for any sign of the man as we went. When we got to the place where we'd found Spinner's crab pot, we slowed but the line was gone. Ida Belle cruised up the bayou until we reached the tree line, and I jumped out.

"Give me just a sec to check."

"You want backup?" Blanchet asked.

"No. I'll be quicker alone."

I quickly found the path that Spinner had used and followed it deeper into the woods. It wasn't long before I found a clearing with remnants of a campfire and markings of tent stakes in the dirt. A clothesline still hung between two trees. But it was clear that Spinner had abandoned this site recently.

I headed back to the boat and found them tucked behind a cypress tree, ducked down. Ida Belle signaled, and I looked up the bayou and saw the sheriff's boat. Crap. The last thing I needed was a run-in with that idiot. He'd take the opportunity to arrest all of us now that we'd not only upstaged him but exposed his complete and utter incompetence to the state police.

I got low and eased into the boat, then peered through the moss with the others. Hermes had stopped about thirty yards away and was standing in the middle of the boat, looking down, but not at the water, at the bottom of the boat. It all made sense when he stepped to the side, and I saw Blair Johnson in the bottom of the boat and the flash of metal in Hermes's hand.

"Holy crap," Ida Belle whispered. "Do you think it was her running away from the camp and not another man? The women hadn't seen everyone there."

"But they thought it was a man's voice," I said.

"Maybe he's trying to get her to tell him where that last guy is," Blanchet said.

"Regardless, we can't sit here and watch him shoot her, and I wouldn't put it past him," I said. "If she's involved, I want her to go to prison and mourn that BMW and designer handbag, but only after she's told us everything she knows about the drug running. Start up the boat and head over there. He can't do anything stupid with four witnesses."

As soon as Ida Belle fired up the engine, Hermes turned around. When he caught sight of us, he snarled.

"Just keep going," he said as we approached. "You've already made enough trouble for me today, but I'm going to be the one who wraps this all up. Then we'll see who gets the credit."

Blair looked at me, her eyes wide, and I could see mud and leaves caked in her forehead. From running through the swamp? Or was something entirely different going on here?

"Get going!" Hermes ordered.

I lifted my pistol at them. Something was off. Way off.

Then I saw the flash of pink.

"I don't think so," I said and fired.

CHAPTER TWENTY

I caught Hermes in the right shoulder and sent the pistol flying out of his hand and over the side of the boat. Ida Belle gunned it and I leaped into the boat before Hermes could go for another weapon. I twisted his right arm up behind his back and forced him down into the bottom of the boat. Blanchet jumped in behind me with rope and tied him up. When he pulled up Blanchet's sleeve, he saw the pink paint.

"It was you," Blanchet said. "All this time, it was you. You weren't blowing off the investigation because you're incompetent. You were covering for them."

"I got nothing to say to you. When the ADA hears that woman shot me, it's going to be hell to pay."

I shook my head. "I don't think so. Not if Special Agent Johnson has anything to do with it."

Blair jerked out of her shocked stupor and stared at me. "How did you know?"

"Just out of the academy, right? They thought since you hadn't developed cop habits no one would catch on. But you weren't counting on one of the bad guys being law enforcement. Hermes was tipped off that the FBI was working this, and he locked onto you because he'd heard a fake social services woman was asking questions."

"Yes, but that still doesn't explain how you knew."

"Because your presence here didn't fit. But to be honest, it didn't dawn on me who you were until I saw Hermes holding a gun on you. Then there was that flash of pink, and I was certain we'd had things backward all along."

"If I bleed out, you're going to the electric chair," Hermes said.

Blanchet kicked him hard in the stomach.

"That's assault!" Hermes yelled.

"Look, he finally got the law right," Blanchet said. "Unfortunately, no one saw it happen. And when you're trying to cover up being a human-trafficking, drug-running, woman-and-child-abusing piece of crap, accidents occur. I think you tripped trying to get away and fell on a stump."

"Seems plausible," I said.

Blair's shoulders slumped as it finally started to register that she wasn't going to die.

"Thank you," she said. "Thank you for saving my life."

I nodded. "Let's get this idiot turned over to the state police. I'll follow in the sheriff's boat. Blanchet, you can take point."

Blanchet sat gleefully on the bench in front of Hermes, clutching his pistol. "If you so much as break wind, I'll shoot you and claim you were going for my weapon."

Hermes took one look at Blanchet's face and knew he wasn't joking.

"If you don't mind," Blair said, "I think I'll ride with the ladies."

I fired up the boat and followed Ida Belle out of the channel. Gertie had sent Harrison a text and he was going to contact the state police and give them our position. We'd just reached the point where the main bayou connected to the lake when I spotted one of their boats speeding our way.

Blair stood as they drew alongside and immediately identified herself, then told them that Hermes had been about to shoot her when I tagged him in the shoulder. One of the cops called someone and then gave us a nod.

"The captain is thrilled," one of them said to Hermes. "He's insisting on booking you himself. You've really burned a lot of bridges."

He looked over at Blair. "Captain says as soon as you're fit for it, give him a call and he'll set up an interview."

The other cop grabbed Hermes by the injured shoulder and pulled him up. Hermes yelled as if they were killing him. The cop smiled. "You think that hurts? Just wait until you get to prison. How many guys have you put in Angola, Hermes?"

"The real question is how many actually belonged there," I said. "Oh, and something I forgot to tell you earlier. That girl we've been looking for? She's safe. I'll reunite her with her mother when we get back to Sinful."

Blair's jaw dropped and one of the cops whistled.

"You've been busy," he said with a grin.

"Do you want to take the sheriff's boat?"

"If you can handle it, then we can get this guy straight to lockup."

I nodded. "Then we're happy to help. We'll take it back to Sinful for use by *real* law enforcement."

The cops headed out with a now-sullen and slightly scared Hermes. I think it was just now dawning on him that this whole farce was truly over. I looked over at Blair Johnson.

"Are you up for some of the state's best boudin?" I asked. "I'd like to have a chat and I figure a bathroom and something to eat and drink would be better than quizzing you in these boats."

"That sounds great, actually," she said.

We headed for the General Store, and I noticed Otto wasn't behind the counter when we went in. "Otto off today?" I asked.

"He had a doctor's appointment in New Orleans," the guy behind the counter said. "Should be back this afternoon, though."

"No problem. We're going to grab some drinks. Hook us up with some of that boudin."

Five minutes later, we were sitting at a picnic table outside and Blair was eating her first bite of the state's best boudin.

"So how did you wind up on the other end of Hermes's gun?" I asked.

"The FBI was tipped off last year about heroin coming into Louisiana from Mexico, all supplied by one of the major cartels, and everything tracked back to this area. We didn't find anything and started to expand our search when some loose talk about the Brethren among inmates at Angola made it back to us. Hermes got on our radar a couple days ago by anonymous tip. The person knew enough that wasn't common knowledge for us to take them seriously. Then when we heard he'd gone straight to the governor to get the temporary sheriff's position here, we thought it would be a chance to bring down the whole group."

I nodded. It was mostly what I'd figured, but something was still troubling me. "The problem is, I don't think for a minute Hermes was the one running this show. He's too arrogant and too foolish. Look how much attention he drew to himself."

Blair's eyes widened. "You think there's a local plant?"

"Yes. Someone who's been here a long time and has blended with the community."

"Any idea who it might be?" she asked.

"I've had my eye on Otto."

She glanced back at the store in surprise. "The store owner?"

"He had a clandestine meeting with a hermit and exchanged ice chests for cash. That hermit is also the one who told us where to find the Brethren and almost got Blanchet blown up in the process. And he was an explosives expert in the military. He also handed Otto a cell phone. Why does a hermit need a cell phone when he doesn't even have electricity? I'm not saying Otto's your guy, but it looks suspicious."

She frowned. "I agree that Hermes doesn't seem to have what it takes to be the leader of a criminal organization, and all evidence shows it existed long before he would have been old enough to be tasked with that responsibility, but the long-running criminal organizations have a lot of leaders over time. Unfortunately, no one else is on our radar. Maybe the women will be able to identify someone."

"I doubt it," I said. "My guess is if there was a local front man, that person didn't interact with the women just in case anyone ever got away. I doubt Hermes was there often, if at all, until today, so someone higher up in the food chain definitely wouldn't run the risk."

"That's accurate. I've been tracking him since I arrived, and today was the first day he ventured near the Brethren compound. I had a tracker on the sheriff's boat and set out after him. He tied off on one of the coves just north of where you found us and hiked across the swamp. I tried to follow, but I spotted one of the trip wires and decided I needed to call for backup because there was no other reason for trip wires to exist out there."

She shook her head. "Then the flare went up, which I assume was you?"

I nodded.

"And the plane flew over and I went as fast as I could back to the bank, but before I could start my engine, Hermes shot holes in my boat and it sank. He left me tied up on the bank and left. I know now he was trying to get the state police out of the area so he'd be clear. He returned later and threw me in his boat, probably wanting to get me out of the area before the state police found me."

"Why didn't he shoot you on the spot?"

"He wanted to know how I'd zeroed in on him."

"So he realized someone had tipped you off and wanted to know who it was. Makes sense."

"I have no doubt he would have shot me as soon as he got that information or realized I was telling the truth when I said I didn't know. If you hadn't shown up, I wouldn't have made it out of that swamp."

I struggled to tamp down my frustration. Pieces of the investigation whirled around in my mind. But there was something I was missing. Something important.

"You said you found the girl?"

"Actually, she found me. She's very clever and resourceful."

"When I first found out about her being pulled out of the swamp, I hoped she'd be able to provide me with information on the Brethren, but I guess we have everything we need now."

"Was it you sneaking around June's house that first night?"

She nodded. "I was going to sneak in, explain who I was, and that I was there to help. And I was really hoping her memory came back so she could give me some direction."

"Oh, it never left," I said.

"What?"

"I told you she was clever. I assume you didn't get to talk to her because June spotted you."

"I wouldn't have been able to anyway. The window was nailed shut."

I jumped up from my seat. It couldn't be, right?

June, who got control of Mariela when Hermes forced her release from the hospital. June, who had a 'sick sister' that she left for weeks at a time to tend to. June, who had her windows open the day we visited to 'air out her house' but had nailed shut the window on the girl's room.

And then it hit me—I'd been unable to see inside the structure the women were locked in, but I'd been able to see the man with the dynamite from inside clear as day. The screens were the same ones June had on her porch.

"We need a vehicle! Where's your car?" I asked Blair.

"Just down from here at the marina. I rented the boat there. Why? What did you figure out?"

"It's June Nelson."

"What?"

"No way!"

"Are you kidding me?"

"How?"

They all spoke at once.

"I'll explain on the way, but if I'm right, we have to get to her house before she clears out. Hermes would have already tipped her off about the sting."

We practically ran to Blair's car and as she made the drive to June's house, I told the others what I thought.

"It's thin," Blair said.

"But it all fits," Blanchet said.

Blair pulled into June's driveway and parked in the middle to keep her from getting her vehicle out of the garage. We hurried to the door and knocked, but there wasn't even a hint of sound coming from inside.

"I think I hear someone calling out for help," Blanchet

declared, even though there wasn't a single sound, then kicked the door open.

We rushed inside, guns drawn, and ran through the rooms. When I stepped in the bedroom, I let out a cry of frustration when I saw we were too late. Clothes had been pulled out of the closet, hangers strewn all over the room, drawers on the dresser were still pulled open, and there were gaps on the floor of the closet where shoes had previously been.

I cursed. "She's headed out of the country."

"Her car isn't in the garage," Ida Belle said.

"Boat or plane?" Blanchet asked.

"She can afford either," I said.

"But she'd drive somewhere to meet them, right?" Blair said and pulled out her cell phone.

"This is Special Agent Blair Johnson. I need you to track June Nelson's car."

I stared. "You put a tracker on her car? I thought you didn't suspect anyone else."

"I was hoping for an opportunity to get to the girl, maybe at a doctor's visit."

"Yes," she said into her phone. "And you're sure? Okay, I'm about to hand you over to a contractor working with us while I drive. Her name is Fortune Redding. Keep her informed of June's progress and call for backup by air. Suspect is assumed to be armed, extremely dangerous, and about to flee the country."

Blair passed me the phone, and the agent on the other end of the line gave me coordinates, which I gave to Ida Belle. Ida Belle took a look at the current location and surrounding area.

"There's an FBO about ten miles away from here. Small aircraft only, but the runway's long enough for a lite jet. And there's a shortcut. It won't be nice to your car, but we might be able to get there before she lifts off."

"I can buy a new car. That whole trust fund thing wasn't a lie."

Ida Belle gave her directions and Blair stomped on the gas.

"BMWs have excellent crash test ratings," Gertie said.

"Can you call the FBO and tell them to stall her plane?" Blair asked.

"I could, but most civilians are horrible in these kind of situations," I said. "If the pilot or June catches on, they'll just shoot them and take off anyway. I seriously doubt she booked that plane through a broker. My guess is the cartel she works for sent it."

"Crap. You're right. God, I have so much to learn."

"You're doing all right," I said. "That tracker on June's car was genius and might be the reason we catch her."

Five minutes into the drive, Ida Belle pointed to a dirt path and instructed Blair to turn onto it. The BMW slid on the slick dirt in a move that Ida Belle must have been proud of, then hit a huge dip and gave us all a good jolt. I heard something crack and hoped to God it wasn't anything we needed to keep driving. Blair responded by decreasing her speed by about one percent.

"Maybe you're related," Gertie said to Ida Belle.

I still had the phone to my ear, listening as the other agent gave me updates. "June just turned into the drive for the FBO. Ida Belle, how far out are we?"

"She's got the jump on us. It's going to be close."

"Backup is five minutes out in a helicopter," I reported.

"Tell them to shoot down the plane," Gertie said.

"This isn't Iraq," I said.

"We never get to have any fun," Gertie grumbled.

"You just bombed criminals with pink paint and glitter and jumped out of an airplane wearing a Supergirl cape," Ida Belle said.

Gertie waved a hand in dismissal. "That was at least an hour ago."

Blair cast a questioning glance in the rearview mirror. "When we have more time, you're going to have to tell me about this bomb thing."

"Turn left!" Ida Belle yelled.

Blair yanked the wheel to the left without hesitation and we found ourselves on a narrow, barely dirt, path through the woods.

"Hold on," Blair said as she clutched the wheel as the car bounced along the path.

"Sorry," Ida Belle said. "I couldn't make out the turn."

"Where does this come out?"

"At the side of the airfield. You'll be able to cruise right on the runway and to the hangar. Except, hold on... There's something I can't see well. I think it's a power line, which shouldn't be a problem. No, wait! It's a fence! Right as you clear the trees!"

As the car tore around a curve, I saw the opening and the hurricane fence just past it. I looked over at Blair, who clenched her jaw and the steering wheel and pressed down on the accelerator.

Here we go!

The car tore cleanly through the fence and hit the runway with a slide that Jason Statham would have been proud of, and she floored it as we straightened.

"There's a plane on the runway!" Blanchet yelled.

Gertie pointed at the hangar as a woman ran out. "And there's June!"

"We're not going to make it," Blair said. "That jet will be in the air before we get to them."

"Open the sunroof," I said and pulled out my pistol. "Ida Belle, you're up. Take the jet."

CHAPTER TWENTY-ONE

As soon as the top slid back, we popped up and locked in on our targets. But the pilot had already seen us coming. He stepped out of the plane with an AR-15. We ducked as he showered the car with bullets, and Blair yanked the steering wheel side to side, trying to avoid a direct onslaught.

I popped up and fired a single shot through the pilot's forehead, but I could see another man moving inside the plane. June was halfway to the plane now, and a second man came out and grabbed the AR-15 from the dead guy.

I knew the red tape on this was going to be longer than the Mississippi, but I fired a single shot into June's leg and sent her sprawling onto the tarmac. I heard several rounds go off beside me and saw them crack the front window of the plane, but they didn't penetrate it. They could still fly.

"Center console!" Blair yelled.

I ducked down as Gertie popped open the center console and squealed when she saw the Desert Eagle inside. I grabbed the gun, deciding I would wonder later about why the FBI agent was carrying this much firepower. Then I popped up, took aim, and blew a huge hunk off the front of the plane.

Two more men ran out, showering us with bullets as they ran for the woods, but a helicopter appeared over the tree line and lowered right in their path, two men pointing automatics at them from the doors. The men stopped running and dropped their weapons. It was officially over.

Blair slammed the car to a stop in front of June, who was collapsed on the tarmac, unmoving, and jumped out with a set of handcuffs. I saw the flash of her pistol from under June's chest before it even registered with Blair and raised my gun and fired again. My only choice this time was a kill shot. Blair stopped and spun around, clearly shocked, and I saw the blood drain from her face.

"I thought she was unconscious," she said.

"Yeah, the bad guys do that sometimes," I said as I walked up and checked to make sure June was dead this time.

"I'm never going to be allowed in the field again, assuming I'm not fired altogether."

"Are you kidding me? You just took down a decades-long-running drug cartel."

"No. You took them down. You and your friends."

"Johnson, you drove that car like a pro. You never hesitated, even when driving into the path of an AR-15. You've got heart and bravery, and neither of those can be taught. You'll do fine."

"Thank you. I know the amount of problems this is going to cause for you, especially as the ADA is not a fan, but if he gives the FBI any pushback, I'll hire you the best attorney. I'll pay for it myself. I won't let them punish you for what you did for me and those women and children."

I threw my arm around her and smiled. "My attorney is Alex Framingham."

Blair laughed. "Of course he is."

―――――

It took some time for the FBI and the state police to sort everything out, and I knew in the coming weeks and even months, we'd be called on time and again to tell our stories. The women and children were questioned first, but no one wanted to hold them for long given what they'd been through. While the FBI was getting the basics from them, we prepared them transport to their temporary living quarters—with Harrison and Cassidy.

It took a bit of rushing around but while we were all tied up with the FBI, the Sinful Ladies put together clothes, toiletries, and other necessities for the women and helped prep the bedrooms at Harrison and Cassidy's huge home. It was important that they felt comfortable and most importantly, safe. With a deputy and a doctor in residence, I was certain they would get both. The relief on their faces when I explained where they'd be staying until we could figure out permanent places for them was overwhelming. Most cried all over again.

As the women were being transported to their new living quarters, Ida Belle, Gertie, Blanchet, and I caught a ride back to Sinful. Ida Belle had already called Walter and given him the rundown and he'd sent Scooter and Dixon over to Mudbug to retrieve my boat. Ronald was overwhelmed with everything that had happened and especially with the news that Hermes was part of it all. But he was most thrilled about Mariela's mother being safe, and I could hear both him and Mariela squealing with happiness when I hung up.

When we were dropped off at my house, Mariela came running out of Ronald's front door and threw herself at me. I squeezed her hard and heard Ronald sniffling.

"Good God, this isn't the waterproof mascara," he said.

I released Mariela and we all laughed. She looked lovely. Ronald had found her a pink jumpsuit and had fixed her hair in a fancy braid with silk flowers running through it.

"Mr. Ronald did my nails and toes!" she exclaimed. "I've never had that before."

"You look wonderful!" Gertie said to her, and we all nodded.

Mariela beamed. "Mr. Ronald knows everything about makeup and hair and clothes. He's a genius."

"That he is," I said, and mouthed a thank-you to him.

"I told Miss Mariela that lip gloss is enough for now because she's got all that young beautiful skin, but when she gets old enough, then I'll give her a complete makeover."

"Well, now that you're all prettied up, would you like to see your mother?"

"Yes! Yes!" She jumped up and down and clapped.

It was a happy group that made the drive to Harrison and Cassidy's house, and we were even happier when Mariela jumped out of the car, running for Lara, who must have been standing at the door watching for us. The reunion between mother and daughter was absolutely priceless.

Cassidy came out to give us all hugs and invited us in, but we declined, stating the obvious need for a shower and some rest. Plus, the Sinful Ladies were already there helping her get everyone settled.

"That's fine," Cassidy said, "but as soon as everything is more normal here, I'm going to have a little get-together. You guys and Kenny, Lottie, Ronald, and Blair if she can make it. I think the women are going to want to thank all of you. It's finally starting to register that they're safe. That their lives are about to begin again, and it's incredible to watch."

"Thank you again for taking them in."

"I'm just furnishing the space. The Sinful and Mudbug residents are bankrolling it. The donations have been overwhelming. So thank you guys for getting word out. People are already talking about offering the women employment. It's going to be huge."

I nodded. It was already huge.

But I still held out hope that it was going to get huger.

———

A WEEK LATER, WE ALL GATHERED AT HARRISON AND Cassidy's house for a celebration. The dead guy at Nickel's camp had been identified by the women as one of their captors. The first of the pink-glittered men who'd decided to tell all in exchange for a lesser sentence said the rumor was their 'big boss' was going to retire and needed to put someone else in charge. He didn't know who that boss was, though, and had been dumbfounded to find out it was a little gray-haired lady who fostered kids and made prizewinning preserves. June had carefully cultivated the perfect cover.

Hermes, of course, had been gunning for that job and a quick check had revealed that he was June's nephew. June's sister, as I had suspected, had never existed. It had also revealed that June didn't appear to like Hermes much and thought he was an idiot, like the rest of us. The dead guy had been trying to posture for the promotion to boss and had last been seen leaving with Hermes to take care of some unexplained business. The cops couldn't match the slug pulled out of the guy to Hermes's weapon, but there was little doubt who'd killed him. I figured he'd dumped the body at Nickel's camp, figuring it would be easy to pin the crime on a convicted felon.

The FBI had investigated Hermes' flunky, but finally determined he didn't know anything about the Brethren or Hermes' connection to them. He was just incompetent and hoping to get a promotion by sucking up to Hermes. Blanchet had dismissed him as soon as he was back in charge and his home department had launched an investigation into his actions in Sinful. He'd been placed on leave, pending that investigation, and I had a feeling that leave would turn out to be permanent.

Two of the pink-glittered men were the ones who'd caught Lara in the boat when she'd been headed to Sinful to try to get help, and they were the ones who'd scared Mariela into the swamp. Hermes had been trying to deflect any form of investigation into Mariela, planning to get her back to the compound before her memory returned.

Years back, Lara had overheard the captors talking about Nickel's camp and the easy access when they'd gotten caught out in a storm and used it. One of them had been a roughneck living in Mudbug for a bit, and he had gotten the information through fishermen. Nickel hadn't been lying when he said everyone knew, but he'd since changed the locks and no longer left a key there.

The last drug run Lara was on, she'd borrowed a lady's cell phone in the restroom to pull up satellite images of the area where the compound was located and had memorized them so if she and Mariela ever got away, they would know how to get to Nickel's camp.

The ADA hadn't made so much as a peep. I suspected it was because he didn't want people looking too hard at his relationship with Hermes. Unfortunately for him, the press had already latched onto it and his move into the DA position didn't look nearly as secure as he'd originally thought. I had no reason to suspect he'd been involved or even aware of the Brethren and their real reason for existing, but as the saying goes, you're known by the company you keep.

Blair was still trying to put all the pieces together to make the case, and I gave her one last theory of mine that I couldn't prove but was fairly certain was true. I thought June was the one who'd tipped off the FBI. Blair wasn't convinced but trusted me enough to go on a deep dive and finally found a way to connect June to the pay-as-you-go phone that had been used to make the call. A voice modulator found hidden in her garage sealed the deal.

Everyone had been shocked at the revelation, but to me, it all made sense. June had spent years caring for abused foster kids, and I didn't believe it had all been to establish a cover. The fact that kids who had lived with her for only a brief time still kept in touch as adults told me she'd really cared about them. The dichotomy of caring for some kids while enslaving others wasn't lost on me, but some people's ability to compartmentalize was astounding.

My guess was that when Mariela came to stay with June, the original plan had been to fake the attack and Mariela's kidnapping, and then that problem would be over. But then Mariela escaped and although June wasn't exposed as far as the cops were concerned, I think Mariela's nightmares brought a lifetime of guilt to the surface.

When we were visiting, Lottie had said, '...guilt is a powerful thing. Almost as powerful as love.' I think she was right.

So June had decided to 'retire,' as one of her soldiers had said, but instead of turning over the organization to the next generation, she planned to dismantle it and leave, probably hoping the cops rescued the women and children held there. What she didn't count on was our surprise attack on the compound and rescue of the women. That had sent her scrambling and asking the cartel for favors, like sending an emergency plane for her. Blair had also found a one-way charter she'd booked for Brazil for the next weekend. We'd been just in time.

And as I'd predicted, Blair had gotten a nice promotion and a commendation for her role in bringing down a long-standing criminal organization. She'd also traded her bullet-ridden BMW for a shiny Mercedes G 63, citing the need for a vehicle that could handle rough terrain. And Bomber Bruce had reported a sharp uptick in his skydiving business, everyone wanting to imitate Gertie and Blanchet. The first two glitter paint targets had been Celia's house and Farmer Frank's llamas.

The women and children looked so happy as they milled around Harrison and Cassidy's backyard and were thrilled to have a chance to hug and thank everyone who'd played a role in their rescue. There was a lot of crying and so much smiling that I was certain people's faces were going to hurt. Finally, everyone settled down with plates of food and Ida Belle, Gertie, Blanchet, and I moved off into our own little group. Ronald was holding makeup court with the women, as he'd brought them bags of samples he'd received and was promising to give them all a makeover. Blair had been unable to make it but had sent chocolate-covered strawberries and flowers.

"I got some information on Otto," Ida Belle said.

I perked up. "Really?"

Since I'd told my original theory about Otto to Blair, she'd taken a hard look at him and Spinner, even though we'd already bagged June as the boss. As I suspected, they were unable to make a connection between the two men and the Brethren. But no matter how you looked at it, their behavior was still suspicious.

"So this has to stay between us but since the cops couldn't make a connection between him and Spinner and all this other mess, I took a drive to Mudbug yesterday and confronted him straight out. Told him what we'd seen and how it looked."

"And what did he say?"

"He got all sheepish and begged me not to rat them out. Apparently, the FBI and state police had already questioned him and he'd lied to them."

"What is he up to that he has to lie to the cops?"

"Mushrooms. Spinner found rare and very tasty mushrooms out in the swamp. Otto's brother owns a restaurant in NOLA and has practically launched his business using them. But Spinner doesn't have the proper credentials for acquiring the mushrooms, and the sales are under the table..."

"So no taxes and no licensing."

Ida Belle nodded. "And therefore, no way for anyone to clue in on where his brother is getting such an excellent product. Apparently, he's cleared out his last location and was scouting for a new one, which he found in Brethren territory."

"Which wasn't a problem for him because he'd been an explosives expert," Blanchet said.

"Then why did he give us their location?" I asked.

"He didn't say, but I have to wonder if he was hoping we'd clear the Brethren out so he had easier access to the mushrooms."

"And the cell phone?"

"Found it in the swamp and gave it to Otto. It had been in the bayou, so it was ruined."

I shook my head. "Mushrooms. Unbelievable."

"So for once, coincidence was actually coincidence," Gertie said. "Go figure."

My cell phone buzzed, and I checked the text, then smiled.

"Blanchet, I have a special delivery for you," I said.

Despite the FBI's attempts to locate Maya Delgado, they'd come up with nothing, especially with a less-than-cooperative Mexican police force, who were already coming apart at the seams as some of them had been exposed as part of the cartel.

But the FBI didn't have the resources I did. When it came to putting people in prison or getting them out, no one trumped the CIA.

I pointed at the back door of the house as a CIA agent I'd worked with years ago stepped out with an older woman beside him. Blanchet took one look at her and dropped his entire plate. Then he jumped up and ran across the backyard and grabbed the woman, likely squeezing the life out of her.

"Maya! Is it really you?"

He released her from the stranglehold, but still clutched her shoulders as he studied her face. She stared at him in shock, and then huge tears fell down her face as she reached up with one hand and placed it on his cheek.

"My Andy. I never thought I'd see you again."

"Why did you go back to them? I would have protected you."

She shook her head. "Because they would have killed you, like they did your father. I was their best transporter, and they didn't want to lose me. So they wouldn't kill me, but they made it clear what would happen if I didn't return. Your father was a warning. You would have been next. I was selfish. My staying cost you your father. Can you ever forgive me?"

He gathered her in his arms again. "There was never anything to forgive."

"Mama?" Lara's voice cracked, and Andy released Maya so she could reunite with the daughter she hadn't seen in over ten years.

Gertie looked at me and smiled.

"Best. Day. Ever."

CHAPTER TWENTY-TWO

I JOGGED UP THE PATH TO EMMALINE'S HOUSE, PRACTICALLY pulling Tiny behind me. Emmaline hadn't been lying when she'd called him lazy. At one point during our jog, he'd lain down in the middle of the sidewalk, and I'd had to wait ten minutes for him to get up. The sad thing was, he wasn't in horrible shape. He just hated to exercise.

Ida Belle and Gertie were sitting with Emmaline on the front porch, drinking iced tea as we came up. I put Tiny in the backyard with a bowl of fresh water, filled my own glass, and headed out to join them.

"Thank you for trying to get that dog moving," Emmaline said. "If I so much as take his lead out, he goes and hides under the bed."

"He doesn't fit under the bed," Gertie said.

"He thinks if he sticks his head under it that I can't see him."

We all laughed.

It had been ten days now since I'd gotten the text from Carter saying, 'I'm sorry'. Neither Emmaline nor I had heard another word, and although we were both doing our best to remain positive, I could see the strain showing on her face, and I felt it myself with my lack of sleep. Carter's best guess for the mission had been two to three weeks. We were approaching the two-week mark, but I knew that didn't mean anything. Those estimates almost always changed and rarely in a good way. They either called off the mission altogether or they had to make changes at the last minute, which often doubled the time.

"I met Maya yesterday," Emmaline said. "She was visiting Andy and he brought her by. Such a lovely woman with an absolutely horrible story. You three are my heroes—rescuing those women and children, bringing Maya back to Andy."

"Thanks," I said. "Andy is doing a great job filling in."

Gertie nodded. "He really is, and it's so sweet to see how happy he is."

"How are the other women doing?" Emmaline asked. "I'm on schedule to help out tomorrow."

"They're doing really great," Ida Belle said.

The Sinful Ladies had made up a schedule and rotated cleaning and cooking among local volunteers, but the women and children were happy to pitch right in, especially now that they had access to modern conveniences. Truth be told, they probably didn't need the volunteers' help any longer, but the socialization was good for them, so Cassidy had encouraged them to keep coming if they wanted to. Everyone had wanted to.

"Big and Little are helping them find jobs," I said. "Good jobs, with education and promotion prospects. And they're offering up free rent for a year at several of his NOLA properties for anyone who wants to move to the city. I think most of them will eventually make that move."

Emmaline nodded. "It's got to be hard staying here,

knowing that hellhole they existed in for so long is just a boat ride away."

A car pulled up to the curb and my heart dropped as I watched a man in dress blues climb out. Then Nora's words echoed through my mind.

I don't see your heart stopping. I see it breaking.

Emmaline was already out of her chair when he stepped onto the porch.

"Emmaline LeBlanc?" he asked.

"Yes."

"I'm Colonel Kitts. I'm sorry to inform you that your son, Master Sergeant LeBlanc, is MIA."

WHAT MISCHIEF WILL SWAMP TEAM 3 GET UP TO NEXT? WILL Blanchet be able to hold down the fort in Sinful? And what will happen to Carter? The answers to these questions and another mystery are coming later this year.

DID YOU KNOW THAT JANA HAS A STORE? CHECK OUT THE books, audio, and Miss Fortune merchandise at janadeleonstore.com.

FOR NEW RELEASE INFO, SIGN UP FOR JANA'S NEWSLETTER AT janadeleon.com.